Sweet Life 2

Erotic Fantasies for Couples

Sweet Life 2

EROTIC FANTASIES FOR COUPLES

EDITED BY

VIOLET BLUE

CLEIS PRESS

Published in the United States by Cleis Press Inc., P.O.
Box 14684, San Francisco, California 94114.

Printed in the United States.
Cover design: Scott Idleman
Text design: Frank Wiedemann
Logo art: Juana Alicia
First Edition.
10 9 8 7 6 5 4 3 2 1

Acknowledgements

Like real life, this book is a celebration of love, hot sex, and lasting connections. And like life, none of these things—including this book—would be possible without the love and support of those near me. This book in particular saw me through an amazing trial of just plain weird luck, and through it all the people around me never wavered in their support, never tired of surprising me with warmth and generosity, and really, really helped me a lot. Simple thank-yous seem trite.

Felice Newman, the laughter, the lunches, the keen eye, and the ability to at once solve problems and make me better at what I do: Working with you is like getting a great big basket full of sweet surprises. Our professional relationship is absolutely inspiring. Thank you. Don Weise: Your excitement and enthusiasm are boundless, almost as much as your sharp wit. Thanks for letting me bug you when my (insert electronic device here) crashes, and telling me when and where, who, and how to get there. Frédérique Delacoste: Every time we meet you make me laugh, and I can always count on sharing at least one conspiratorial smile with you. Thank you for your mirth, and support.

If life is like sex, friends are the lube. Thomas Roche, this chapter of my life has you as a major character: a source of unending support, assistance, deeply dark humor, and guidance through murky literary seas. It's a good thing we're both insomniacs. My admiration for you is gigantic; thank you for helping me when I really needed it. Annalisa, Annalisa, Annalisa—four syllables that mean "true friend." Your skill and ability astound me, and I am thankful that you are in my life—thank you, and drinks are on me. Constance, thank you for reminding me just by being my friend how important it is to stop working and enjoy myself, and also for letting me do my laundry at your house when my stress meter went into the red zone.

My family in Survival Research Laboratories is the most beautiful, complicated, crazy, scary, tight-knit, deeply caring, and loving type of family I could ever wish for. Michael and Melanie: Thank you for giving me so much support, being such wonderful friends, and loaning me a vehicle when mine was nearly totaled. During the writing of this book, so many SRL members fed me, made me laugh until body parts ached, and on some occasions even made sure I wore enough sunscreen. I love you, and thank you, my friends. But no thanks to my family in SRL would be complete without thanking Mark for being sweet, generous beyond measure, fiercely supportive when I most needed it, teasing me mercilessly when I also needed it, and being one of the funniest people I know. Plus, you kept me coffeed-up and let me crash on your couch when I worked too late (on manuscripts and machines) to go home. Thank you, Mark. Again, on the SRL note, but far more personal: Thank you, Todd, my dear friend, ex-husband,

and confidante. What we have done with our relationship is amazing; we have had a deep love relationship, and when it changed we allowed it to grow into a fantastic friendship. Your support, advice, and help when I needed it are things beyond value—thank you, as always.

This book saw me through an auto smash, a motorcycle drop, a friend's suicide, theft, loss of property, and just about everything else that could've gone awry (and often did). That's why these acknowledgments are so damn long. But there was one person who saw me through the entire roller-coaster ride and was at my side every time I needed him, and even when I thought I didn't—but really did. I not only made it with your help and support, Courtney, but I have also had the time of my life. Thank you for the driving, grinding, kissing, baritoning, massaging, "research," squeezing, giggling, pranksterism, and spanking. Thank you for looking for my keys when I lost them. And thank you for finding the key to my heart, when I thought that was lost, too. *Uz jsme doma.*

Contents

Introduction: Uz Jsme Doma

As the spasms of orgasm gently subsided, my lover and I nes-
tled into a comfortable sideways position, arms entwined, the
lengths of our sweaty bodies touching beneath the sheets. We
were winded, sticky, and smiling. He looked into my eyes and
asked, "What are you thinking?"

"I'm thinking how good I feel," I answered. "How nice it
is to be as close as two people can be. Not just physically, but
to have someone to open up to completely, to share intimacy
that comes from deep inside, intimacy that is so powerful and
overwhelming that sometimes it feels as if it's a death-defying
act just to be having sex. It seems like everyone is afraid to
really open up to each other, afraid of rejection or acceptance,
or both, as if the moment you show them what's inside, you'll
be thrust into a life-or-death situation.

"Suppose you were on an airplane, going on vacation
with your lover to some long-sought-after tropical destination.
There's a commotion in the row of seats behind you; you turn
around just in time to see some crazy guy with a knife lunge
for the flight attendant. The attendant escapes down the aisle,
but that puts your lover right between the lunatic and the

attendant. Your lover is out of her seat, trying to get away, so the madman goes after her instead. You have to think quickly if you want to save her, and saving her would mean putting yourself in danger; you might get stabbed, or worse. Do you risk it? They would in the movies.

"Heroism like that is a lot to expect in real life. As little kids we learn to try and blend in, not to make waves, especially when someone might be judging you. Especially when the person who might be passing judgment is someone you really want to impress, or someone whose opinion of you is important to you. 'Don't do anything different.' 'Hold still and don't make any sudden movements or the T-rex will get you.' It's as if we're trained from birth to be helplessly stuck doing things the way some imaginary 'others' think we should be doing them. Asking for what we want in bed is even scarier. So in what we perceive to be a no-win situation, it's easier to just resign yourself to suffering. Fear holds us back from asking for what we want, like a steel cage.

"We have these fantasies all the time about saving our lovers, about being the ultimate hero in their lives. She falls down a cliff, broken and bleeding, and you rescue her. He gets into an auto accident, and you pull him out of the car just before it blows up. This type of fantasy about our lovers has become a modern archetype of sorts, a fantasy of gaining total acceptance and love in the instant of one act that shows them who you really are, and they love you completely. David Lynch uses the hero-lover fantasy theme a lot in his movies, and it was in the film *Heavy*, too. But where do you go from there? What if the fantasy is true and they really do love you completely—can you still be brave enough to ask for what you really want, desire, or need in bed? And how do you stay the hero in love?

"I was just thinking about the nature of love in general, I suppose. I mean, I'm best friends with my ex-husband and I see him every day, spend quality time having drinks or going shopping with his great new girlfriend, and every single day it blows my mind how love can change. It has to change, in order to survive, just like us. I think too many people cling to the notion that love is this static thing that is always the same frequency, and will always be the shape, flavor, and size you thought it was last week, or even last year, and when they see that it's changed they think something's wrong. That 'different' means 'less.' When the truth is that love between two people is like a plant you grow together, and though you can't always predict how tall or into what shape it's going to grow, you can cultivate a direction together, and fertilize the plant with new ideas.

"You're giggling—I know it sounds cheesy. But everyone's afraid of love changing because it might mean the end, on one level or another. People are scared that nothing lasts forever, that there are no happy endings for love relationships. That's what the fear is: that you'll get fed up, that I'll get fed up, that someone will die, or find someone else, or move on, and that it won't be mutual. That it will hurt. It's happened to all of us, everyone, and no amount of drinking, crying, smoking, eating, TV watching, or Prozac will make it hurt any less, no matter who left whom. Gone, like a pack of matches. True intimacy in a long-term relationship is really scary because a change in direction, such as asking to try something new sexually, could mean heroic fantasy-fulfillment, or death.

"The funny thing is, I can't help but think of couples

who are worried about making love last, like someone who is looking around for their sunglasses when the glasses are sitting on top of their head. There's a Czech saying, 'Uz jsme doma,' which you use when you're looking for something and it was with you the whole time, literally translated as 'We're already home.' Great, hot, intense, and satisfying long-term relationships occur between couples who know they're 'already home,' and are unafraid to court the dangers of death-defying sexual intimacy. Fantasy is the cornerstone of human sexuality, and nothing is more intimate or arousing than confessing a fantasy—or making one come true.

"I'm practically swimming in sexual fantasies right now, and the ways couples can make them come true. Putting together *Sweet Life 2* has pushed me further into couples' fantasy-realms, giving me no small amount of inspiration. Some of the stories are sweet and succulent as a ripe peach, such as Emilie Paris's 'Breakfast in Bed,' where a woman's handsome musician boyfriend literally makes a delicious confection out of his girlfriend. In 'Auto Erotica' by Alison Tyler, an unrestrained couple creates an outrageous sexual game that verges on exhibitionism, with the aid of a few traffic lights. 'Good for the Goose' by Jesse Nelson is what happens when boyfriends get caught with the lipstick, and must learn what it's like to reverse roles. And 'The Real, Real World' by Alexandra Michaels shows us a couple whose reality TV show will never be on cable—though we can make one of our own, just like theirs, if we want.

"Some of the stories are intensely dirty, and flirt with danger. 'Round One' by Dante Davidson puts a man in a precarious situation at the hands of his dominant girlfriend, who wants to explore her newly discovered penchant for dressing—and fucking—like a man. Elle McCaul's 'Lucky' takes a highly taboo fantasy into a public parking lot, and we get to see a naughty girl's hide get tanned—that's what happens when you make Daddy mad. 'Mile High' by Simon Torrio shows us how to join the club of the very same name—with a twist.

"Many of these fantasies are tense, explicit explorations of sex pushed to the limits. 'Special Occasion' by Felix D'Angelo shows us a woman who will give her husband anything he wants—including sex with a stranger. And 'Bad Doggy' by Julia Moore takes the phrase 'be your dog' literally, as a woman endures an unusual obedience school at the hands of her loving master.

"I can tell you're getting excited—I am too. There's more: voyeurism, spanking, threesomes of every combination, and some activities I was surprised to learn about. And I want to try them all."

He sighed. I could feel his arms tighten around me.

"Violet, you are awfully long-winded. And I love you for it."

And he kissed me goodnight.

Violet Blue
San Francisco, California
January 2003

Round One

DANTE DAVIDSON

Toni and I met at the mall during our lunch hour. She claimed that she wanted my opinion on an expensive new business suit she was planning to buy. "Deep gray," she told me, "with micro-thin white pin-stripes. It'll look so fucking hot with a pair of spectator heels." Although extremely flattered by her request, I couldn't fully fathom the concept. Toni has impeccable taste. She rarely asks my opinion about anything she puts on her body. In fact, I have very little say in the matter unless it's my fingers, mouth, or cock, against her naked skin.

I should have known. Usually I'm not this slow.

We had planned to meet at a location by the escalator. I was early, and I watched as she cut through the crowd of shoppers. Toni is always noticeable. She wears her short red hair slicked away from her high forehead, revealing the mastery of her sharp features: lovely wide-set green eyes, a haughty jaw line, perfect nose. She's tall, especially in her signature skyscraper pumps, and she favors man-style suits. Not that she wants to hide her curves—no, not at all. An authoritative goddess: That's Toni's fashion statement. Even in a suit, she's all woman.

As I gazed at her approaching figure, I felt my cock stir to life. Toni can make me hard with a look. Now, she wasn't even glancing in my direction, but I found that radiating power of her sexual energy truly palpable.

"Ready?" she asked, when she reached my side.

I nodded, and I had the distinct feeling that I was signing up for more than a viewing of a new item of clothes—but I still couldn't figure out Toni's plan.

With a smile, she led me, like a kid tugging a puppy on a leash, to the women's department of an exclusive high-end store. The salesclerk quickly located the suit for us and set it up in one of the fancy private dressing rooms. Because we were in an area reserved for those special sort of people who spend oodles of money on clothes, we were allowed to go in together. No questions asked.

"Let me know if you need any assistance—" the iced-blonde saleslady crooned to us. I thought I could actually see the dollar signs of her impending commission in her light blue eyes.

"Oh, we will," Toni promised, ushering me in with her. This is where my sensors should have started ringing. But for some reason, I was still lost in the concept that Toni actually wanted me to advise her on an article of clothing. I'd even gotten a look at the price tag of the suit. The figure was enough to make anyone want a second opinion.

Sitting on the edge of the padded peach-colored bench, I waited for her to get undressed. I had turned to glance at my own reflection in the mirror when I realized that Toni was standing directly behind me with her suit still on, waiting for me to pay attention to her. Confused, I turned around, and as soon as I did, she slid her hands behind my head, fingers twining in my dark curly hair, and brought my mouth forward, to the crotch of her slacks.

Oh, I thought, as I instantly obeyed her silent demand. *Ohhh,* I thought, that mental moan stretching out as my mouth opened and I began to lick along the length of her plastic prick, still concealed within the rich fabric of her suit slacks. Suddenly, I understood completely. Toni was acting on one of my darkest fantasies, a concept I had described to her late one night, when we were at the private mental place where couples can truly confess. I'd wanted her to fuck me. That's all I really said at first. *Just fuck me.*

"Tell me more," Toni had urged, fingers stroking along my strong chest as she looked up into my face.

"You know," I'd said, bashful, "you take charge."

A glimmer of understanding had shone in her green eyes, and then she'd snuggled against me under the sheets, her hand moving down from my chest, working lower as she'd insisted I continue the fantasy. As she'd wrapped her fist around my cock, I had done what she requested: I'd told her every single thing I wanted.

Now, she was making that fantasy come true. And because she'd understood my desires, Toni wouldn't let me do the work myself. She rubbed my face firmly against the split between her legs, letting me know the power of her passion.

I've never sucked cock before, but I know what I like when Toni goes down on me, and I transferred that knowledge to how I pleased her. Using the whole of my mouth, I suckled her through the suit pants. I could tell that beneath the slacks she had on only the harness and cock, and I couldn't wait to see what this toy looked like. But when I brought my hands up to her fly, she shook her head, and said, "No. You wait. Wait until you really want it—"

"I really want it," I assured her.

"No," she said again, and she started to fuck her cock against my face. I sighed and let her, loving the feeling of that ripe toy caressing my cheeks, brushing against my parted lips. My own cock was doing its best impression of a steel pole in my pants. I wanted release and relief.

"Take off your clothes," Toni said, her voice harsh. "I want to see just how much you want me."

Quickly, I stripped without a word. Heart pounding, I stood and undid the fly of my slacks. I kicked off my shoes and stepped free from my pants and boxers, aware of exactly how hard my cock was. I'd just noticed how the trio of mirrors worked, and I turned to see my body reflected to infinity: the hard muscles of my thighs, the strong plane of my back, ridged stomach, unbelievably hard cock. Toni trailed her hand along my rod, and I realized that she wasn't wearing nail polish today, that her nails were cut short and buffed to a clear glassy shine. She had on a heavy, man's-style watch I'd never seen on her before. When I looked into her face, I saw that she wasn't wearing makeup, or jewelry. And was that a man's spicy cologne I smelled?

Suddenly, I started to really get it. Toni had transformed

for me. That was fair, wasn't it? Because I was undergoing a transformation of my own, from dominant to submissive in sixty seconds or less. From tough guy to neophyte.

Toni pushed me back down on the bench, then finally she undid her slacks and revealed the answer to my fantasies. Yet as I saw the toy, questions bloomed in my head. I started to ask her where she'd gotten it, *when* she'd gotten it, but the moment I parted my lips, she took immediate advantage of the situation, silencing any queries I might have had with a huge mouthful of cock.

"I had this fantasy the other day," she said softly, rocking back on her heels as she moved in and out of my mouth at a slow and steady pace. "I was trying on the suit and I imagined you in here with me, doing just this. I actually made myself come all alone in the dressing room. That's when I knew I had to bring you back with me."

That image made me even harder, even more desperate to please. I sucked her cock as if it were a true extension of herself, a living part of my lady's body. The fact that she was still entirely dressed turned me on even more. I was serving her—and then, as I looked up at her and saw her suit, I mentally edited that phrase—I was serving "him." Tony. Some man that my lady had brought for me to fuck. For me to get fucked by.

Mouth full, cheeks indented in an instant sucking motion, I still had the wherewithal to wonder where the salesclerk was and what she might say if she knocked on the dressing room door and we were unable to answer. From a recent article I'd read, I recalled that many department stores have cameras guarding against shoplifting. I considered mentioning this to Toni, pointing out that we might be in the process of being videotaped, but then I had second thoughts. Knowing my filthy-minded girlfriend, I realized Toni would probably be turned on by the possibility.

Regardless of what could happen to us, I couldn't deny my own intense need. I didn't think I'd ever been that turned on, and I knew that Toni was deeply aroused as well. I could sense just how excited she was from the sensuous scent of her sex in the air. That part was still all woman. The more I sucked on her toy cock, the hotter she seemed to be getting. She twisted her fingers in my hair, pulling me more firmly against her. I used my tongue the way I like her to go down on me. I cradled the head of her cock in my mouth, then ran the very tip of my tongue along the veiny underside of her well-developed tool.

"That's my boy," Toni murmured as I slid one hand along her naked thigh, moving steadily upward. It was my goal to reach under her black leather harness and tickle her clit, but she had other plans. "I want to fuck you," she said, her voice hoarse. When I pulled away and looked up at her, I saw the yearning in her eyes. "Yes," she repeated, nodding, "you heard right. Now, turn and put your palms flat on the mirror."

I did as she said, offering my ass to my lover, certain she'd take care of me. Toni always does. I knew just what it would feel like when she took control, and I tried to will my nerves to stay steady.

Toni had come prepared. After rummaging around in the outside pocket of her satchel, she emerged with a bottle of lubrication. She tilted her head at me, daring me to watch as she poured out a handful of glistening lube. Gently, she parted the cheeks of my ass and strummed her fingertips along my crack. Now, I groaned and felt my hips arch backward automatically at the instant flush of pleasure her fingers brought.

"You like that?" she asked.

I nodded.

"Then say it."

"What, Toni?"

"Say what you want me to do."

Could I? I'd have to. Swallowing over the instant lump in my throat, I managed to murmur, "I want you to fuck me."

"How?"

"Hard—"

That's exactly when she slid her wet, warm cock into my ready ass. As she did, she met my eyes in the mirror, continuing to describe what she'd daydreamed about on her previous visit.

"I thought of paging you at the office," she said, "of telling you that it was a dire emergency and just giving you the address...nothing else. Demanding that you be here in ten minutes."

"You could have gotten me fired," I said.

"At the time, it almost seemed worth it."

I glared at her, and she gave me an open-handed smack on my ass for the look. That made me cringe—the thought that other shoppers might have heard the spank, but Toni didn't seem to care. She continued fucking me, tightening the muscles of her thighs and really working me in and out.

"I didn't, though," she said, "did I? Instead, I planned this—planned on having you meet me, to give me your opinion." Now I caught the sarcasm in her voice and realized exactly how fucking slow I'd been. *My* opinion about her clothes. Toni practically dresses me every day. She knows which ties to place with which of my shirts, what color socks I'm supposed to wear with each of my suits. I'm not the most coordinated person when it comes to fashion.

But I'm very adept at other things, like squeezing her thick, plastic cock with the muscles of my ass, making my own rhythmic contractions that brought a look of confusion and ecstasy to my sweet girl's face. Yes, the cock was synthetic, but the way I pulled on her had to have an effect on her pussy beneath the toy. She swallowed hard and held onto my flat waist with her hands, jamming me back against her, slamming me against her body so that our skins smacked together. Now, I *knew* other customers would be able to hear us, was sure that it was only a matter of seconds before some burly security guard burst into the haven of our dressing room.

But no, we were safe. No knocking, no horrified voices, just the pleasing, steady rhythm of Toni's cock driving inside me, the look of flushed and feverish pleasure on my face, the glow in our eyes when we glanced at each other.

As we finally found the stride I needed, she gripped onto my cock, working me with the pumping-fast motion of her hot little hand. I couldn't believe how intense that felt. I watched in the mirror as she jerked me off, and then I bit down hard on the cry that wanted to escape as I shot my river of come toward the mirror, splattering the glass with sticky white semen.

I tried to catch my breath, but it was difficult. Just too surreal thinking about what the next poor person would find in the dressing room after we left. That wasn't really my concern, though. My concern was taking care of Toni. I turned around and quickly worked to slide down her slacks and unbuckle the harness of the strap-on, letting the toy fall to the ground. Then I went to my knees on the plush gray carpet and brought my mouth to her pussy. Her cunt was positively swimming in juices. I licked up and down along her outer lips, then thrust my tongue between them.

Again, Toni wrapped her fingers in my hair, holding me close. I rubbed my face back and forth, using every part to work her. My chin dug against her skin. My cheeks pressed into her. Toni was so excited that it was only a matter of seconds before I'd gotten her to the verge. Now, I cradled her asscheeks in my hands and lifted her off the ground. I wanted her to feel weightless as she came, and I wanted to remind her that I can be in charge of her pleasure as easily as she can be in charge of mine.

As she sank slowly back down to earth, she gave me a look of total, sublime delight.

"That wasn't easy," she said, wiping her face with my undershirt.

"Which part?"

"The whole thing. The planning. The paying off of the salesclerk—"

"Was that why she gave me such a strange look?" I'd thought I'd seen dollar signs, when really I'd seen sex.

Toni nodded, and when she saw me reaching for my clothes, she motioned for me to sit back down.

"I still want you to see the suit," she said.

"Seriously?"

"You've got good taste, you know. You picked me,

didn't you?"

I gave her a look—she can be so pompous at times. But then I settled down to watch her dress for me, pretty sure that she was only stalling for time…before round two.

X-Rated Eden

CRAIG T. VAUGHN

Eden and I sit side-by-side next to each other in the movie theater, trying our best not to touch one another. Trying, because although we're both desperately aroused, we are out for a date with her extremely conservative parents. This means that we have to exhibit our most dignified manners—what I like to call our "boy scout and girl scout behavior." Amazingly enough, Eden's folks still don't know we live together, don't seem to understand modern couples at all. Whenever they have a chance, they wax poetic about how perfectly Eden's name suits their innocent, flaxen-haired girl.

If they only knew…about Eden's tattoos, about her penchant for doing tequila body shots, about her innate ability to talk dirty.

Of course, the fact that we have to behave for the next two hours means that whenever Eden shifts in her seat, simply the innocent brush of any part of her body against mine makes my rig throb fiercely in my cleanly pressed khaki pants. Every time she waves her long hair over her bare shoulders I am caressed by a whiff of her subtle sandalwood perfume. The simple pleasure of her scent makes me want to lean over and kiss the soft skin of her neck, to bite along the rise of her collarbones, to sink my teeth in deep and make her squirm. I am unable to even share the crimson velveteen-flocked armrest with her. For the first time in my life, the touch of an elbow against my bicep makes me want to shoot.

Who knew arm-sex could be so intensely erotic?

Midway through the picture, I realize that I have no fucking idea what the movie is about. When people around us begin to laugh, I look up, startled, having forgotten that we're even watching a comedy. For me, there is nothing funny about the situation at all. In fact, if I were to classify the genre, my life is currently bordering on tragedy—the waste of a perfectly fine bone-hard erection due to being in the wrong place at the wrong time. If we were here on our own, we'd skip the screen climax in favor of a good, old-fashioned fuck session at home.

I see it all—our clothes on but open. Eden's dress pushed to her waist, panties off, her legs thrown over my shoulders as I slam into her to the hilt.

"Be good," Eden whispers to me when she sees me shifting uncomfortably in the seat. I've got blue balls like you wouldn't believe. "Please, Charlie. You only have to do this once every few months."

After the movie, when I'm ready to drag my honey home for an all-night encounter on our California King, Eden's mother suggests a late dinner at a nearby Mexican restaurant. No idea has ever sounded worse to me, but my brain is so sex-soaked, so totally consumed by images of me and my lady in a tight and powerful clinch, that I can't think of an excuse. Usually, I'd be able to say, "That would be wonderful, but I've got an early court time in the morning." Something, *anything* to be able to drag Eden home with me and fuck her until she creams.

She's got on this whisper-thin strapless dress tonight. Multicolored flowers bloom all over the fabric. A rich heady bouquet, so suited for "Eden." But I want to plunder my Eden. I want to drive inside the heavenly garden between her legs and make her moan with delight. When I look at her, I see her shining hair pulled out of her face, see every one of the freckles that decorates the bridge of her nose. She has on a thin golden chain around her neck, and I want to bite on it, tug on it. Raging hormones have turned me into a hungry animal. I know nothing except my urgent desire.

"What do you say, Charles?" Eden's father asks. My silence is bordering on the bizarre.

Desperately, I look over at my baby, but even though I'm certain she reads the serious longing in my eyes, she doesn't make a single effort to save us. Instead, she smiles sweetly at her mother and nods, saying we'd be more than happy to join them. Her parents walk ahead of us to the restaurant, and now Eden twines her fingers in my own, and finally I understand just what she's doing. She's teasing me, and it's exciting her immensely to be in charge. Power has changed even the way that she moves. Her confidence has skyrocketed.

"Why'd you do that?" I whisper anyway, pressing my lips to her ear and feeling her golden hair tickle my skin.

"Because you're on fire."

"You're right," I say. "Just walking is torture."

"And you're going to be that much harder when we finally fuck—"

Her mom turns around then, missing by a millisecond the moment when her preciously angelic daughter has used vulgar and inappropriate language. I lose myself in thoughts of exactly how obscene Eden can be. I picture her bent over our coffee-colored sofa, her own hands reaching back to part her asscheeks for me, waiting for me to drive deep inside. "Fuck me, Charlie," she always says. "Fuck my ass hard. Make me feel it."

Then I see her standing in the center of the tiled floor of our kitchen, drenched in olive oil, wrists tied tightly together with twine and fastened to a hook in the ceiling. Slowly, I circle her, my belt doubled, waiting, just waiting, for her to give me the excuse to strike. She always does. Eden can't keep quiet to save herself. And when she lets loose and says filthy words, my cock stirs immediately. How someone so coolly beautiful can speak in such heated dialogue turns me upside down.

"Just wait," she says now. "I'm going to screw your brains out."

"Here we are, you lovebirds," Eden's mother coos at us, ushering us in ahead.

Dinner is hell. Pure and total hell. Eden is in ripe form, dragging her stockinged foot against my crotch under the table. Leaning down to pick up her *accidentally* dropped napkin, and then grazing my cock through my slacks with her long, rose-pink nails. When I feel her actually try to unzip my slacks, I give her a stern look, my jaw clenched, and she smiles at me, then licks her lips. What I'd do to feel those lips around my cock. Pursing, tightening, swallowing. What I'd give to be able to push all of the half-filled dishes onto the floor, lift her up on the table, and just fuck her in the dead center of the restaurant. I can hear the crash of breaking porcelain in my head, and when Eden's father asks me a question about a recent case, it takes me a moment to decipher the language of his words. I want to tell him, "Excuse me, if I could just fuck your daughter for a moment—quickly, I promise—I'd be able to get myself under control. Then I'd be a much better dinner guest."

After about a thousand years, the check arrives. I pay with cash, drastically overtipping in my hurry to get it over with, and then finally we say our good-byes, excuse ourselves, and hurry from the joint.

"You're in for it," I tell her.

"Oh, really? Am I, Charlie? What exactly am I in for?"

I hold onto her hand, pulling her down the escalator to the parking lot, but now I'm so hot that I can't remember where we fucking parked the car. Walking is a nightmare. My cock needs release, needs to be inside Eden's sweet cunt, and I finally just stop and stare at her.

"Poor baby," she says, stroking my dark brown hair away from my eyes. "It's that bad, is it?"

Visions blur in my head. Pictures of what we've done together in the past and what I want to do right now in our present. We live only ten minutes away, but that's ten minutes more than I can handle. And even though we've never done this before, never done anything close, I pick the happily squealing Eden in my arms, throw her over my shoulders, and find a concrete pillar nearby. This will protect us, if only slightly, from the prying eyes of any curious passerby. Protect us enough, as far as I'm concerned. I set my sweetheart down, flip her around so that her palms are flat on the white plaster, and lift her innocent-looking floral sundress in back.

And, Jesus fuck me, she doesn't have any panties on. Not even one of the tiny, floss-like pastel lace thongs that she favors. No panties. No stockings. No nothing. I'm so shocked by her bare skin that I stand there like a fool looking down at her.

"This whole time?" I ask, trying to figure out if there was a moment during the evening when she could have ditched them.

"This whole time."

And at this exact moment, one of the mall's security rent-a-cops goes strolling by. I quickly lower Eden's dress and do my best to talk to her in a casual tone, as if we're discussing the fact that we've misplaced our car.

"You folks need any help?" the heavyset man asks us. I can tell from his raised blond eyebrows that he thinks he knows just exactly what we've been up to, and that he's caught a multitude of sexually excited couples in similar positions in the past. We're obviously not the first lust-filled couple to look for a little love-tryst in the parking garage beneath the mall.

I shake my head and Eden says to the guard, "We thought we'd lost our car. But now I remember that it's on a different level—" Her voice is so sweet and so calm. How could the security guard help but believe her? Yet I notice the way his eyes seem to skim over the naked skin of her shoulders, the tight cinched-in waist of her dress. He takes his time before answering, and I am infinitely aware of the thunderous sounds of cars driving by around us, the way Eden tilts her head slightly to add to her honest effect, the way my cock throbs animatedly within the confines of my slacks.

"Happens all the time," the man says, moving on. And now Eden and I have to move on, as well, but we only make it as far as the next pillar.

"That was close," I tell her.

"Not as close as I want you to be."

"Meaning?"

"Fuck me, Charlie. Just fuck me."

I run my fingers along the back of her dress, and now I feel the dampness there, caused by her arousal combined with her lack of undergarments. She's chosen well, though. The multicolored pattern of the fabric hid the wet spot so well that all evening long I didn't notice.

"So you knew what you were doing from the start," I say, unbuttoning my slacks now and releasing my near-desperate cock.

"Exactly what I was doing," she agrees.

"And you knew what I was going to do when I found out?"

"Exactly what you'd do," she sighs as she feels me enter her. Then she leans her head back, and her rich blonde hair cascades in a gold-foil river down her back. Her body tenses as I thrust and release, holding her hips and pulling her back against me. I think about the way she teased me in the movie theater, playing on a fantasy that we'd discussed often in the past, but never done. "Maybe we can do it on the beach," she has whispered to me in bed. "Or at the movies," I've countered, knowing that this sort of conversation makes our at-home times even hotter. In reality, it's difficult to find public places to misbehave in Los Angeles. You're never entirely alone.

As we're not entirely alone, now. Even behind our pillar, at the rear of the parking garage, we could be spotted at any moment. And this is what further fuels my passion. The thought that someone might walk around the corner and see. That someone might uncover our secret and gaze at us beneath the fluorescent lights, watching for a moment, as if we were putting on a show for their pleasure.

But we're not. We're putting on this show for our entertainment only. I slip-slide my way into Eden's wet pussy, and then I bring my hands down in front of her body to tap her trembling clit. She is so excited, even though she was playing the ice princess all through the movie and dinner, playing cool. I've never felt her this wet before. My thumb drags along her clit and she shivers in my embrace. That shiver works through my own body as her pussy contracts on my rod. I use my fingers to spread her pussy lips, holding them wide apart, and she groans. The noise is loud enough to reverberate around us. My immediate moan echoes hers. I can't believe this is us doing this. And then she starts to talk, my X-rated Eden, saying those dirty words that always take me higher.

"Come on, Charlie," she urges me. "Fuck me, right, baby—"

"Like this?" I ask her.

"Yeah," she sighs. "I like to feel your big cock inside me. Gives me something to squeeze on when you touch my clit—"

I do. Each time my fingers flick over her hot little gem, she pulls me tighter inside her. She's gripping me as hard as I can possibly imagine, when she freezes.

"What?" I hiss.

"Just stop—"

So there I am, midthrust, moments away from coming, and I have no idea what's going on. No idea until I hear the familiar sound of Eden's mother's voice. Then I freeze as hard as she is, and we hold our place like statues. I am not even breathing anymore. We watch, immobilized in a sliver of time, as Eden's parents walk by only yards away. I don't dare to move at all, not to withdraw, not to slide forward. I'm caught inside Eden, and I feel her body grip into me even tighter. Then finally her parents disappear from range, and Eden sighs and releases.

We continue our motion together, and then I let her take me over the edge. I do nothing, just stay inside her, not thrusting, not withdrawing. Her tight powerful muscles milk me, and when she comes, the inner embrace of her cunt is like a form-fitting sleeve, like a fucking machine. She drains me until I am completely spent, pressing forward against her, sealing her up against the concrete pole and shuddering.

"You think you know," she says, as she pulls off me and turns to gaze into my eyes. I see her pretty face, her pale glossed lips, slim nose, dark blue eyes like the sky at dusk.

"Think I know what?" I ask, because right now, fumbling to get my cock back into my slacks, I honestly don't feel as if I know much of anything.

"Just like my folks," she grins, motioning with her head to where our silver convertible is parked, only several feet away. It's suddenly obvious to me that she knew exactly where it was this whole time. "You think you know me, but you don't."

"But I'm constantly learning," I say, reaching for her again and holding her tight before she can get away from me. "I'm discovering more and more every day." And it's okay if it takes forever for me to discover all of Eden—because that's time I'm willing to spend.

Smoking in the Boys' Room

PAUL ROUSSEAU

Michelle was dressed for the occasion: short, tight plaid skirt decent by only a couple of inches, white stockings, high-heeled shoes, loose white blouse with just a hint of her white, lacy bra showing where she'd carelessly let a button or two come undone. Her blonde hair was in pigtails and she was wearing heavy eyeliner and lipstick. My twenty-eight-year-old girlfriend was dressed up in the height of Catholic schoolgirl drag, pretending to be the naughty slut she always wanted to be, the slut she'd begged me to let her be for an evening—and I planned to comply, eagerly.

I regarded her from behind the big oak desk, tapping the 18-inch ruler on my palm.

"Don't sit down," I snapped. Michelle stood nervously in front of the desk, popping her gum and shifting from side to side. "Miss Peabody informs me that you were caught smoking. Is this true?"

"Honest, Sir! I wasn't smoking, honest I wasn't!"

I stood up, moving toward her quickly. Michelle took a step back and I snapped, "Stay still!"

I came close to her, bending down so that my face was just inches from hers. I grabbed a pigtail and sniffed it. It reeked of smoke—ten points for realism.

"Not only smoking, but lying," I growled.

Michelle exclaimed: "The other girls were smoking, but honest, I wasn't!"

I bent closer to her face, sniffing.

"You weren't smoking? You swear?"

She shook her head quickly.

I put out my hand.

"Spit out your gum, Michelle."

Nervously, she leaned over and let her bubblegum fall into my hand.

She looked into my eyes, fear crossing her face as I leaned close. Suddenly I grabbed the back of her head and pressed my mouth to hers, forcing my tongue between her lips as she whimpered and tried to pull away. I held her fast, probing her mouth with my tongue and tasting the telltale residue of tobacco: sharp, rich, nasty.

I pulled back and stared at her. Michelle's red lipstick was smeared across her mouth now; I wiped my mouth on one of her blonde pigtails and saw its tip rouge faintly red.

"Your excuses fall part under investigation, Michelle. I recommend that you start telling the truth." I sat on the edge of the desk and tapped the ruler on my palm.

Michelle blushed fiercely and looked down at the floor in humiliation. Her pigtails hung past her shoulders; just underneath them, the peaks of her nipples had begun to stand out quite plainly under the blouse.

"You know the punishment for smoking, Michelle."

She nodded. "Yes, Sir," she said miserably.

"If you'd like, you could encourage me to lessen the punishment a bit. Say, by telling me who gave you the cigarettes?"

She looked up at me, her blue eyes wide and bright. "Sir?"

I took her chin between my thumb and forefinger and held her fast while she tried to look away. "Who gave you the cigarettes, Michelle? You know full well that you can't have bought them—you're not old enough. Now, who gave them to you?"

Michelle stared into my face, putting on a beautiful show of being too scared to talk. I could already feel my cock hardening in my pants, and Michelle's nipples were more evident than ever under the blouse.

"Miss Peabody said you were smoking in the boys' room. Is it one of the boys who gave you the cigarettes? Andy Taylor?"

"I…I…I," she began.

"Your parents already told me in our parent-teacher conference that they cut off your allowance because they caught you drinking. So you couldn't have given Andy money for the cigarettes. What did you give him, Michelle?"

Michelle was a gorgeous actress. She looked on the verge of tears.

"I thought so," I said. "You sucked him with that pert little mouth of yours, didn't you, Michelle? He smeared your lipstick all over that pretty face, didn't he?"

Shifting nervously, Michelle nodded.

"Uh-huh," she said.

"Did he have you service his friends, too, Michelle?"

"Just a few of them," she whimpered pathetically. Her nipples were now even more clearly evident.

"How many?" I asked sternly.

"S…six or eight," she said.

"You're sure? Not more?"

"Well…maybe ten," she whispered.

"Ten boys, all using that mouth of yours, just for a few cigarettes. Tsk-tsk, Michelle. Don't you know that even whores your age get cash? What have you got to say for yourself?"

"I…I don't know," she said.

"Open your blouse," I told her.

"Sir?"

"I said unbutton your blouse, Michelle. Right now."

Michelle began to fidget with her top button, looking at me for reassurance.

I tapped the ruler in my palm. "Go ahead," I told her.

She unbuttoned her blouse slowly, letting it fall open to reveal the creamy mounds of her breasts imprisoned in their too-tight, too-low-cut bra. Her nipples peaked out quite clearly. Tucked into her cleavage was a cigarette.

"I thought so," I said. "Give it to me."

She took the slightly crushed cigarette out of her cleavage and handed it to me.

"Anywhere else you're hiding the cigarettes your boyfriends gave you, Michelle?"

She shook her head.

"We'll see. Lift your skirt."

"Please," she said, tears forming in her eyes. "Please don't make me...."

"Lift your skirt, Michelle. Right now."

She took hold of her tight skirt and snugged it up over her thighs, revealing the lace tops of her stockings where they hitched to her garters.

"Higher," I said.

She lifted her skirt up over her crotch, revealing smooth-shaved pussy unhindered by panties. Tucked between her thighs, in the top of her stockings, was a pack of Marlboros with matches in the cellophane.

"I thought so. Give them to me."

She took out the pack of cigarettes and handed them to me. I took them and got one out, lighting it while she watched.

I took a drag and blew smoke at her.

"Would you like one?"

She shook her head nervously.

"I'll bet you would, but you're too ashamed to ask for one. Now, Michelle, care to tell me why you're not wearing any panties?"

"He...he doesn't like me to," she said.

"Andy?"

She nodded.

"Does he like you to shave your pussy, too?"

"N...no," she said. "That was my idea."

"I'm sure it was. Do you like the way it feels?"

She nodded.

"You do realize that only strippers and prostitutes shave

down there, don't you?"

She shook her head.

"Well, they do. Which are you, Michelle?"

She looked at me dumbly. I blew smoke in her face.

"You're a whore. At least, that's what your clothing tells me."

"Please, Sir…I'll try to be good."

I took a drag off the cigarette, walked over to the couch, sat down.

"Over my lap, Michelle."

She began to pull her skirt down and I said, "Leave your skirt up."

Nervously, she came over to the couch and lay across my lap, her skirt pulled up so that her pretty derriere was exposed.

"Legs spread."

"Sir?"

"Legs *open,* Michelle. I don't want to tell you again."

She parted her thighs. I set the ruler in the small of her back and let my hand trail up her inner thigh. I was still holding the cigarette.

I placed it close to her pussy, so close that she could feel the heat, but not close enough to burn her. She squirmed, her belly pressing against my hard cock.

"Can you feel that, Michelle?"

"Uh-huh," she said.

"Does it scare you?"

She nodded.

"I'm going to spank you, Michelle. But the next time I catch you smoking, do you know where I'm going to put out this cigarette, Michelle?"

She shook her head.

I chuckled. "Oh, I think you know."

I dropped the cigarette on the floor and crushed it out with my foot. My hand returned to her thigh and lingered an inch from her pussy.

The first blow shocked her, made her yelp. She squirmed as I hit her sweet spot again, my fingers curving under to give her exactly the right amount of thud, an amount I'd calibrated in years of spanking her—though never in a schoolgirl's skirt.

"Say 'Thank you,' Michelle."

"Th...thank you, Sir."

I spanked her again, my hand beating her firm ass in a slow, mounting rhythm. Michelle began to squirm in earnest, writhing and wriggling in my lap with each blow on her butt. I spanked her faster until she was moaning in pain, whimpering with each blow.

"Th...thank you, Sir," she said, without being prompted.

I slipped my hand between her legs, touched her there. She gasped as I slid one finger into her. A thin dribble of juice ran onto my hand.

"You're not a virgin," I said.

She shook her head.

"And you're very, very wet," I said.

She didn't nod.

"Was Andy your first?"

Michelle shook her head again.

I slipped two fingers inside her, curving my hand down to massage her G-spot. She gasped and then moaned, pushing her ass back against me, forcing her pussy onto my hand.

"You're enjoying this, aren't you?"

Shaking her head, quickly: "No, Sir. Please stop."

I worked my fingers in and out of her pussy, making sure that the pads of my fingers hit her G-spot with every thrust. Her wriggling felt incredible on my cock, and I knew I would come before she did if I wasn't careful. When I eased my thumb down to touch her clit, she let out a wild, uncontrolled moan of pleasure and looked up at me with her bright blue eyes.

"You want it, don't you. Want me to do to you what Andy did."

"No, Sir," she said. "Please...."

"If you don't want it, Michelle, why are you so wet?"

"I...I don't know, Sir!"

I started spanking her again—slow at first, then faster and faster as she whimpered and squirmed. I could tell she was very close—she could come from spanking alone if I did it right, but I wasn't about to let my schoolgirl get off that easy.

"Ask for it, Michelle. Ask for it or I'll tell Andy you tattled on him."

"No, Sir, please...."

"Then ask for it."

"P...please, Sir. Please do it to me...."

"Do what? You know the word, don't you, Michelle? Surely a slut who gives head for cigarettes knows the word for what she wants done to her?"

She said it so softly I almost couldn't hear her: "Fuck."

"Louder."

"Fuck, Sir." Louder.

"Ask me for it."

Again, so soft I couldn't hear: "Please fuck me, Sir."

"Ask me!"

Louder, almost a groan: "Please fuck me, Sir!"

"You want it from me the way you got it from Andy? Then beg for it!"

"I want it, Sir! Please fuck me, Sir!" She seemed to break through a barrier and whimpered hungrily, "Please, Sir! Stick your thing in me, Sir! I want it, Sir!"

"Show me what you did to his cock before he put it in you! Show me what you did to Andy and his friends in the boys' room!"

She had definitely broken through the barrier. She was down on her knees in an instant, between my spread legs, groping at my belt and pants. She got them open and took my cock out, began licking the glistening pre-come from the tip. Then she took it in her mouth, sucking it fiercely, leaving lipstick traces down the length of it. She gulped me down, moaning with hunger as she slid it down her throat.

Michelle was an expert. I knew I would come very soon if I didn't hold back. I fought my orgasm, not wanting to lose it before I fucked my naughty schoolgirl. She lavished her love on my prick, sucking desperately.

I knew it was coming soon—I couldn't hold back any longer. It was hard to pull her off my cock—she was so desperate for it, her breasts heaving under the open blouse as she sought after my hard prick.

"Turn around," I told her. "Turn around and put your ass in the air."

She scrambled around, getting on all fours and wriggling her ass back toward me. Her gorgeous ass curved around my cock as I fitted the head between the lips of her shaved sex and pushed it in, hearing her gasp of release.

She came before I did—just. I heard her moaning, felt the spasms of her cunt as it gripped my cock, as I drove it into her rhythmically, and the contractions inside her milked the orgasm right out of my cock. I came, moaning myself as my cock spent itself in her.

My cock slipped out of her. Michelle remained on her knees, moaning, her ass swaying back and forth as she begged for more.

"You're headed right back to the boys' room, aren't you?" I asked. "You can't wait to get back there."

She looked over her shoulder, and smiled.

Girls' Night Out
GISELLE PARKER

You've been lying to me. When I asked you whether you had gone in my underwear drawer, you said you hadn't. You told me you had no idea why some of my sweet nothings might have been in the wrong place, folded incorrectly. You even told me you didn't know why my panties might have smelled funny. You think you fooled me, but I saw your face reddening, noticed the sense of indignation in your voice when I suggested that maybe you were just looking around in there, out of curiosity. You told me you didn't know what I was talking about.

That was your second mistake, lying to me. Your first was assuming I didn't know what to do with a boyfriend who likes to wear my lingerie. I know exactly what to do with you, and you're about to find that out.

Naturally, I lied to you, too. I smiled sweetly and told you of course you hadn't been in my underwear drawer. I must have been mistaken; I was in such a rush that morning to pick out my clothes for work that I didn't notice I was putting things in the wrong order. Silly me!

But you believed me, even if I didn't believe you. You didn't think anything was unusual when I pushed you down on the bed and pulled your pants open, caressed your cock, molded my mouth around it, and sucked you until you were moaning. You didn't think twice about how wet I was when I climbed on top of you and pushed your cock into my pussy; I was dripping, gushing, and I came almost the second your cock was inside me. You didn't think anything of it—of course, I was just turned on because you're so devilishly sexy.

But you were wrong. I was so turned on because I was thinking about what I'm going to do to you, now—tonight.

I lied to you again. Earlier, I told you I was going out with some girlfriends, that we'd be going dancing in clubs. That wasn't a lie; we went to a strip club and got in the mood for what we're going to do to you later. Strippers always love it when other women come in, especially when they're all tarted-up like me and my friends, wearing tight sexy clubwear and hip fetish outfits. From the moment we entered the strip club, the sexy young women were all over us; guys couldn't get a lap dance to save their lives. Feeling our pussies rubbing against our thighs, wet through our thongs, made my friends and me horny for what we had in store for you. The strippers got us good and wet so that we'd have more energy to do what we'd planned.

You told me you were going to stay at home and work on our taxes. That wasn't a lie; I saw you working on the taxes as I left, and I'm sure you worked hard for a good five minutes, until you were sure I was gone.

The lie I told you tonight was a simple one: I said we'd be out late.

I selected this group of four friends carefully; I know they're all women who can appreciate the pleasure of putting a man in his place. You know them all; two of them, Julia and CJ, work in your office with you. They're your supervisees; you spend your days telling them what to do. That's about to end. Pandora lives next door to us with her husband, Dan; I know from experience that Dan's already found out what you're about to discover, that a man's place is on his knees. Tracie, the last woman in our group, is your ex-girlfriend. You were a little dismayed when you discovered her and me forming a friendship—as you should have been. Tonight, you're going to find out how dangerous it is to let your women talk.

We're very quiet as we sneak in the sliding glass door; you've got the music on loud, dance-electronica like you might hear at a rave or a hip dance club. You've left the door to the bedroom open. You're standing in front of the big mirror at the foot of the bed, the one you like to watch yourself in when you're fucking me. Except now you're not fucking me. You're standing there, swaying in time with the music, a bottle of cognac on the end table. Good: I like the idea of having you drunk for what's about to happen. Drunk and helpless.

You don't notice me standing there at first. I just watch you as you watch yourself, dancing with the music. You're only a little bigger than me; that's why you can squeeze into my white lace thong and you can fit my white garter belt around your waist. The garters descend to the white lace tops

33

of my favorite fishnet stockings. Your feet are bigger than mine, though, which is probably why your feet look a little uncomfortable crammed into my white six-inch heels. You're also wearing my favorite wig, the black bob I put on when I'm going clubbing. Your face is painted thick with my makeup, your lips cocksucker red, the pancake on thick to hide your five-o-clock shadow. You're wearing my white push-up bra, the D-cups stuffed with extra pairs of my panties. Your cock hangs out of the thong, hard and drooling.

CJ kills the music like I told her to. You look away from the mirror, eyes wide, terror overcoming your whore's painted face.

I cross my arms in front of my D-cup breasts.

"What have we here?" I snap.

You begin to make up some lame excuse, but then you see my friends crowding in behind me, laughing as they see how ridiculous you look dressed up like a little teenage tart. Who is the most humiliating for you? Who are you most embarrassed to have see you degrading yourself, dressing up like a cheap street hooker on the prowl for a $20 date? Is it Tracie, who caught you once before? Or is it CJ and Julia, because usually *you're* the one in the position of power, patting their butts and feeling them up as they bend over near your desk? Or is it Pandora, because she lives next door and you have to see her every morning as you back the car out of the garage?

Or is it me, because I'm your wife and you know, now, that there's no more hiding it?

"Don't bother making up excuses," I growl at you. "Just admit it. You've been wearing my clothes since before we got married, haven't you?"

34

Your face is beet red. You turn and start to move toward the bathroom, which is when Julia and Pandora dash into the room and grab you, holding you, turning you toward the rest of us so that we can see you in your pretty lace panties.

"Admit it," I tell you.

Looking down, too humiliated to speak, you nod. I see tears glistening on your cheeks. Sobbing just like a teenage whore.

"Do you know what happens to boys who wear girls' clothing without permission? Tracie already did it to you once. Didn't she?"

Still sobbing, you nod. Maybe you've noticed that behind me, CJ's got our camcorder out, ready to videotape everything we do to you so that I can remind you of what's waiting if you're not an obedient husband, so that she and Julia can remind you of what the board of directors will see if you don't give them their promotion. Not that it matters—I already discovered the cache of videotapes you hid under the floor of the garage. No wonder you were so insistent on buying a high-end camcorder instead of a car stereo.

Julia and Pandora drag you toward the bed. Your ass looks so good in my little white thong, the crotch cradling your balls and your distended cock. Julia is wearing a tiny little spandex skirt and a halter top; Pandora's got a pair of tight leather pants on, and maybe you've noticed the bulge in them. The strippers in the club loved it; they whispered to her how much they adore it when their girlfriends fuck them with their strap-ons. You're about to find out how good it feels.

Julia's not wearing panties; when she hikes up her spandex miniskirt, her bare, shaved pussy is ready for you to service. She drags you onto the bed as Pandora bends you over the edge. Julia tangles her hand in your hair and shoves your face between her spread thighs. You begin to work your tongue, servicing Julia as Pandora unzips her leather pants and takes out her big, flesh-colored rubber cock. CJ comes around the side of the bed, running the camcorder from Pandora's cock to Julia's pussy as if she can't decide which is hotter. Pandora produces a tiny packet of lube from her pocket and drizzles it on the head of her cock before pulling the thong out of the way and guiding her cockhead between your spread, hairy cheeks.

You yowl as Pandora pushes her cock into you; I know for a fact you've taken it this way before, years ago when Tracie caught you in *her* lingerie. But it's obviously been a long time, and Pandora's cock is much bigger than you're expecting. Your whole body shudders as she pushes the strap-on dildo deep into your ass, shoving you hard against Julia so that she can grind your face mercilessly against her shaved pussy. I can tell from the look on her face that you're doing a good job; you eat great pussy when you do it, which isn't nearly often enough. That's just one of many things that's going to change—you'll be eating my pussy every night from now on.

Pandora keeps reaming your ass good, her body pumping furiously as you open up for it, against your will. Julia grabs your hair and wrenches your head up so that CJ can bend down and get a close-up of the humiliation on your face, careful to focus on the way your mouth and chin glisten with the juice of Julia's sopping-wet pussy. Then Julia shoves your face back between her thighs, where it belongs, as Tracie helps me strip off my tight little cocktail dress and buckle into my own harness.

Julia comes with a shudder, moaning and gripping your head to make sure you don't back off at the last minute. When she's done coming, she and CJ kiss, hungrily, their tongues intertwining as you continue your oral service until Julia's good and ready for you to stop. Then, she pulls your head away and gets up off the bed, handing you over to Tracie.

Tracie's wearing a little cocktail dress like mine, and she doesn't have to pull it up very far to expose her bare pussy. But she takes her time, bending over and pushing your head back so that she can talk to you.

"Remember what I told you when this happened before?" she growls. " 'If I ever catch you in lingerie again, you'll get the same treatment.' You thought when we broke up that you didn't have to worry about that, didn't you?"

You nod, your face still dripping with Julia's pussy juice.

"You were wrong," says Tracie, and crawls under you, spreading her legs wide and shoving your head down, forcing your mouth onto her pussy.

Your tongue starts working as Pandora fucks you harder, the base of the dildo rubbing her clit so that she can take her pleasure with your pussy. She fucks you faster and faster as you go right to Tracie's clit, knowing from many years of experience exactly what you need to do to make your ex-girlfriend come. Soon Tracie is moaning as Pandora plows your ass viciously, working toward her own orgasm. But you're a talented pussy-licker, so by the time Pandora throws back her head and lets out a moan of orgasm, Tracie's coming, too. They both come for long minutes as they hold you down and use your body; when they both collapse, panting from their pleasure, you know what's coming next.

CJ gets a good shot of your face as the terror registers on it. Tracie gets off the bed and Pandora pulls her huge cock out of your ass, glistening with your lube. You look over at me and see me there, ready to teach you what you'll be doing every night for the rest of your life, or until I get tired of you. I've taken off all my clothes and I stand there wearing nothing but my high-heeled boots and the leather harness that holds the biggest dildo you have ever seen, several inches longer and thicker than Pandora's. You look at my D-cup breasts and I know you're wishing you could suck them as if I was your mommy. But I have other plans for you.

CJ giggles as she catches you sobbing in fear. A surge goes through my pussy as I realize that terror has really begun to set in. What am I going to do to you? I think you know, and that's what has you so frightened.

I climb onto the bed, pulling your face close so that you can get a good look at my flesh-colored rubber cock. Your tear-shiny eyes look up at me, wide.

"Suck it, bitch," I tell you. "Show me what a little cross-dressing whore does when a big cock's in her face."

You do it so good, I think maybe you've sucked real cock before. You take the thick head of my cock in your mouth, having to stretch your lips around it, it's so wide across. I've got your hair so that you know you'll be expected to swallow it all, or I'll hold you down until you do. You begin to suck my cock.

When I wrestle it against the back of your throat, you gag. I have to try three more times before you take a deep breath and let me push the shaft of my cock down your throat. CJ, Pandora, and Julia utter a cheer and say, "Show 'im, girl!" Tracie's too distracted playing with your balls, crouching

38

behind you so that she can watch as she swats them with her hand. Every time she does, your body jerks and you try to gasp, but your throat is filled with my cock. When I let you come up for air, you're gasping. That's when Tracie balls up her fist and gives it to you once, hard, in the balls. You stifle a sob, and I laugh.

"What do you want?" I ask you.

"I…I don't know. Please let me go!"

"I don't think that's it. You know what you want. Now tell me."

CJ's close with the camcorder, recording the color of your face as it goes deep, deep red, taping your humiliation so that I can enjoy it later.

"Your cock," you say.

"Ask me for it."

"Please give me your cock."

"Where?"

"Up…up my ass."

"Think you can take it, little bitch?"

You know better than to say you can't. You nod, your face wet with tears, with your spit, and with the juice of Julia's and Tracie's pussies.

I come around behind you as CJ settles down on the bed, pushing your face between her spread thighs and videotaping you as you eat her pussy. Tracie takes over the camera so that she can get a good close-up of your ass as I violate it. Your hole is already wide open and slick with lube from Pandora's buggering, but my cock's much bigger so it's still going to hurt. I fit the head into your asshole and push. You groan into CJ's pussy as the head pops in.

I push hard, violating you in one stroke. You have to struggle to take it all, but I offer plenty of help, holding your hips firmly as I shove my cock deep into you. Your body spasms with each stroke deep into your back door; soon you're panting and whimpering into CJ's shaved pussy. She growls at you to keep eating, and you follow her instructions, burying your tongue deep between her folds. She's going to come soon, and so am I. My harness holds a second dildo, thrust deep into my pussy, and the ridge of the one in your ass rubs against my clit as I fuck you. I pound your ass faster and faster as CJ grips your hair, warning you against slowing down now. When she comes, she looks at me, her mouth wide open in a smile, and my orgasm follows moments later. Tracie focuses the camcorder on your face as CJ pulls it out from between her thighs, showing everyone how juicy her pussy was.

I pull my cock out of your ass and present it to you. You look up at me in terror, not knowing what's coming next.

Tracie hands me the camcorder. I take out the cassette and hand it to Julia. "If my husband acts up at work, be sure to show this to the board of directors," I tell her. "I'm sure they'll find it very interesting."

"I'm sure they will," says Julia.

I smile down at your tearstained face.

"Especially since he'll be wearing panties to work," I say. "Panties and a garter belt under that suit, every single day. You'll take him shopping tomorrow, won't you, girls?"

"Definitely," says CJ, giggling.

"Buy him some really sexy outfits. Oh, and Pandora, bring Dan over—I'm sure he'd like to see my husband getting the same treatment he does."

"Yeah," says Pandora. "I'm sure he would."

"From now on," I tell you, "I'm in charge. Me and my friends are going to do whatever we want to you, and you're not going to complain one little bit. You know what happens if you do?"

You nod, miserably, the humiliation evident on your face.

I sigh and smile, my pussy throbbing with anticipation of the many long nights ahead.

Special Occasion

FELIX D'ANGELO
FOR KATRINA

Julie led the stranger by the hand as they entered the motel room. As soon as the door was closed, she grabbed him and forced him up against the wall, pressing her lips to his and kissing him deeply as she let her hands drop to his hips, feeling the weight and texture of his belt against her fingertips. *I'm going to fuck this guy,* she kept thinking as she felt his tongue probing back against her own, as she felt his hands reaching for her ass, squeezing her cheeks, pulling her miniskirt up over the curve of her buttocks. *I'm going to get on my knees and suck his dick. I'm going to wrap my thighs around his face. I'm going to let him put his cock inside me.* As she thought these things, her body responded tangibly—her nipples grew harder than they already were, which was very hard; her pussy seemed to pulse and throb more than it was already pulsing and throbbing. She knew that if her lover put his hand up her skirt, he would find her dripping, hot, swollen—ready for him. *I'm going to go to bed with this guy,* she thought. *This is wrong, so wrong. So very wrong.* She could feel her husband's eyes on her, accusing her, watching everything, knowing every moment, every texture of her transgression—close to her, knowing the taste and smell of her betrayal, the sight of her with a strange man's body against hers.

Unable to hide her excitement, Julie glanced toward the closet door, which was open just a crack. Brian crouched there in the dark, but she couldn't see him—just a narrow strip of black where her husband hid and waited, watching his wife fuck a stranger. His cock was probably hard. Maybe he was stroking it.

The stranger's lips parted. She was panting, frightened but exhilarated. She could feel his cock hard, stretching through his jeans against her belly. Their eyes met and she saw hunger, desperation, a certain exuberance at being about to score with a hot chick. He smiled.

Without warning, Julie dropped to her knees. She could almost feel Brian's eyes on her as she pressed her face against the strange man's crotch, inhaling the scent of him through his well-worn Levis. Her hands were shaking as she pulled open his belt and unzipped his pants; she felt his fingers going through her hair as she reached into his open jeans and found him without underwear, felt his cock, hard for her, naked. She didn't have a single thought to think; instead, she bent forward and took it in her mouth, hungrily. There was no teasing, no invitation—just the spinning of her head as she opened up and slid the stranger's cock down her throat, holding her breath and feeling him there, fucking her throat. She could feel the beat of his heart deep inside her as he gripped her hair and let out a loud, rapturous moan. She could feel her cunt pulsing in time with it.

His pants slid neatly down his slim legs, bunching around his ankles and telling Julie that she'd been right, he really wasn't wearing any underwear. She came up for air and went down again, wrapping her fingers around the base of his shaft so that she could lavish affection on the head, running her tongue and lips all over it. She moaned softly as she licked her way down to his balls and took them in her mouth, savoring them as she rubbed her thumb over his glans.

"Fuck, Julie," he gasped. "It seems like you've been waiting ten years to suck cock! How did you learn to do it like that?"

"By doing it a lot," she said. "And it's been too long."

"Doesn't your husband like getting his dick sucked?"

Julie stiffened, her pussy clenching as she thought of Brian, hiding in the closet, watching, stroking himself.

"He loves it," she said. "I do it every chance I get. But it's still been too long."

"Fuck, Julie. Suck my cock anytime you want."

She took the stranger's cock back in her mouth, both thrilled and haunted by the fact that he'd called her by name. She gulped him down again, into her throat, but she could sense that he was going to come already—and she wasn't finished with him yet.

Gracefully, she slid up his body and pressed herself against him. She could feel her breasts falling out of the thin minidress, her nipples poking through and rubbing against his rough shirt. She kissed him, feeling a rush of excitement as she felt his tongue going into her and understood that he had no compunctions about kissing her right after she'd sucked his cock. She wanted him, she wanted him inside her, against her. Their lips parted slightly and she looked into his eyes again.

"What was your name again?" she whispered. She knew he'd told her in the bar—it was Dave, Tom, Ed, Mike, one of those manly one-syllable names—but all she'd been able to hear were the words Brian would say if he knew, the words he would say if he discovered her in the arms of another man. The fear and excitement had prevented her from hearing anything except Brian's voice in her own head.

The man didn't answer her, didn't tell her his name. Instead, he grabbed her and spun her around, slamming her against the motel room wall and kissing her again, harder this time, while he yanked up her skirt and slipped his hand between her legs. Her arms went up, reflexively—not in front of her, to ward him off, but straight up, against the wall, palms spread, in a gesture of desperate surrender. She felt him plucking the crotch of her skimpy thong out of the way, felt two of his thick fingers sliding into her, discovering her wet, wetter than even she thought she was. He kissed her harder, slid his fingers deeper into her, and with his other hand grabbed the front of her flimsy, almost see-through minidress. She didn't believe it was going to happen, didn't believe he'd really do it—until she heard the long, low rip and felt the fabric falling away in two pieces, leaving her revealed, exposed, wearing nothing but her barely-there push-up bra her tits were already falling out of, and a tiny, tiny thong. A shudder went through her as the air-conditioned air hit her nipples and the gooseflesh spread suddenly across her breasts.

"Oh, fuck," she panted. "You ripped my dress." She didn't mean it as an accusation, or a complaint, but simply as a statement of overwhelming fact—this stranger had literally ripped off her clothes, and now he was going to fuck her.

While her husband watched.

The remains of the dress blew in the draft from the air-conditioning vent as the fabric hung in tatters around her. The stranger bent low and took her nipple in his mouth, sucking hard and bringing a sharp gasp from Julie's lips. His tongue flicked over first one hard nipple and then the other, his unshaven face prickly against her breasts as he pulled the cups of her bra down, tucking them under the curves of her full breasts. His fingers went into her again, three this time, his thumb pressing expertly on her clit, and Julie knew she was going to come—she always came eventually when someone played with her nipples and clit at the same time. She knew it was close, so close, and she begged the stranger not to stop. But there was no need—he wasn't going to stop, not by a long shot. Julie felt herself dissolving into what felt like sobs as she came hard, her upthrust arms curving around the stranger's muscled back as he fingered her deeply and suckled on her breasts, as his thumb pressed her clit in time with the rhythm of her orgasm. She wanted to scream, "I'm coming!" because she wasn't sure he'd know she was—but she couldn't. Instead, she collapsed against him in a shuddering mass of release.

She felt as if she was floating as his hand slipped out of her and he cupped her ass, lifting her against his big body and swinging her around to set her down on the motel room bed. Julie lay there staring up, the afterglow of her orgasm bringing on a sudden thrill of guilt and fresh arousal—*Brian. Brian can see me. He knows. He knows I'm with another man. Oh, god, this is so wrong.* She felt the stranger's hands on her thong, pulling it down her thighs, over her knees and calves, over her feet. Then she felt the stranger gently pushing her legs open, felt the rush of desperation from not knowing if he was going to fuck her or eat her out—and the ecstatic pleasure as she felt the scratch of his face against her inner thighs, felt his fingers opening her up, separating her lips. Then she succumbed to the push of his powerful tongue against her clit as his fingers slid into her again; he fingerfucked her as he started to go to work on her clit with the tip of his tongue.

"Oh, god," Julie gasped as she felt the rush that told her it was too soon after her orgasm—she was too sensitive. She wanted to tell the stranger to stop, it was too much—but she didn't. Instead, she spread wide and accepted the intense sensations as they flowed through her body, as she ached and moaned. His tongue flicked faster and she knew she was going to come again. She never came this soon. Never. Never with Brian. *Brian,* she thought. *He knows. He knows I'm cheating on him.*

She was right on the edge of orgasm, and she would never know if the stranger sensed it or it was merely a fortuitous coincidence that he chose that moment to slip his fingers out of her body and mount her, sliding his body up hers until the head of his cock slipped neatly between her pussy lips, his cock sliding into her body. He was thick, thicker than Brian, though shorter—and he had an unusually bulbous cockhead, shaped not unlike Julie's favorite dildo. Her back arched and she came as she felt the head popping in, and the slide of his shaft all the way into her made her utter a desperate moan as her climax heightened with each millimeter he entered her. He started fucking her slowly, and she kept coming until she was almost delirious with the pleasure, totally dissolved into the sensation of being done. She wrapped her thighs around his body and clutched him tight, coaxing him deeper inside her as he pumped, holding back in case she wanted to come again. But she was quite finished coming, her pussy swollen and sensitive, her clit raw from sensation. She gripped him tight, wrapping her arms around him, and whispered, "Come, baby. Come inside me." It felt strange to call him "baby" when she didn't even know his name—or, more to the point, when she'd known it and forgotten it. But she didn't care—she just wanted him to come inside her, to sow her with his stranger's seed. She begged for it, and he kept thrusting until he let out a shuddering groan and she whispered, "Yes, yes, yes, come inside me, baby, please, I want it." When he sighed and went limp on top of her, she knew it was over—and she knew that Brian knew, knew every moment of her transgression, every instant of her violation, every sight and smell and taste of what she'd done—or, at least, he would.

The stranger rolled off of Julie, kissing her politely and embracing her tentatively. She kissed him back, but didn't move to cuddle him. Instead, they lay there in the sweaty darkness as Julie imagined Brian watching, understanding that she'd done this for him.

"Listen, I gotta get back to work," the stranger said. He got off the bed and pulled up his jeans, buckling them. Julie realized she'd never even unbuttoned his dark-blue work shirt; it was still fastened, the silver-white "Cross-State Trucking" logo glistening in the slanted light from the window.

"All right," she said. "Thanks."

He stood there, looking at her, his eyes nervous as they took in Julie, stretched across the bed, her dress ripped and unraveled, tangled around her mostly naked body.

"Sorry about the dress," he said.

"I liked it," she smiled. "No problem."

"Do you have another dress or something?" he asked.

"Sure," she said. "Don't worry about it."

"Well, I'll see you," he said.

"Yeah," she said. "Thanks."

He came over and bent down, pressed his lips against hers, his rough hands slipping between her legs, cradling her pussy.

"Bob," he said. "My name's Bob."

"Nice to meet you, Bob," said Julie, and patted him on the crotch.

Bob turned and left the motel room, closing the door behind him gently.

As soon as he was gone, Julie got up, turned the deadbolt, slid the chain home. When she turned around, Brian had slipped out of the closet and was lying on the crisp, starched motel-room bed, his cock hard against his belly.

Julie moved to slip off what remained of the minidress, but Brian said, "No, don't. Leave it on."

She reached the bed quickly, not even stopping to kiss her husband before taking his cock in her mouth. She took him deep, his taste mingling with that of the stranger. She felt his fingers going through her hair, caressing her as she let his cock slip out of her mouth and mounted him, spreading her legs as she fitted his cockhead into her come-slick pussy and sank down on top of it, moaning.

"Oh, god," Brian moaned as Julie began to fuck him. "Thank you. Thank you, thank you, thank you."

It had been Brian's fantasy, his whole life. To watch his wife fuck a stranger in a motel room. It had never been Julie's—until she had done it.

Just once, she had told Brian. *I'll do it just once. Once, for you, because it's our anniversary, and I love you.*

"Thank you," Brian whispered as Julie pressed him deeper into her. "Thank you thank you, thank you...."

"Happy anniversary," she moaned softly. But she knew that in the instant she'd felt that stranger's lips on hers, her gift had ceased to be for Brian—and she knew such behaviors would never again be restricted to special occasions.

As they fucked, as she felt Brian's cock inside her, felt herself coming again, felt Brian coming too, releasing himself inside her, Julie imagined the bar across the street, the long line of semis parked, desperate men sleeping in the cramped cabins inside—desperate, horny men.

"What time is it?" she asked as they finished, their bodies still entwined on the bed.

"It's early," said Brian, and smiled.

Lucky

ELLE McCAUL

It's only eight o'clock in the morning, and already I'm making goo-goo eyes at the older man sitting across from me at the chrome-topped diner counter. He's distinguished-looking, with silver-white hair combed back off his head and the air of a rebel about him, even if he has probably outlived most of the rebels of his generation. There's a certain movie-star style to the way he moves, a self-assuredness that I find incredibly attractive. He's like Gene Hackman in *The Firm,* or Paul Newman in *The Color of Money.* Sure, matinee idol Tom Cruise was in both of those flicks, but I've never gone for guys my age. I always crave a man who has seen the world, who has the real-life experiences to know how to take care of a trouble-making minx like me. Because I *do* like to make trouble. Everywhere I go.

After enduring several minutes of my teasing glances, he walks to my table and pulls out the red vinyl chair opposite from where I'm sitting. This restaurant is one of my all-time favorites. Not an updated version of a '50s diner, but an actual diner from the '50s. The sparkly red chairs are now considered vintage. The menu is filled with real, hearty American food— big portions, blue-plate specials. The man fits easily into the surroundings. Even without a verbal invitation, he makes himself comfortable at my table, stares at me, and waits.

"You're very forward," I say, my lips pursed coyly.

"No," he disagrees, and I catch the edge of dark humor in his voice, see the crinkles around his intense green eyes from years of smiling. "It's you, naughty girl. You're the one who made the first move. That's not appropriate behavior at all."

"Oh, really?" I ask, knowing that I sound exactly like the smarty-pants brat I am, but unable to change my tone. "In your world, I'll bet girls are expected to be sweet and shy and demure, right? So who makes these rules up? Do you?"

He won't rise to the challenge in my voice. He sits there patiently for a moment, then lifts my heavy white porcelain coffee cup and has a sip of the hot liquid as if he has all the time in the world. I get the feeling that he's not going to speak again until I behave myself. But I won't apologize, and he can't make me.

"A girl who comes on strong seems desperate," he says finally. "You don't want to appear desperate, do you?"

Now I run my fingers through my short black hair, pushing it off my face. I hold his gaze, telling him my response with my expression alone. No, I don't want to appear desperate—but there's no man around who would think I was. Looking away, I catch my reflection in the polished silver mirror behind the counter. I've got smoldering dark eyes, full red lips, the rarest pale skin. My hair is glossy and thick, cut in a boy's style with a lock that falls intentionally in front of my eyes. As I reach to push my hair away again, he shakes his head once and does it for me. The brush of his warm fingers against my skin makes me tremble.

Still, he's lucky to be sitting across from me, and I tell him so.

"Lucky," he repeats. "You think I'm lucky?" He almost laughs at the ridiculous quality of the question, and then he reaches into his pocket for his battered leather wallet and sets down enough cash to cover my meal. I watch him, mesmerized, as he stands and reaches for me, not helping me by the hand, but solidly grabbing me by the wrist in his firm, powerful grip.

"What do you think you're doing?" I ask, and now there's a vicious sneer in my voice, a hard-edged timbre that I can't shake. Even *I* want to give myself a smarting smack across the face for that tone of voice.

"This way," he says, pulling me after him. I only have time to grab my cinnamon-brown leather hobo bag, and then he leads me from TJ's 24-Hour Diner, out the back way to the gravel parking lot. The gray slivers of stone and rock crush under his heavy footsteps. "Lucky," he repeats again, practically spitting out the word, "do you believe for a second that I'm lucky to be the daddy to a bad girl like you? The games you play. The way you misbehave. Girl, do you honestly think I'm lucky?"

My heart is pounding so hard that I find it difficult to breathe. We've played out versions of this scenario in our bedroom before. James always is in charge when we fuck. He's been my master, and he's been my "Sir"—as in "Yes, Sir," and

"No, Sir"—but he's never been my daddy before. That's the one taboo—the *last* taboo—left for us to cross. Now, my pussy spasms with urgency as he drags me toward his car.

"Misbehaving," he sighs, "just asking for a spanking. *Asking* for it with those dirty looks of yours." He glances skyward dramatically as he poses a question to the heavens, "And she thinks I'm lucky?"

Then the back door of his huge American car is open, and he has me over his lap across the deep blue back seat. My short, red-and-black plaid schoolgirl skirt is hiked up in the back, my white cotton panties are tight on my ass. He strokes me once, twice, before he lets his firm hand connect fiercely with my panty-clad bottom. "Such a tease," he says, "and so fucking forward."

He doesn't swear very often, and I stiffen when I hear the obscenity because I know what that means. It means I've pushed him to his limits, and I'm in for a long, blistering-hot session over his sturdy lap. My bottom is going to be red and raw when he's finished. I recall from experience just how much heat he can bring to my nether regions. James knows how to do it. He concentrates on spreading out the blows evenly—punishing the whole of my ass so that it's hot and throbbing when he's done. Spankings from James last much longer than the actual time of discipline. I feel the aftereffects for hours—sometimes days.

Not caring at all that someone might see us, he slides my panties down past my lean thighs and begins to truly spank my ripe, round ass. His calloused hand connects firmly with my bare bottom, and I can tell that he's not holding back. My ass quivers with the blows, and I close my eyes tight and try to absorb every sensation. Although each spank stings, I raise my hips upward to meet his hand, and I kick my heels out when his palm meets my blushing asscheeks.

As he punishes me, I think about our first time together—me standing outside of the hair salon where I work, catching a quick smoke break between clients. I had long sapphire-blue cornrows back then, and an attitude that was as wildly willful as my hair color. The day we met, I was wearing my favorite pair of skin-tight shiny black leather pants and a long-sleeved metallic silver sweater with no bra beneath. My nipples were cold and hard from the chill in the air, but I refused to go into the salon for warmth until I'd finished the butt.

When he saw me standing there, he pulled the huge red Cadillac into the space in front of me and got out. Without a word, he walked to my side, then stood looking me up and down. When you live in the city, you learn how to deal with strangers. Without a thought, I adopted my best go-fuck-yourself expression, and I stood erect, readying myself for anything. But I wasn't ready for what he did. Gently, he reached for the cigarette from between my lips, and then crushed it out onto the cracked gray sidewalk.

"You're killing yourself with those," he said. "Someone ought to be looking out for you."

"Someone?" I snarled. "Someone like you?" My hand was already on my half-empty Marlboro Reds, fingers ready to pluck the next fag from the pack.

He smiled, as if he could read my every thought with perfect ease. "You need a little authority in your life, don't you, bad girl? You need someone to take care of you." He was so close to me, and I thought I saw dark promises in his eyes. The way they gleamed with a hidden knowledge, as if he understood me. My clothes had suddenly felt far too restrictive. All of my cocky, hardcore confidence had disappeared, and I looked down at the ground, stammering something incoherent. He'd transformed me from savage to servile in seconds.

"No," he said, tilting my head upward. "You don't look away from me. Not when I'm talking to you. Not unless you want to feel the kiss of my leather belt against your naked skin." That's all it took. Dinner at a fancy restaurant that night after work and a spanking back at his home afterward. He made sure my ass was warm and red all over before fucking me. Made sure that I was on the verge of tears before sliding his cock between my legs.

I quit smoking that week, but I retained enough attitude to ensure that I was in for many more spankings, both planned and unplanned. Yet although he's continually given me what I crave, we'd never played like this before. He'd punished me, yes, in public and at home. But it had taken me curling up in bed next to him, and whispering my most secret fantasies, to bring us to this erotic point.

"I need—" I'd started.

"What do you need, baby doll?"

"I need a father figure—" I murmured, blushing, hoping he'd figure out exactly what I was asking for. I shouldn't have doubted him for a second. James seems to read my desires before I fully understand them.

Now, his hand smacks fiercely against my bare skin and I cry out, even though I'm not anywhere close to my pain threshold yet. It takes a lot to make real tears come. But I am close to my pleasure threshold. And so is he. I feel the insistent pressure of his cock straining up at me from underneath. I think about all the careful choreographing that went into this morning's encounter. We drove separately: him arriving first; me coming in late and sitting across the room, ordering my standard breakfast fare of black coffee and well-buttered wheat toast. The flirtatious looks that I sent him were pure concoction on my part, an impish way that I tested his will.

Now, I'm a bad little girl and Daddy's punishing me.

As he does, he taunts me with his words, knowing exactly how much I get off by the way he talks to me. "What did you think would happen to you?" he asks.

I say nothing, because that will get me extra-heated spanks.

"When you act like a royal brat, you get treated like a brat," he continues. "And in my book, your behavior requires the sternest form of punishment."

"Your book," I repeat, my head turned to face the rear of the car. My cheek rests on the smooth seat, and I breathe in the smell of well-cared-for leather. I know I should just bite down on my full bottom lip to keep silent, but for some reason, I can't. I want to talk, want to bring down his wrath down upon me. For every stroke of his hand on my ass, my pussy will flood over with an undeniable pleasure. "Your book," I say again. "Did you write that, too?" I ask. "Along with all those other chauvinistic rules?"

"Oh, baby girl," James sighs, as if deeply saddened by my sorry state. "You really do need it today, don't you? You're craving a punishment that you'll be able to remember later. When you walk. When you try to sit down. Whenever you move."

My pussy clenches at his words, and I kick out again, just to see what he'll do. "Girl," Daddy says, "Don't make me take off my belt."

Oh, I will—and he knows I will. I'll make him take it off. Make my daddy put me over the seat and punish me with his oily black leather belt. I'll make him spank me until my skin is a hot, rosy blush. And then I'll make him fuck me. Because I know my daddy understands. He'll make it all better with a few steady caresses, and then he'll push me up, so that I can sit on his cock, and he'll bounce me to the outer limits of pleasure that erase every wash of pain.

But to get there, I have to push him just a little bit further.

"You think you can make me cry—" I dare, and that's all it takes. James is instantly in motion, pushing me roughly onto the seat. He stands next to the car looking in at me as he slides his belt free from the loops. My heart thrums at an insane speed as I watch every move.

Still without a care that people might see us, he hauls me over the back end of his car and begins to wield the belt with the graceful finesse of a true sadist. He knows how to hit the mark, how to make me shift from one foot to the other. When he admonishes me, I realize that I'm honestly trying to stay in place for him, but unable. Pain blooms with each stripe of the belt. The sensation spreads throughout my body, radiating. Images before me seem clearer, as if suddenly the world has come into sharp focus: the smooth lines of the Cadillac, the rough gray gravel beneath my feet, the ruby-red neon sign of TJ's. Pain is clarifying. James knows.

He makes sure to land the belt on the roundest part of my

ass, striping me there. Then he lines up the next stroke above and the next stroke below. I hold onto the car, searching for purchase. I lower my head and grit my teeth. And I feel the tears start to fall, heavy drops that splatter on the rocks and on my polished patent leather high-heeled Mary Janes.

The rest of this has just been a game. The teasing. The misbehavior. Tolerating the pain of the hand-spanking…but this is real.

"Your ass will be on fire when I'm done," my daddy says, "so don't bother squirming. I'm not going to stop until I know you're truly done."

I try to tell myself to give in. To let it all just happen, wash over me, wash through me. But because I'm a defiant one, all the way to the core, I feel myself start to stand upright, and James is right on me, pushing me back over the car. Holding me in place while he lands the last few sizzling strokes. And then he's behind me, his pants open, his cock out, and he's fucking me against the rear of his car. I feel how hard he is, feel how aroused he is when he reaches one hand up under my white blouse to stroke my breasts.

"You need to be a good girl," he hisses, mouth against my ear as he drives his cock on home. "You need to behave for Daddy." I sigh and close my eyes, feeling the wealth of bliss start to unravel within me. Filaments of pure white-hot pleasure slip through my body, and I half-sob, half-sigh as I sense the climax emerging.

I called him lucky. But maybe I was wrong.

Maybe it's me who's the lucky one, after all.

The Real, Real World

ALEXANDRA MICHAELS

"The Real World," Loren snorts when he catches me watching my favorite MTV series. I'm a decade out of high school, but still I'm addicted to the teenybopper show. I don't even bother to look up as Loren sits on the edge of our raspberry-colored velvet couch and critiques the very concept of the popular program. "They consider *that* the real world?"

"Sure, why not?"

"Being put up rent-free in some fabulous loft in one of the coolest cities in the world while cameras film their every move. Yeah," he sneers, voice drenched in sarcasm, "that's what real life is all about."

"Sounds pretty good to me," I say, not paying much attention to his rants. I don't want to miss even one minute of the show. I adore the soap opera–level drama of the kids' lives, love losing a bit of my daily routine in the fantasy of their world.

"But it's *not* real."

"Doesn't make the show any less fun to watch," I tell him. "In fact," I continue, finally looking over at my dark-haired, dark-eyed husband, "it's the fantasy aspect of the whole concept that I like."

After another moment, he leaves the room, and then I hear a series of odd noises from the bedroom closet. Although curious, I wait for a commercial break before padding barefoot down the hall after him. The emerald-green '70s-style shag carpet tickles the bottoms of my feet.

The door to our bedroom is shut, which is strange. We are an open couple with no secrets between us. I don't bother closing the bathroom door when I do my magical makeup routines, when I highlight my hair, or even when I floss. Loren doesn't shut me out when he's writing his screenplay, or cutting his toenails, or jerking off.

For some reason I find myself knocking on the whitewashed wood rather than rudely flinging the thing open.

"Come on in, Tyra," he says. "I'm just about ready—"

"Ready for what?" I ask as I open the door.

"Your close-up," he says with a grin, and I see that he's set our video camera up on a tripod, and the lens is aimed in my direction.

"No way," I say, but he just stares at me, so I have to add. "You've got to be kidding."

"*This* is the real world," he explains, pointing to me, then back to the camera, then to himself. "This is what real life is like." Although I hear the sounds of the show coming back on in the other room, I've suddenly lost all interest.

"Filming your wife in the bedroom is the real world?"

"No," he says, shaking his head. "I just mean that this—" and now he spreads his arms wide in a dramatic gesture to indicate the whole apartment. As he does, one of our heavy-set upstairs neighbors clomps across the floor. It sounds as if she's wearing clogs. "*This* is the real world. Where the neighbors are inconsiderate slobs who can't keep the noise down. Where people actually work and pay rent and do their laundry at the Spin 'n Dry and sleep and eat and—"

"Fuck—" I interrupt.

He laughs softly, and I notice the camera has a red light on. "Yeah," he says, pulling his navy-blue T-shirt over his head to reveal his fantastic physique. "And fuck."

I think about the different X-rated videos we've watched together, giggling under the covers like naughty kids who've stayed up past their bedtimes. "We're better than that," we often promise each other, but we never have acted on this concept in the past. Not even when Loren insisted that he wanted to watch my face while he fucked me doggy-style, the way I like best. "You make these sounds," he told me afterward one night, "these amazing, dark moaning sounds. I wish I could see your face when you come like that."

And now, maybe, he will—

"I just thought," he tells me, "that since you're addicted to *The Real World*, perhaps you'd appreciate a starring role in your very own reality show."

"I would," I nod, as if agreeing to something deeply serious. "Yes," I continue, pulling the sparkly pink band from my ponytail, so that my white-blonde hair falls loose past my shoulders. "I think that's a stellar idea." As I speak, my hands are busy on my thin white pajama bottoms, and it takes no time at all to peel my pale-blue princess T-shirt over my head.

"Slower," he says, indicating the lens. "Let's see you work a little slower—"

No, that's not right. If this is a reality show, then the camera should catch the real thing, not me doing a faux strip-tease for the hungry eye of the lens. And the real thing is so different from pornos. The real thing is me, pushing my lavender lace panties down my thighs and stepping out of them, then lunging onto the waterbed and making the raucous ripples bounce Loren against the wall.

"Nice," he says. "Classy—"

"Maybe not," I grin, "but this is real."

"So is this—" he says, gesturing to his hard-on, concealed only by a pair of gray flannel boxers. I move my way up the bed until I am situated between his thighs. He looks down at me, strokes my hair gently, then waits. Immediately, I bring my mouth to his cloth-concealed cock and suck him through the material. Myself, I like the way a barrier feels. When Loren goes down on me through my panties, it makes me crazy with yearning. I'm lost between two conflicting sensations. Part of me wants him to keep up the action, while another can't wait for him to push the fabric aside and let me feel his wet mouth against me.

Loren's the same way. He arches his hips forward, begging with his body, and I take pity and slide my hands along the waistband and then pull his boxers down and off. Now, we are both naked, and ready. So ready that for a moment, I actually forget that a camera is catching our every move. That's the wonder of reality shows, after all, isn't it? The moment when people forget they're being filmed, and (to steal from MTV's cult-classic show) start acting real.

"Real" to me and Loren is hard and fast. I climb his body, straddle him with my legs spread wide and my pussy directly on top of his cock. I rub sweetly up and down, up and down, getting his rig wet and slippery with my sex juices. I fuck my vibrating clit with his shaft and he stays still on the bed and lets me work. He knows my favorite ways to do it, and he also knows that I'll never let him down. I cream my body against his until I just can't wait another second, and then I grip his rod firmly in one hand, squeezing exactly the right way, and guide him between my legs.

"Oh, Tyra," he sighs. "Jesus—"

And I buck up and down, using the powerful muscles in my thighs to get the leverage I crave. I want to fuck his brains out. That's my goal: to fuck him until he comes and then just sit there on his cock until it gets hard enough to fuck again. I don't know why I'm this hot, this entirely too horny, but I am. Maybe it's because every few seconds, I remember that we're being filmed, and I imagine what it will be like when we retreat to our living room to watch our own home-made production.

I can see it easily—the two of us on the floor right in front of the TV set, as close as we can possibly get to the screen and still take in the movie. We'll watch, critique, pay careful attention, until the action becomes too intense and we have to re-create the scenario a second time. Real life will echo art as we fuck on the green shag carpet. And if we decide to film *that* round, well, the whole thing will become too complicated to sort out. Where does real life start and fantasy end?

Loren has his own plans, and after a few minutes of letting me ride him, he slips me around in the bed and drives in hard. Missionary-style. His body pulses with electricity. Each time he slides in, it seems as if he fucks me deeper. I'm like a sleeve that perfectly fits his cock, like an elastic band that hugs him tightly with each thrust.

"Jesus," he says again, when my pussy engulfs him and tries to hold him within me. "You're so fucking tight."

Squeeze and release, squeeze and release—it's what I do best. What I do, at least, until Loren moves us both again, and I find that I'm on my hands and knees, rocking with the turbulent currents in our waterbed, and he has taken his position behind me. We're going to do it doggy-style and he's finally going to get to own the image of what my face looks like when I come.

But I find myself suddenly self-conscious. From this position, I can too easily see the camera. I know that the lens is focused on me, and I can't get off while that blind eye is staring in my direction. I feel exposed, and I'm unable to shake the urge to perform.

"Relax," Loren advises. "Let it happen, Tyra."

"Can't—" I tell him.

He grips my hips and drives further inside me. I try to concentrate on the way his rod feels when it pushes into me. His skin is warm against mine. The head of his cock rocks within the mouth of my cunt, creating the most delicious form of friction. I work to pay attention to every subtle sensation. The thickness of his cock has a wicked feeling when it swells within me. The head presses right against the back walls of my pussy, then grinds back out again, leaving me breathless. The rhythm of his choosing is mesmerizing. I find myself starting to relax, starting to lose myself, and right then I see the camera and tense up all over again.

Loren recognizes my problem and diagnoses the cure. Softly, he slides one hand along my thigh and under my body, working to find my happily twitching clitoris. He taps that little hummer with his fingertips, knowing from our years of experience how to tease me up to climax. But even with his sweet caresses, I can't reach the limits with him.

"Forget the camera," he tries.

"No way." Because there it is, watching us, and I suddenly wonder if those kids on *The Real World* ever truly forget about the camera crew. How could they? How could anyone on any of those reality shows every really forget? It would always be a concept in the back of your mind. "Don't say that. Don't do that. People are watching." Maybe Loren's right to be so cynical. Maybe the entire thing is scripted, from start to finish. Every fight. Every frame.

"Don't look at the camera, Tyra," Loren tells me. "Close your eyes and focus on how good you feel."

I *do* feel good. The way his cock pulses within my body takes me to a higher level. Takes me almost all the way there. But I know that we're on film, and I freeze up right at the moment when I should be screaming with release, right at the moment that Loren pulls out and groans as he spreads his come along my naked ass and back. And then he's pushing me down on the bed, on my stomach, and spreading my asscheeks wide apart. I feel his tickling tongue between my legs, flicking from my clit to my ass, bathing that edgy line in sweet heat and wetness.

"Oh, god," I groan, because that sensation is almost too good to handle. I love the circles that he makes with the tip of his tongue, the way he takes his time, rubbing his face against my skin so that I can feel the sharp sting of his five o'clock shadow.

Then he flips me over so that he can get deeper inside of me with his tongue, and he tells me to put my arms over my head and lock my hands together. I obey automatically, and he rewards me with the magical powers of his knowing tongue. And as he plays endless hide-and-seek games with his tongue in my pussy, I start to lose myself. To *really* lose myself. The pleasure is too much to deny. My self-conscious act dissolves. I wonder if this is what it's like for porn stars. Suddenly, you forget you're on tape. You have to forget. Because the sex is just too damn good. I raise my hips, lower them back again, and start to tremble.

When I come, the bed shakes with my orgasm. Our tempestuous waterbed ripples like the ocean, and I climax in a rush, gripping Loren against my body with my legs. Holding him to me. As I open my eyes again, I see the camera and I realize that I really did lose my knowledge of it. For the wondrous moment that Loren made me come, being filmed was the last thing on my mind.

"You ready?" Loren asks, grinning at me.

"Ready?" I repeat, an echo of our conversation before. "Not for my close-up."

"No," he says. "For the viewing."

"Viewing," I say, but this isn't a question.

"First episode ever," Loren smiles. "You know. *Our* Real World."

"The *Real*, Real World," I correct him, as he pops the video and heads down the hall to the media center. I follow one beat behind, entirely naked, ready to witness the transformation of life into art. Ready to experience the transformation in myself. Ready to see myself for real.

A Recent Favorite

Rose Kelley

John Fleck <jfleck@labridge.com> wrote:
> There could be more to the fantasy. But I like
> yours, with the first time we meet in
> person. Explain and elaborate, please.
>
> But maybe there are other fantasies to explore.

> Suzanne Ramsey wrote:

A recent favorite:

I come over to your house for the first time. As we walk in, small talk is made, a little awkward smiling and laughing. You are seeing me for the first time; you like that I wore a skirt and blouse to meet you. I walk across your living room and make a point of checking out your couches. Light comes in through the window, revealing my legs, ass, and breasts through both skirt and blouse. I'm not wearing a bra.

Your telephone rings. You excuse yourself and answer. You're watching me look around the room as you talk. I wander over to the bookcase and pull out a title, thumbing through. It's important to you; you don't like people to be casual with that title. You put your hand over the phone and ask me to be careful. I look directly at you, and drop the book on the floor. It's loud. The person on the phone asks you what the noise was. You make a flustered excuse and hang up quickly. I am still looking at you.

Calmly, you walk over and ask me to pick up the book. I cross my arms and look out the window. You move very close to my face; you could kiss me if you wanted to. We have never kissed. I can smell your skin. I imagine that I can smell your anger. You can definitely smell my fear, but I do not move.

You slowly smile and reach behind me, snaking your hand up into my hair. It's soft. It feels good to me, your hot hand cradling my head. You squeeze your fist and get a handful of hair. I stiffen, unable to move. You move in closer, and your lips brush mine. You say, "Pick it up."

The light from the window on my face shows a veil of sweat beginning to cover my brow, nose, and upper lip. You step back and lower my head down toward the floor, toward the open book with its pages folded underneath it. I reach, and pick up the book. Bent over, you can see the rounded curve of my asscheeks where they come together in the center. You bring me back up to standing. I look into your eyes, and I drop the book again.

More?

John Fleck <jfleck@labridge.com> wrote:
> Definitely, more.

> Suzanne Ramsey wrote:

There is no sound. You look at the book, pages crushed again, then back to me. My breathing seems loud. A struggle of sound erupts in your apartment as you yank my head, leading me face first by the back of the head toward the nearest couch. I wiggle and push away at your body, making little grunting noises, and my feet scrape the floor. You've got my head fast and firm and I trip, falling onto my bare knees. You haul me back up, wailing now, dragging me on faulty legs. My knee is scraped, and my face is flushed red.

Jerking my head around, you sit on the couch. I am half-crouched, pitifully trying to stand. I can't see it, but your free hand finds its way to my blouse, my teacup breasts. One rough squeeze on one breast, the other hand pausing to pinch and pull my nipple. I give a little squeal. You pause, as if to appraise the noise, then move your hand to the center of my chest. With one rip, my blouse comes open. I gasp, and my eyes are wide as saucers.

Your lap roughly abrades my now-erect, pencil-eraser nipples. I'm trying to move away, but I can't. This angers you further, and you haul me over your lap. I struggle and kick in the air in futility. I can feel your erection through your pants, poking me in the stomach.

You switch hands and press my face into the couch, where my sounds become muffled. With the other hand, my skirt gets hiked up over my bottom, with a little difficulty. I'm wearing sheer white panties, and the movement has settled them into the crack of my ass. Suddenly I've become still. I'm frightened.

Shall I go on?

John Fleck <jfleck@labridge.com> wrote:
> Nah, that's enough.
>
> Are you crazy? Of course go on!
>

> Suzanne Ramsey wrote:

I'm trying to be perfectly still, but you can feel me trembling a little. My hips are moving slightly and you can feel them moving against your cock. The heat from my pussy is radiating into your lap. You reach to cup a cheek in your hand and I jump, startled at the soft touch. You grab a handful of my ass and move it, so that my panties go further into my crack. My breathing is now labored, my mouth is open against your couch.

You grab the other cheek, and I start again. This annoys you. I feel your hand move away, and you pull back and deliver a hard smack, square on both cheeks. Crying out, I arch my back and kick my feet into the couch like a petulant child. I'm moving around on your lap, trying to somehow get away from your monstrous hands. You grab the waistband of my panties and lift me off your lap for a second: I hear a ripping sound. You yank them off my hips, leaving angry red scrapes as I try to make it more difficult for you. Your cock is merciless, poking me every time I move.

The panties are shoved down around my knees and keep my legs together. I'm still wiggling, and you plant another hard slap on my ass. The color is changing, and you can see two faint, almost abstract red hands emerging in my white skin. I'm gasping for air, and I arch my ass higher off your lap. It's as if I want more. You comply.

I moan when the third blow is landed, muffled and wet, into the cushion. But you hit my ass harder the next time and I try to move away from you again. You pause and admire the color, rising and deepening. You pass your hand over it and feel that the skin is hot: I hiss from this sensation on my raw skin. You let go of my head and grab the back of my neck, still pressing me down, and deliver a series of sharp spanks, one after another as I yell, scream, and sob. I'm moving all over the place, I won't stay still.

You stop as I cry and take shortened breaths, but only to push the panties down more and shove one of my knees over your lap. My legs are spread now, and you have a full view of my ass and shaved pussy. It glistens. You put your whole hand, flat, over my vulva and cup my pussy. The wetness seems ridiculous, it's everywhere. You take two fingers and trace them over the puffy outer lips, drawing the wetness around. I'm finally quiet and still.

Your two fingers dip into the fold alongside my clit and you press: I stiffen. You slip your fingers to my slit; it feels velvety. I relax. Your fingers slide inside me and I gasp. You leave them there. I wait. You do not move. I can't help it, I start to buck my hips toward your fingers, trying to fuck myself on your hand. You allow it for a moment; when I'm really losing myself you pull your hand away. I whine. You pull your hand back, and begin to spank my exposed pussy.

Had enough?

John Fleck <jfleck@labridge.com> wrote:
> Continue, if you please.
>
> Suzanne Ramsey wrote:

On the first blow, your hand hits my spread pussy with a wet smack. I jump and you have to grab my neck again, and though the spanks are lighter than the pummeling you gave my ass, I'm making mewling noises and breathing hard. On the third spank, my leg slides further to the floor, making my pussy wider. Next spank, you feel the soft, smooth wetness of my outer lips, and the bud of my swollen clit impacts your hand. You stop, push my body up so that my pussy is centered on your lap, and reach to open your fly.

I feel your hand under me as you unzip, move slightly, and your hot, hard cock presses against my pubic bone. The skin is so soft. You move so that your cock is between my outer lips and presses against my clit. With a slow, deliberate movement, you close my legs around your erection, engulfing it in the sticky wetness of my vulva and thighs. With my legs closed, you spank my ass, hard.

I scream and buck, inadvertently plunging your cock up and down the outside of my pussy. I can feel your heat, and I've gotten you all wet. You strike again, and when I writhe I keep my legs together, making a delicious suction around you. Again, and I howl, moving against you. Again, and I sob while your penis rubs my clit in pleasure that's practically unbearable.

You realize you don't need to hold my neck down anymore. That's no fun for you. You roll me off you, onto the floor. I look up at you on my knees, unable to sit down completely, so that my lags are parted and my ass juts out obscenely. You tell me to come to you and lick you clean. You survey me: I'm red-faced, my makeup has made black rings under my eyes, my lipstick is smeared, my blouse is torn open, and my skirt is around my waist. I move forward and begin to gingerly lick your sticky cock.

Are you still awake?

John Fleck <jfleck@labridge.com> wrote:
> Although this is a very soothing and relaxing sort
> of bedtime story, I am, oddly,
> still awake. Continue, if you're up to it.

> Suzanne Ramsey wrote:

My little tongue flickers and grazes your cockhead. I jump when you bolt forward and grab my head with both hands. You put your face very close to mine. You inhale, and force a kiss on my mouth, deep and hard. Your tongue is unrelenting, and you crush my lips. You stop and say, "Like that."

I smile, and stick my tongue out at you. Forcing my head down, you press your cock on my lips, forcing them apart. I finally yield, and open my mouth, sliding all the way down until your pubic hair touches my nose. I choke and sputter. And suck.

You let go of my head and I start working your cock up and down in my mouth. I press my lips together to make a tight fit, and my cheeks go in slightly as I bob up and down. I'm enjoying it, devouring you. But I'm not supposed to like it too much, so you grab my hair again and pull me off, leaving my mouth in an open O shape. You hold me still while you stroke your cock with the other hand, pulling and squeezing, pausing.

You let go and push me hard back onto my ass. I cry out from the pain and try to scuttle away to the side. I turn slightly to crawl but you're fast, on top of me, and I yell again from the rough fabric of your jeans on my tender skin. On my stomach, I reach to claw the floor for traction but can't move. You've grabbed my hips with both hands and dragged me back to you, and I feel your cock nose the opening of my pussy. In one rough thrust, you're in. And you stay there, still, while my pussy convulses around you.

You begin to move inside me, in short, hard thrusts. I'm breathing harder, balling my fists on the floor. You have my hips like handles, jerking me onto you, jerking you off into me. One hand releases and I feel your fingers press my clit, hard, and I start to buck on your cock, trying to make you go faster. You won't. I move harder, until I'm the one pushing into you. The pain of the skin on my ass is lost—until you let go of my clit, grab my hips again, and hold them down as you pull out. I begin to beg you to fuck me.

With both hands you grab my asscheeks, and I squeal. You part them and I know what is next. The slick, fat head of your cock pushes against the opening of my ass, nuzzling. Wetly, you begin to slide in, slowly at first, and my breath is coming in heaves. Your head pops in; it's so tight in there, and you can feel the muscles constricting around your cock. You pull my hips up off the floor, onto your cock, so that you enter me all the way and I shriek. Leaning over, you reach in front of me to grab my breasts, and you roll my nipples between your fingers. I start to grind on your cock, and this time you oblige me, fucking my ass in a forced, jerky rhythm. Within a minute, you can feel my muscles getting tighter around you, and my breathing has quieted. My nipples are very hard between your fingers; you know I'm about to come. Your cock stiffens further inside me as the constriction becomes almost enough to push you out. You shove your fingers in my mouth, and at that instant, I exhale hard and you feel my ass and pussy squeeze down on your cock again and again as I rock back onto you, coming on your cock. The contractions milk you, pull the come out of you, and you go over the edge of your orgasm. You explode and lose control. I feel your cock shudder and your come shoot into me, hot and wet.

Yours,
Suzanne

Auto Erotica

ALISON TYLER

"Red light," Molly announces gleefully, resting her hand on top of Jason's thigh and squeezing. He removes his tie and tosses it at her, and she giggles and uses it to pull her hair away from her face, knotting the expensive scarlet silk in a bow beneath her ebony mane.

How pretty she looks in the pale twilight, her face kissed with a fever-flush of excitement. He smiles at her, and nearly runs the red, but she stops him in time, saying, "Red light," and flicking her bangs out of her face with a triumphant little nod—the same look she wears when she creams him at tennis. Jason unbuttons his blue shirt and pitches it into the back seat where it comes to rest on top of his loafers, belt, slacks, and socks. The only items of hers in the pile are a crocheted white sweater and her high-heeled sandals.

"Red light," she says, "Red light, Jas." He's already down to his striped boxers, still a good ten miles from home. But now his luck changes. They zip through two greens in a row, and Molly, giving him the sweetest smile ever, a light pink color to her cheeks, takes off her white thigh-high fishnets, one at a time, and adds them to the pile. Jason speeds through a yellow—obviously hoping she'll remove the dress—but she calls "Foul!" and rightfully so.

There are rules to this game. Silly rules, admittedly, but rules, nonetheless. It's a spicy, after-work game, a summer-night-on-the-way-home-from-a-show game, an anytime-day-or-night game, if you're in the mood. And the rules are as follows: Driver removes one article of clothing at every red light (full stops, only—if the light changes as the driver pulls up, it's the passenger's turn). Passenger removes an item of dress at each green light. It's safer that way, if you think about it.

But what happens when one is left without any more pieces to remove, and you're still miles from home? That, of course, is where the real fun begins.

"Foul," she pouts. "You cheated. Off with the boxers." He gives her a sly smile, wondering to himself, *Does she really think I mind losing this round?*

"Next stop," he says, "I can't take 'em off while I'm driving, you know."

"At the next light, Jas, you *owe* me. The boxers, plus...."

"Plus...?"

"I'm thinking." The light ahead turns amber, then crimson, and she blushes as she says, "Take them off, and kiss me *there* until the light changes."

There...his sweetheart, his darling, Molly, so shy with the words, but so bold with her actions. She has a difficult time saying "pussy," would never say "cunt," can barely say "cock." Although it makes it that much more exciting for him when she does.

Jason plays fair, now, sliding out of his blue-and-white boxer shorts. As he removes them, Molly hits the "recline" on her seat and he bends and buries his face under her dress. It's a long light, a three-way, and he has time to run his tongue the length of the seam of her panties, from the waistband down and up again, tasting her fragrant honey through the thin white cotton.

"Go," she whispers, and he sits back upright, a nude man tooling along in a black VW, grateful, not for the first time, that he doesn't drive a convertible. They make the next light, and Molly casually peels off her floral sundress. She's sitting at his side in a matching underwear set that he bought her for Valentine's day: white bra and panties made of the sheerest cotton, trimmed in delicate eyelet lace. The car is filled with the scent of heat, the intoxicating perfume of her sex rising. The heady aroma makes him dizzy, near-desperate to stop at the next light so that he can taste her again. But he cruises through, despite slowing, and Molly, sitting up again, slides out of her bra. Her pert breasts are a wonder to see, perfectly round and proud, the way they seem to perch on her slender frame. The man in the next car can't take his eyes off them, either.

"Look at the road," she admonishes, and Jason works his best to follow her command, although he can't keep himself from snaking one hand out to touch her rose-petal skin, the softness of her creamy flesh amazing to him as always. How someone could be that soft, that supple, never ceases to astound him. To thrill him.

"Oh…" she starts, as he makes the next light, because now they're even. Her panties are at the floor by her feet. Her cheeks are the color of the sky outside, a summer palette of colors, ranging from pink to scarlet. She is lovely when she blushes.

"Call it," Jason says, watching the light ahead go red.

"No, wait." And she's right. This light is a quickie, and it turns green before they make it to the intersection. He putts through it, saying, "Down on me, girl, now," and she quickly obeys, moving her slender body in the seat to comfortably reach his cock, drinking him down her sweet throat and suckling. "Keep it going 'til the next light," he tells her, twisting one hand in her dark curls, stroking her naked back, casually losing his hands in the curves, the secret places of her body.

"Dmn't lmine…" she mumbles, her mouth filled with cock. But he speaks her language, knows what she's trying to say. She's warning him not to lie, and he won't. To trick her, he'd have to go through a red, and safety is important in this game. (Let this be a warning to all you lovers out there making mental notes: You don't want to be pulled over by a cop for reckless driving. Not with your ID in your wallet and your wallet in your slacks and your slacks in the back seat of the car.)

She feels him ease up on the gas and move to the brake, but it's only a stop sign, which doesn't count either way. You have to stop. There's no chance to it. No fun. They continue, nearing the residential area by the beach where they live, the streets well-shaded with purple-blossomed jacaranda trees. There are only a few more lights until their turn-off. He misses the first one.

"My turn," she sighs, "Or rather, *your* turn."

He assumes the position, reaching over her to hit the lever that sends her seat all the way back. She giggles as he tickles her pussy with his tongue, then moans at the feel of his stubble brushing the outer lips…then she sighs as he finds the right spot, the perfect spot, and begins to make those dizzyingly tight circles around her clit.

"Mmm," a dark moan, and the sound of her voice gone husky and whisper-soft works to excite him even more. He dips his tongue deeper inside her, going for the very source of her pleasure.

"Green," she sighs, stretching the word out as if it's some kind of release, "Greeeeeennnn." He swallows hard, sits upright, and hits the gas, pulling into the intersection as the car horns behind him begin to blare. Molly stays in the same position, sprawled out in the passenger seat, one hand in her lap, covering her nakedness, like Venus as she stepped free from the ocean, her hand so modestly in place.

He makes it through next light, the last light, and without a word from him, Molly swivels around and takes up where she left off. Her mouth is hungry and open and willing on his cock. She takes him in deep, one of her little hands squeezing the base of his shaft, the other caressing his balls. What he wants most to do in this world is close his eyes and wrap his hands in her hair, letting her work him until she's finished.

But instead, he makes the left turn into their complex. In effect, it's still his turn because he won the last round. Molly blushes becomingly, waiting for his command. He could make her cross the parking lot to their apartment totally nude, if he wanted. He could hand her the keys and follow a few steps

ALISON TYLER

behind her, watching the pretty jiggle of her hips as she tried
not to run.

He doesn't, though. Instead, he says, "Get back to work,
darling," and he revs the engine, switches into reverse, and
backs the car out of their space. She shoots him one puzzled
glance, but doesn't question him, and in an instant he is back in
heaven, with her head bobbing up and down between his legs.

"That's the girl, that's my sweetheart."

He drives down Seventh Street in Santa Monica, looking
for a place to stop, and finds it, finally, a cul-de-sac off the
road, in one of the unknown pockets of wealth. There are no
sidewalks here, just huge houses surrounded by acres of trees.
He misses the second to last light, and at Molly's instant smile
he buries his face between her legs again and feels her pressing
down on him from above, holding him in place with both
hands, rocking her hips forward and hard against his tongue.
She has a difficult time murmuring the word "Green," and he
has a harder time leaving that warmth, the delicious feast, and
sitting upright again. But he does.

The tables are turned again. Molly is now the winner. He
can tell from her smirk that she's got a few things planned once
they stop. That is, if they miss the last light. It turns yellow as
he cruises through, and he doesn't bother to meet her gaze.

They both know what yellow means....

They turn at a stop sign and park beneath a pepper tree,
and Jason motions for Molly to get out of the car. She smiles
as she does, moving quickly. As he gets out of his side and
walks around to her, she turns quickly, facing the car and
offering him her ass—her beautiful, perfect, heart-shaped ass.
Jason grabs her around the waist, not checking to see if she's

84

wet enough. He can smell her scent from where he stands. He thrusts forward, impaling her instantly, and they begin a new ride. Beat for beat, her hips swivel against his, and her breathing catches each time he pushes forward.

She tries to regain her balance by leaning against the car, but he lifts her off her feet and pulls her back down on him, impaling her on his cock. How she sighs when she feels him enter, how she moans when he finds that perfect spot within the tight walls of her pussy, the pleasure spot that takes her to a higher level.

As the ride escalates, she calls out his name, bucking against him wildly. She fucks like that only when she is really turned on: aggressively, dominantly, even with him behind her. It makes his cock grow harder to feel her pulling at him, squeezing with the powerful muscles of her pussy.

Before he knows what is going on, she pulls off him and turns, face to face, motioning with a flick of her coal-black hair for him to switch places. He does, without speaking, and she comes into his arms and then nearly climbs his body, straddling his rock-hard cock, wrapping her legs around his waist.

"Now," she says, moving him against the car, pounding into him, the blush of her cheeks caused by lust, not embarrassment. The glow to her eyes pure and simple, golden in the fading light, violet with the heat of it all.

"Yes," he says, more of a sigh, a whisper, than a spoken word. "Oh, yes, Molly, yes."

They come together, holding each other, moving back and forth with the rhythmic pounding of their climaxes. A sweet, soft breeze picks up around them, stirring leaves and fallen flower petals into a gently fragrant whirlwind. They can smell the ocean. They can smell the heat of their bodies and the silver scent of their sex, mingling. Jason's arms are tight around her body, and for a frozen moment it seems as if he'll never let her go.

But then a car pulls down the street, and they hurry to get into the VW, to hide themselves in the flurry of dressing. As Molly pulls her dress over her head, she smiles at him. "I like that best," she says, crashed out beside him, reaching for his hand.

"What?"

"I like it when the game works out like that."

He grins at her and strokes a wispy curl away from her glistening cheek. And together they say, "A tie."

Domestic Service
N.T. MORLEY

When Heather agreed to take the job as my maid, she knew she
was going to get fucked.

Maybe it was the way she looked during the interview,
flirting with me as if she wasn't sure she was flirting. The
way she would lock her green eyes in mine and then drop
them shyly, not turning her face down—just dropping her
eyes, humbly, meekly, as if to beg for the job. Her tight little
sundress was too short and too low-cut; I could see the outline
of those gorgeous tits of hers right through the fabric, and her
smooth, slim legs looked so good crossed nervously as she sat
on the living room sofa. I never took my eyes off her, though
she kept her eyes down most of the time; whenever she looked
up, she'd see me eating her alive with my eyes. She looked so
cute, hungry for approval, desperate for the job. I could see
her nipples hardening through the thin fabric of her sundress,
and something told me she was wet under that little dress. She

wanted the job bad—and she knew, I could tell, that she wasn't getting hired for her skills at dusting.

Just to make sure, though, before I said she could have the job I mentioned that she might like to try out the pool. She giggled and said she hadn't brought her suit. When I told her that wasn't a problem, she blushed deep red and said she'd pass—this time. She was breathing hard.

I knew she'd be skinny dipping before too long. And not in the pool.

Do you think me a bastard? I am one, I suppose, but the temptation to manipulate and degrade such a luscious piece of faux-innocent ass was more than I could take. If you consider me a ruthless, horny, dirty old man and a heartless, hateful son-of-a-bitch, I'm flattered. But you've got me all wrong. I swear you do.

Because the little cunt was asking for it. Begging for it, from the first moment she laid eyes on me. If I know one thing, it's that my new maid's pussy was gushing wet from the first time she rang my bell. And, however hard-to-get the little tease liked to play, she was aching for the time when I would ring hers.

I offered her the job at a salary of $20,000 a year. It was a stretch with my salary, but more than worth it. I would provide room and board, all meals, and she would have the servant's bedroom on the first floor. I also told her she could use the pool anytime she wanted, and not to bother bringing a suit. "I'm very casual around the house," I told her. "The neighbors almost never look."

It wasn't until she moved in that she found out there wasn't a lock on the door to her room. Or that I provided a uniform for her to wear—clean, starched, black cotton muslin too small through the bust to avoid the gaping I found so fetching, right between her breasts. And short, torturously short, decent by perhaps an inch. Or that I expected her to shower in the pool house, where there just happened to be no curtain on the shower stall and no door on the hinges. Or that the only towels I provided for her to use were just a bit too short to wrap around her slim body, just a hair too narrow to cover her from nipples to crotch. Or that I planned to watch her as she cleaned.

She accepted this all meekly, glad to have a job—and finding, despite herself, that this arrangement sat well with her unspoken needs. She never complained about the way my eyes followed her everywhere, or that I expected her to bring me a nightcap each night while I lay in bed, naked, my hard-on evident underneath the single white cotton sheet as my eyes followed her across the master bedroom. Even if she'd already changed into her night clothes.

She didn't complain, either, when I came up behind her while she was bending over the Queen Anne credenza to adjust the painting behind. She gasped and yelped when my hand drew slowly up the inside of her thigh and slipped between her legs, my middle finger stroking up her slit and finding it bare.

"You're not wearing any underwear," I said, which I'd noticed several times before—the uniform I'd provided for her was exceedingly short and her job required a lot of bending over.

She blushed. "You won't let me do my laundry in the house washing machine," she said meekly.

She stood up and I spun her around, popping away the already strained buttons of her top. They rolled across the hardwood floors audibly. She shied away. I left her like that, her dress hanging open wide enough to show me the full swell of her cleavage, but leaving her nipples barely covered by the edges of the neckline. She blushed a still-deeper red.

"You know the rules," I said. "Only house linens, my clothes, and your uniform."

"Yes, Sir, I know," she said. "I ran out of clean underwear last night. I've never been to a laundromat before. Perhaps I could bend the rules and do just one load of panties?"

"I don't think so," I said. "Rules are rules. But I would be willing to provide you with uniform underclothes, as well. You could wash those in the house machine."

"That...that would help," she said. "I...I would appreciate that."

I left her to do her work and went to make a phone call, then quickly sought out the sewing needles and thread in the kitchen utility drawer and locked them in the safe. The next day, several large express packages arrived at 8:00 A.M. I signed for them and went into her bedroom while she was out skimming the pool. I opened her top drawer, now empty since all her bras and panties were in the hamper. I unwrapped the packages, filled the top three drawers of her dresser with the new items, upended her hamper into a black garbage bag. I looked through the remaining two drawers of her dresser, finding T-shirts, jeans, shorts, sweat pants, socks, two sets of flannel pajamas, a white string bikini for sunbathing, a one-piece swimsuit for swimming or beachgoing. Tucked into the bottom drawer, and wrapped in a T-shirt, I found two battery-powered vibrators, one sheathed in a large-headed phallic sleeve.

I took everything out and dumped it into another black garbage bag, then added the casual dresses that hung on wire hangers in her closet, along with the flats, ankle boots, and tennis shoes from her closet floor. I took her terrycloth robe from the peg near the door and stuffed it in, as well. She'd purchased the garment with her own meager funds on one of her trips to the drugstore—shortly after she discovered I intended to watch her entering and leaving the shower regardless of the insufficiency of the household towels in covering her body. I thoroughly disapproved of the garment.

I knotted the black garbage bags securely and left them by the front door. I could hear the roar of the garbage truck as it edged down the suburban street, servicing the houses leading up to mine. I waited until its mechanical arm was lifting our big black garbage can into the great maw of filth.

"Heather, the garbage needs to be taken out," I called out to her as she bent over the edge of the pool, seeking the company of a struggling bee. "Hurry—the garbage truck is coming!"

"Yes, Sir," she said agreeably, and trotted past me into the house. She ran fast enough that I could see she still wasn't wearing underwear. She had safety-pinned her uniform closed, as I had broken off the buttons when I tore it open the day before. She picked up the bags and ran down the concrete path to the street, a challenging task in the four-inch heels that were part of her uniform. She caught up with the garbage truck and handed the workmen the bags as they leered at her. She walked back to the house, breathing hard. I watched her come up the path, flushed and glistening with sweat.

"Thank you, Heather," I said.

"Yes, Sir," she told me.

Heather never mentioned the discarded clothes, nor did she mention the reading material with which I had filled the third drawer down—probably proving quite problematic since I had taken away her vibrators.

Heather did, however, thank me for my kind gift of underwear to match her uniform. Though, she said with a blush, "they don't exactly match."

"Show me," I asked her.

She lifted her uniform dress and displayed, her embarrassment as obvious as her excitement, the see-through white mesh G-string I'd provided for her.

"You've shaved," I said.

"Otherwise it shows," she said. "My hair, I mean. They're very see-through—the things you bought me."

"Indeed they are," I said. "Show me all of it."

She unfastened the safety pin holding the top of her dress together. I took it out of her hand and tucked it in my pocket. She held her dress open, showing me the push-up bra I'd given her, its bottom half, of white lace sprinkled with pink flowers, stiff to assist in the elevation of her already perky C-cup breasts, its top half, of white mesh, as transparent as her sexual needs.

"All of it," I said.

"Yes, Sir," she whispered, and began to wriggle out of her uniform. With the garment as tight as it was, it took quite some doing, but I didn't move to help her. I heard the hint of a tiny rip as she pulled the skimpy thing down over her shapely hips. She looked down, no doubt frightened of a reprimand from me for damaging domestic property.

When the black garment pooled like midnight around her high-heeled shoes, she stood in it awkwardly as I looked at her, glorious and pale in her high-priced white and pink lingerie, so virginal in color, so slutty in presentation.

"Turn around," I said.

She obeyed, making several circles, each one slower as I instructed her. The back of the G-string barely rose to the top of her rear cleft; it was so thin that it disappeared quite fully even between Heather's slender cheeks.

"I think they match just fine," I told her.

"Thank you," she said, and reached down to pick up her dress. When she pulled it on, I saw the place the rip had occurred—at the terminus of the neckline, the place where the top of the dress met the waist. It was a small rip, perhaps an inch long, but I could tell Heather was worried I'd noticed.

She held out her hand for the safety pin, to pin her uniform closed.

I smiled.

"I'll be having a swim if you need me," I told her, and left, the safety pin still safely in my pocket.

Over the next few days, the rip in Heather's uniform slowly grew; though the uniform's tightness was compromised by the top remaining unclosed—and while my employee slept I had scoured the house for any stray safety pins to ensure that it remained so—its waist was sufficiently snug that the slightest bend or twist of Heather's body created an inaudible tear in the fabric, and soon the dress was all but split down the front. It fell awkwardly off Heather's shoulders and left the top of her G-string revealed. I didn't mention it but watched her more closely than ever as she went about her domestic duties. She pretended not to notice, but I could see her blushing as my eyes followed the uniform's open top and the slowly growing rip.

When she finally came to me, her eyes were downcast.

"Sir, I'm afraid…I'm afraid I need a new uniform."

"Why can't you mend the one you have?" I asked, eyes flowing hungrily from the swell of her lace-clad tits to the top of her shaved pubis.

"I can't find any needle and thread," she said. "Or safety pins. You don't still have the one I was using before, do you?"

"I believe the teenage punk rocker next door put it through her eyebrow," I said. "Why not go to the store and buy a needle and thread?"

"Well, Sir," she said, her voice quivering. "You've been having the groceries delivered, so I haven't been out. And… and this is the only uniform you've provided, so…." Heather's voice trailed off.

"Yes?"

She cleared her throat.

"Well, Sir," she said. "I can hardly go to the store like this."

I smiled.

"Yes," I said. "Quite a problem for you. Luckily, the weather's still warm. I'm willing to let you forego the uniform."

Her eyes wide, Heather shifted nervously.

"In fact," I said, "the kitchen floor needs scrubbing, and I believe we're out of rags. Since your uniform is clearly of no use any longer, perhaps you could use it to accomplish that task."

"Sir," she said nervously. "I…I don't think that would be a good idea."

"Why?" I asked her.

"Because…then I'll have nothing to wear," she said.

"You'll have much to wear," I said haughtily. "I recall buying you a large selection of undergarments just a few days ago. Now get to it—that kitchen floor is filthy."

"Y…yes, Sir."

When I checked in on her later, she was bent over on all fours, scrubbing the kitchen floor with the tattered shreds that remained of her black uniform dress. She had taken off her high-heeled shoes and they sat discarded in a corner of the kitchen floor. She looked quite fetching in the skimpy G-string and push-up bra, but when she lifted one leg slightly to get under the stove, I saw that her knees were red and raw.

I made a quick trip to the garage and returned with a new addition to Heather's uniform. I dropped them next to her.

She looked at the knee pads, her eyes wide, her face confused. Her dark hair was sweaty and mussed, tangled about her pretty face.

"Sir?" she asked.

"Knee pads," I told her. "This task will be more comfortable if you wear them. In fact," I added, "many of your tasks will be more comfortable if you wear them. Let's make them a regular part of your uniform."

"Th…thank you, Sir," she said. "But I don't think…I don't think it's necessary. I don't have to kneel all that much."

"Yes," I said. "A recurrent problem in your perception of your job. It probably explains why the floor is so filthy. That, and the fact that the vacuum is on the blink. The repairman comes a week from Thursday, and in the meantime I think the knee pads should help you keep the carpet clean. Oh, and incidentally, the mop's vanished as well. I can't imagine where it's gone, but the laundry room needs scrubbing as well."

Heather's eyes filled with tears.

"Yes, Sir," she said.

"More importantly, I don't know if you think this is a hippie commune, Heather, but I don't expect my servants to go about barefoot, whatever task they're accomplishing. Those shoes are a part of your uniform. I expect you to wear them, and the knee pads, from now on."

"Yes, Sir," she said.

"Here," I told her. "Let me help you get them on."

With my guidance, Heather lifted first one leg, like a dog, then the other as I slipped the knee pads up her calves and tucked them into place. Then I assisted her in getting the high-heeled shoes on, and she bent over again, scrubbing the floor, now fully uniformed. I had to say, I found her even prettier with the knee pads on.

It took me three more days to fuck her. By then, she was begging for it. All the kneeling and scrubbing, her pretty ass high in the air, seemed to be having the desired effect. Her behind looked more delicious every day, and I found myself anticipating each morning to see what color of G-string I would see on that smooth crotch of hers, what hue of push-up bra would mold her pretty tits as she cleaned the house.

That was my entertainment each day, and I'll admit I gave up TV entirely.

I watched her most of the time, sitting casually and sipping a cool drink while Heather scrubbed or picked at the living room carpet, sheened with sweat, moist with anticipation.

I know she was moist—more than moist, in fact—because I insisted on checking each load of her laundry to ensure she didn't sneak in nonuniform underthings.

Those tiny G-strings I bought her had some variety in color, but none at all in construction. Their unifying theme was that there was no cotton to protect her crotch. And the thin mesh didn't prove to stand up so well to repeated day-long soakings.

Within the week, she was begging for it.

The floors were immaculate, but she continued to scrub. She would turn her butt toward me as she did, wriggling it fetchingly and spreading her legs as if in invitation. The G-strings she wore were so skimpy that I could see the shaved, swollen lips of her sex curving around them, inviting me to tug the string out of the way and fuck her. Still, I made her wait.

Her trips into my bedroom to bring me my nightcap grew more pregnant with anticipation, especially since I had instructed her that she was not allowed to sleep in her "uniform." No other garments remained in her wardrobe, so this meant she now slept nude. Since, when I summoned her from her bedroom to bring me a nightcap, I expected it quickly, she would arrive naked and flushed with exertion from the long trip up the stairs from the kitchen.

I began to make her wait while I tasted the nightcap, to ensure that it had been properly mixed. She would stand, naked, beside my bed, waiting for my decree. Often I decided she had done an insufficient job of mixology, and I sent her back to the kitchen after a long couple of minutes while I sipped and decided. Then, and other times, I also felt unsure as to whether I wanted another drink. While she waited through my leisurely enjoyment of my first nightcap, to see if I wanted another, I started asking her to make that time productive by cleaning the bedroom floor.

While it certainly was necessary—it's amazing how many stray flecks of effluvia could show up on a bedroom floor in just the few hours since Heather performed her evening cleaning—it also had the added benefit of having the very naked Heather wear her knee pads to bed. As she cleaned and I sipped, I watched the nude girl crawling around my floor and addressed, in my mind, the question of when the proper moment was to fuck her.

You think me a boor. You consider me the world's greatest cad, to abuse my employee so. You would be right, but not for the reason you think. I'm a cad because a week was much, much too long. By the time I fucked her, the girl was ready to start humping the furniture.

In fact, there were a number of challenging events in that last week before I took Heather. When, once, I awoke in the middle of the night and entered her bedroom to ensure both that she was following my orders by not sleeping in her uniform and that she was wearing her knee pads (in case I should need to call on her in the night), I heard a familiar rhythmic whimpering noise as I approached her room.

When I opened the door, I discovered Heather performing a shocking act. Stark naked except for her knee pads, she had her knees a great distance apart, and as she firmly pinched one nipple of one perfect teacup breast, she fucked herself violently with the four-inch heel of her uniform shoe.

Doubtless it was the only oblong item the poor girl could find for relief: I had scoured her room to ensure that no candles, perfume bottles, or toothpaste tubes could satisfy what I suspected was a quickly mounting need. Clearly, I had overlooked this one critical item.

I could see every detail, as Heather had left the light on. I saw *why* she had left the light on—one of the magazines I'd provided for her was opened beside her on the bed, turned to a page of a girl dressed as a French maid kneeling and giving head to a rather improbably endowed man in a tuxedo.

Her eyes, however, were shut tightly, as the photograph had surely served its purpose and been forgotten as her own physical pleasure took precedence. Her mouth, unlike her eyes, was open, and her lips moved softly as her soft moans of pleasure were punctuated with deafening *Yeah, Daddy*s and *Fuck me, Daddy*s and *Make me scrub the floor, Daddy*s. Heather was so engrossed in her self-abuse that perhaps three long minutes passed before she noticed I was there—and by that time, I could tell by the rising timbre of her moans that she was very close to reaching completion.

By that time, also, I was bent over her, my face quite close to hers as I snapped my fingers. It was perhaps the twelfth snap—and the loudest one—before she heard me over her moans, and I had thoughtfully saved the loudest snap for what I suspected was the very instant before Heather's orgasm.

"Shameful," I said. "I won't have it in my house."

She gasped and looked up at me, her eyes wide. In an instant her face went from lustful pink to humiliated crimson. Her mouth, already opened wide to accommodate her rhythmic panting, worked helplessly as she struggled to find appropriate words to explain her behavior.

I reached down and unbelted my black silk robe, letting it fall open to reveal the length of my hard-on.

"See what you've done?" I asked. "And you call yourself an employee!"

"I'm...I'm sorry, Sir!" she exclaimed.

I plucked the high-heeled shoe from her hand and tossed it unceremoniously into the wastebasket by her bed.

"Clearly you can't be trusted with shoes," I said. "You give me no alternative."

"Sir?"

"We can't have you walking around barefoot," I said. "So there will be no more walking, in the house or out of it. Luckily, you've got knee pads. I suggest you put them to use from now on."

"Sir?"

"Starting now," I said, gesturing toward my hard-on and glancing toward the magazine she'd left open.

Heather's face, already red with exertion and arousal, went deeper crimson in a moment as her eyes ran with obvious fright up and down the length of my turgid organ. I stepped back from the bed and sat in the room's single chair, a simple wooden one near the bed.

"Well?" I asked.

Trembling, Heather crawled off the bed. Clearly the girl could take orders; rather than getting to her feet and then kneeling, she presented herself first on her knees, descending from the bed and putting her knee pads for the first time to the use for which they were intended. Her face found my crotch with expert familiarity.

No sooner was her mouth on my cock than I heard her moan in long-squelched hunger. Her obvious need to suck cock bubbled over and displayed itself in the fervent way she gulped my entire length down her hungry throat. The girl, for all her coquettish charm, had clearly done this before. Whether she'd ever done it with knee pads on was another question, but one I didn't care to address.

I sighed in satisfaction, watching Heather's pretty face as her eyes turned up to meet mine, her lips curved tightly around the base of my cock. She began to bob up and down desperately, her eyes wide and hungry for my come. I had merely planned to take her mouth, but Heather was so lovely I simply couldn't resist. I snapped my fingers.

"Admirable, but not good enough," I said. "If a spike-heeled shoe is good enough for you, surely a hard cock would be more appropriate."

Just the barest hint of the girlish coquette returned for an instant, and then the hungry domestic whirled round, putting her ass high in the air and spreading her legs. When I snapped my fingers, she looked over my shoulders, realizing only after a second displeased gesture that I meant to inform her I had no intention of doing any of the work. She hunkered down on her elbows and lifted her ass higher, scooting back and wriggling her dripping cunt onto the head of my prick. So swollen were her sex lips that she had to reach back to spread them with her fingers before she could wrestle the prodigious knob of my organ into her tight channel. Pushing down onto it, Heather let out a great moan of exertion, then a long, low whimper of pleasure as her wet snatch slid with great difficulty down my shaft. When she'd pressed her pussy lips around the base of my cock, she began to moan the phrases that had been so compelling to her while she'd fucked herself with the shoe. *Yeah, Daddy! Fuck me, Daddy! Make me scrub the fucking floor, Daddy! I'm your whore, Daddy!*

With that, she began pounding her ass back onto me, violently ramming my cock into her. While I certainly enjoyed watching her do all the work, I knew that requiring her to fuck herself onto my cock would ensure that her rhythm would bring the little slut off, proving to her once and for all that the place she was born to live was not in my servant's quarters, but impaled on the long shaft of my cock.

And it did, within moments, the desperate pumping of her hips driving her suddenly and, clearly, almost painfully into orgasm so that her whole body shuddered and the muscles of her sex gripped me rhythmically with a fervor no cunt I've had has ever offered. Her orgasm continued while I lifted my ass off the chair, hoisting myself on my haunches so that my powerful thrusts lifted Heather fully off the floor, rendering her knee pads unnecessary. I grabbed her hips and put one foot down, providing the necessary leverage to elicit a long, inhuman wail from the girl's lips as I fucked her. Then, with a great moan, I pulled my cock out of her and spun her around, tumbling Heather onto her back as I stroked my cock over those lush, firm-nippled tits I'd spent two weeks admiring. Streams of come shot out onto her bosom, and Heather, moaning, rubbed the liquid into her orbs, cooing and sighing as she slicked up her tits with the glistening thickness of my sperm.

With a shudder of my own, I collapsed onto her, locking my lips to hers and thrusting my tongue into her as we both panted, exhaustion seizing us.

When our lips parted, Heather looked into my eyes and said in staccato syllables between great trembling gasps:

"What...the...*fuck* took you so goddamn long, Honey?"

"You loved it," I said with a sneer.

"Fuck you," she said. "I'm going to make you pay for every goddamn minute of the last two weeks."

"Promises, promises."

"Yeah, you *wish* they were just promises," she said.

You think me a cad, perhaps, a boorish low-mannered simpleton who abuses his subordinates and ravishes younger women. You'd be right, but not because I fucked Heather silly, nor because I stripped her of her dignity, humiliated her ritually, and exploited her desperate need for approval.

Rather, I'm a cad because it pleased me so much to make my horny little slut of a wife wait. She *did* love it, I swear, but she'll still make good on her promise.

You see, Heather's decided she needs a butler.

And with her wide hips, she happens to be just my size.

Mile High

SIMON TORRIO

For as long as she could remember, Vanessa had wanted to do it. Ever since the first time she'd heard about it, when she was young, when someone had made some funny comment about the "Mile High Club" and that someone else was a member, implying that anyone who was—a girl, at least—was a terrible slut. Maybe that's what she liked about it—the idea of being a real slut, having sex in the most cramped, risky, dangerous place possible, risking arrest, public humiliation…just thinking about it caused a shiver to start between her legs and go all the way up her spine to the back of her head. She'd wanted to do it ever since.

But just going on a trip with a lover and fucking him in the restroom wouldn't be as naughty as fucking a stranger you met on the plane, would it? That was Vanessa's fantasy, and Daniel was more than willing to indulge her.

Which is why, when she saw Daniel clamber out of his

seat and head back toward the restroom, Vanessa casually got up herself. Making a show of stretching, Vanessa glanced around to make sure no one was watching—at least, no one who would realize that someone else had just gone back toward the restroom. Then she hurried back there.

She reached the restroom just as Daniel went to close the door. She put her hand on the door and glanced over her shoulder as if to indicate that no one was watching. Daniel stood there for a minute, the restroom door open, staring at Vanessa in mock disbelief. He looked at her pretty face, noting the few strands of long hair that fell in disarray from the neat bun at the back of her head. Then his eyes roved down over her full cleavage, the low-cut blouse, the neat, businesslike, straight skirt just a little shorter than it should have been. He had seen her a million times nude, had fucked her in every position possible. But now, she was a stranger to him—a mystery, her body fresh and new as if he'd never seen it, never touched it, never been offered it shamelessly.

Today, Vanessa and Daniel were strangers. Clearly she was traveling on business, like he was—who else travels in a suit and tie, especially on a late-evening flight? And clearly, she liked to show a little leg when she was otherwise conservatively dressed. Daniel smiled his approval and stepped back to allow Vanessa to slip in; she glanced over her shoulder one last time to make sure no one was watching, and then she entered, latching the door behind her.

The restroom was exactly as cramped as it always was in her fantasies; their bodies were pressed together much closer than they would have been if they'd been hooking up in other circumstances. This sudden rush of forced intimacy excited

Vanessa, and she pressed her lips to Daniel's, forcing his mouth open with her tongue as he reached down and began to pull up her skirt. God, was she actually going to fuck him in here? Vanessa was a small woman, but she could hardly imagine making room for intercourse here in these cramped environs. Then again, the mere thought send a shiver through her body. Daniel gathered her skirt over her ass, discovering that she wasn't wearing anything but a garter belt and stockings underneath.

"I never travel with panties," she whispered warmly into his ear. "I have to wear stockings to business meetings, but nobody says I have to wear underwear."

His finger tucked its way between the cheeks of her ass, reaching for her pussy; he discovered how wet she was and seemed to finally accept that she wanted to fuck him—here, now, in the airplane's restroom. Vanessa pulled off his red-and-blue striped silk tie and began to unbutton his shirt as he lifted his fingers to her mouth; eagerly, she licked herself from his fingertips and put her hands in his open shirt to feel his bare chest, reveling in the soft, dark fur there. He unbuttoned her low-cut blouse and found an even lower-cut bra, front clasp. He made short work of it and Vanessa felt his thumbs against her nipples, gently rubbing them into full erection as she gasped.

He dropped the toilet seat and pushed her down onto it, kneeling and curling his body into a ball so that he could get his face between her legs. Vanessa's eyes went wide as she spread her thighs for him and felt his tongue on her clit, pressing expertly against it as he began to finger her. She moaned softly, frightened but unable to stop herself, praying that the noise of the engines and the wind would cover the sounds of her excitement. Daniel's tongue wriggled between Vanessa's lips and lapped at her slick pussy. She whispered, "Yes, yes," but he didn't need any encouragement; he moved from her pussy to her clit and back again, building her up slowly until she was pulsing with anticipation. His hands moved up her body and caressed her tits. Vanessa arched her back and pressed her breasts into his grasp.

She felt his palms against her firm buds and then felt him working them with his thumbs, first rubbing, then gently pinching. Vanessa always came like a rocket when she felt a tongue on her clit and her nipples being pinched; it was as if the "stranger" knew this instinctively. "Harder," she begged him, and he didn't ask whether she meant harder on her clit or harder on her nipples; he gave her both, his tongue pressing roughly and rhythmically on her clitoris as he pinched her nipples so hard it would have hurt terribly if she hadn't been so turned on that all she could feel was pleasure. She grasped at the aluminum handrails as the airplane bucked and swayed a little; was it turbulence or Vanessa's orgasm? They came shuddering on her at the same time, pleasure overwhelming her as the sudden movement of the airplane tossed her easily up in the air. She felt as if she was floating in space, Daniel's tongue and fingers her only connection to the world. She came hard, biting her lip to keep from moaning louder. Then came the sound of the intercom.

"Ladies and gentleman, the Captain has turned on the 'fasten seat belts' sign; we should be experiencing turbulence for the next few minutes. If you're up around the cabin, please return to your seats at this time until the Captain has turned off the 'fasten seat belts' sign."

"Quick," she gasped. "Before they catch us."

She reached down and pulled him to his knees, groping desperately at his belt and unzipping his pants. She reached in and found a very hard, very large cock tucked into his respectable silk boxers. With great effort, Vanessa bent forward and took it in her mouth, tasting the hard cock. All those years of yoga had finally paid off; despite the awkward position, she could get her mouth halfway down Daniel's cock, and it tasted marvelous. She ran her tongue all over the head of his cock; he was already oozing pre-come.

There was a knock at the door.

"Excuse me, the Captain has turned on the 'fasten seat belts' sign. You'll have to return to your seat."

She reluctantly pulled her mouth off his cock, knowing that they had to work fast.

"Just a moment!" she called. "I'm feeling sick. I'll be right out."

She bent forward and licked his cock a few more times, then looked up at him, made eye contact, and whispered, "Fuck me."

It wasn't easy doing so. As petite as Vanessa was, he was rather large—in body, not just in cock. She struggled into position with her knees on the seat of the toilet, her ass in the air, her skirt bunched around her waist. She reached back, parting her lips with her fingers as she felt Daniel position himself behind her, his hard cock pressing urgently between her bare cheeks. Shifting, Vanessa felt her stockings catch on the edge of the aluminum surface and rip. She didn't care; she pushed back against him and spread her legs as far as she could in the cramped space.

"Fuck me," she repeated.

He was inside her in an instant, her pussy swollen and tight with arousal—but dripping wet. As tight as it felt, and as big as he was, it went in easily. She loved getting fucked from behind; she felt as if she could feel every vein of the big cock, every contour of his organ. He reached around and took Vanessa's breasts in his hands, pinching the nipples and making her gasp as he fucked her from behind, faster and faster.

She managed to lean back, put her hand on his face, and kiss him gingerly as he leaned over. God, she wanted him. She wanted him everywhere.

"Do you want to give me more?" she whispered.

He looked at her, eyes wide, and nodded slowly.

Vanessa leaned forward, exhaling as she felt his cock slip out of her. She reached into the pocket of her blouse and found the tiny pillow of lube she'd placed there. Breaking it open with her teeth, Vanessa reached back behind her legs and found the hard cock waiting for her, then drizzled lube over its head.

She lifted her hips and wriggled her ass, guiding his cockhead between her cheeks, helping him find the right place.

"Fuck me in the ass," she whispered.

Disbelieving, he hesitated. Vanessa pushed back onto him, feeling his cockhead, slick with lube and with her pussy, pressing against her asshole. She pushed harder, and finally he started to believe she wanted it that way. The gentle roll of his hips met hers, and Vanessa's eyes went wide as she felt his cockhead entering her.

"Oh god," she whispered. "Yes. There. Right there."

Without any warm-up, it was almost too intense for

Vanessa to take. There was a quick flush of pain, melting into a wave of fear and an urge to pull off him. But Vanessa had been wanting it like this for as long as she could remember. It wasn't just being fucked in an airplane restroom—it was being fucked like this, in the ass, on her knees, in the dirtiest way possible, her begging for it, asking for it, pushing herself onto this "stranger's" cock. Despite the initial discomfort, Vanessa felt her ass relaxing, felt it opening to accept the shaft as the businessman slid it into her, as she pushed back onto him, impaling herself on his cock.

"Yes," she moaned. "Oh god yes."

As good as it felt, she never would have come again with him fucking her pussy. But now, as she felt his cock filling her ass, pushing down into her G-spot, she knew she was going to come—and fast.

The plane lurched, swayed. Another knock on the door. "Ma'am, are you all right?"

"I'll be out in a minute!" Vanessa called. Then, under her breath, "Fuck me in the ass," she begged. "Fuck me hard."

He began to fuck her gently, gingerly. "Harder," she moaned softly, and he started fucking her the way she wanted it. She reached down and started to rub her clit, faster, faster, in circles as he pumped her ass. She had to bite her lip hard this time to keep herself from screaming as she came—it was so intense she thought she might pass out, but it was just the plane swaying and throbbing with the turbulence, forcing their bodies together, forcing her harder onto his cock. She heard him groan behind her, felt his cock, so tight in her ass, pulsing as he came. She forced herself back rhythmically onto him, her body still contracting with her own orgasm as he finished his.

It was several more minutes before she could pull off him, struggle around, and kiss him. She fastened her bra, buttoned up her blouse, and pulled down her skirt. She could feel his come leaking out of her ass, slick and hot between her cheeks.

She kissed him one more time, then opened the door. Squeezing out, she saw the young, pretty stewardess standing close—not quite close enough to see that Vanessa wasn't alone in there, but close enough to give her a head start.

"Are you all right, miss?" the flight attendant asked.

"I'm sorry," said Vanessa. "I got a little airsick."

"Well, let me help you back to your seat," said the flight attendant, irritated. Vanessa made a show of being weak and wobbly on her legs, but it wasn't much of an act. She could feel the come leaking down the backs of her thighs, oozing out of her. She glanced back just in time to see that he had slipped out of the restroom while the flight attendant was occupied. He was now ensconced comfortably in his seat, his tie knotted flawlessly.

As soon as she disembarked, Vanessa rushed to the nearest airport bar and had a stiff Scotch. She could still feel her ass—slick in the center, sticky on the cheeks, with trailing moisture drying slowly down her thighs, sticking her businesslike skirt to her flesh. Just the thought of it made her feel warm again, a surge going through her body as she thought of what had been done to her—in the restroom of an airplane, the naughtiest place possible.

She stopped in a nearby restroom and fished her extra pair of panties out of her carry-on bag. She slipped into them and felt much safer, though a very slutty part of her missed the feel of come dripping down the backs of her thighs. She rushed to baggage claim and found her red suitcase circling forlornly on the carousel.

Outside, she found Daniel already waiting for her in the rental car—an anonymous copper-colored four-door. He smiled as she tossed her suitcase in back, got into the passenger's seat, and kissed him.

"Have a good flight?" he smirked, running his fingers through her hair.

Vanessa ran her hand down the red-and-blue striped silk tie Daniel wore.

"Out of this world," she smiled. "But I can't wait to get out of these clothes."

"Me neither," he said, and put the rental car in gear.

Tonight

ELIZABETH COLVIN

I've been saving it for you. I know it's a big fantasy of yours; you confessed as much after our long first night of making love, when we both lay tangled in the sheets. I've even showed you my cock, watching as you squirmed a little, contemplating what it would feel like to take it inside you. You seemed so titillated that I've done this before, that I seemed so casual about it. Maybe you thought I'd want to do it right away, and in one sense I really, really did. But I've saved it, waiting for the perfect moment to surprise you with it.

I know tonight's the night. It's a Friday night; both of us have had long days at work. While you're downstairs making dinner, I take a long hot shower, feeling my muscles relax and my pulse quicken as I think about what I'm going to do to you tonight. I step out of the shower, towel dry, and take out the strap-on harness. As I fit the dildo into place and step into the harness, I picture you splayed before me, taking my cock into your ass. I can feel the pulse of my pussy as I buckle up the straps of the harness.

I put on a T-shirt without a bra and a faded pair of jeans just tight enough to display the long, hard bulge plainly in front. I go downstairs to the kitchen, where you're chopping vegetables. Your butt looks so good in those boxer shorts you're wearing; I get more excited as I come up behind you, put my arms around you, and grind my crotch against your ass.

You tense against me, then relax. I put my lips very close to your ear and breathe warmly. "I've got a very special surprise for you tonight," I tell you, just as you realize what the bulge against your ass means.

You catch your breath, squirm against me. I reach down under the counter and feel your cock swelling in your boxers. I smile and kiss your neck, satisfied that I've had the desired effect. I back off and go into the dining room to set the table.

All through the delicious dinner, I can see the anticipation and nervousness on your face. I can see you shifting uncomfortably in your seat.

When we've both finished, I smile and ask if you'd like to watch some TV. You catch my drift right away; we go into the living room and recline on the couch. You relax into the soft cushions and I lay alongside you, careful to place myself in the superior position, atop you, leaning hard, letting you know that you can't get away. I know you want this; I know you want it even more than I do. But even if you changed your mind, there's a part of me that wouldn't care. Part of me would wrestle you down, drag your ass up high in the air, and give it to you without lube, listening to you scream as I take your ass with all the force of a heartless, uncaring bastard, the bastard you so sweetly need me to become. I know there's always a chance of you backing out, chickening out on me. And there's a part of me that wants you to, so that I can date-rape you. You think you can flash that adorable ass at me in those tight boxer shorts and then not give it up, you tease? Not a chance. You're going to put out whether you want to or not—you know it and I know it, and that's why I'm so fucking wet.

You seem to be paying extra attention not to touch my crotch—maybe a little frightened of it? But I can see that your cock is half-hard under your boxers.

You pick up the remote and ask what I'd like to watch. "Start the DVD player," I tell you, and you do. The wide-screen TV is filled with an image of a gorgeous guy down on his knees, using his mouth on a woman's strap-on. He's young, younger than you, and she's a standard-issue porn bimbo. But her strap-on is huge, and he's sucking her cock as if it's the sweetest thing in the world. He's sucking her cock as if he's desperate for it. Her cock is peach colored, just like mine, matching her light skin tone so that it almost looks as if she's a hermaphrodite wearing a leather cock ring. Almost like it's a real cock. Almost like she's going to shoot her come all over his face, down his throat. Or is it that she's going to roll him over and shove her cock up his ass, filling him up with her magical sperm? My pussy is tense, so tense, swollen with anticipation and hunger, alive with all the possibilities of having a cock.

I feel you squirming. I put my arms around you and kiss your neck.

I'm a little afraid I've gone too far too fast; after all, I've done this before many times, and you haven't. "Shhhh," I tell you soothingly. "Don't worry, I'll go slow. You'll open right up for me. That ass of yours is beautiful. I'll slick you up right before I ram my cock in you." You tense at my aggressive words—but then you seem to relax, knowing I'll take care of you. I always have, and I always will.

We sink into the couch and begin kissing, my nipples hardening under the T-shirt as you run your hands over them. I stroke you through your shorts, feeling how hard you've gotten—hard, insistent, as you grind your hips against my hand. You want me to jerk you off? You want me to suck your dick? On any other night, that's exactly what I'd do—I'm as hungry, as savage, as much of a little piggy as you are. I want to suck you as bad as you want to suck me—but you need it more. So tonight I'm the one who's going to get sucked. You're the little cockwhore, down on your knees servicing me. You're going to swallow me, deep throat me, and then you're going to roll over and put your ass in the air.

Your hands feel good on my breasts, but I want you to feel the tool that's going to violate you, make you mine. I take one of your wrists and push your hand down into my crotch. Your fingers curve around my bulge, stroking it as if it were a real cock, your body tensing as if every stroke of your hand reminds you of how it's going to feel sliding down your virgin throat, being pushed up into your virgin ass. I moan softly as if it was really my cock; the feel of pressure on the base of the dildo is rubbing my clit and I almost think I could come. I almost think you could jerk me off. And the best thing about my cock is that when I shoot my load it doesn't go soft. It just gets harder, and I get hornier than ever. I stroke your cock as you stroke mine—and then, to my surprise, you bend down and unzip my pants.

You look up at me, a little scared, a lot hungry. God,

you look like a fourteen-year-old girl about to suck her lover's cock for the first time—just like I was, ten years ago, when I did it the first time. It's the sexiest thing I've ever seen—your gorgeous face, about to be penetrated by my hard cock. Your gorgeous face, not knowing if it belongs to a fag or a whore or a little virgin girl—just knowing, beyond the shadow of a doubt, that it belongs to a cocksucker.

"You give head, baby? You suck cock? Yeah, I've been wanting you to suck my cock since I first laid eyes on you. Suck it. Come on, don't be shy. I won't tell anyone. Just suck it. I know you want to."

And you do, looking up at me a little scared at first, but then giving in as a rush of sudden hunger comes over you. You take my cock in your mouth and swallow it.

It's been a long time since I had a lover who was willing to play this way with me; I feel my pulse pounding as I watch you savoring my cock, sucking it. I coax you on with dirty words: "Oh, yeah, you look so good sucking that…you're so pretty with your mouth around my cock." The dirty talk seems to heighten your interest, and you slip your hand down between the straps of the harness to work two fingers inside me, pressing up against my G-string. I run my fingers through your hair as you bring me closer to orgasm, getting still closer when your thumb works its way under the base of the dildo and presses my clit. I could almost believe my cock is real, that you're sucking me off and I'm about to come in your mouth. The thought sends an explosion of hunger through me and I come, unexpectedly, all of a sudden, in an intense rush of sensation. "Oh yeah," I tell you. "I'm coming in your mouth. Swallow it…."

But I'm far from satisfied; my cock doesn't get soft when

you suck it off. Rather, my appetite for more of you has been heightened, and I guide you onto your back so that I can lift your legs up over my shoulders and raise your ass off the couch. I put my mouth on your balls, totally ignoring your cock though my mouth is watering for it. Tonight I want to pleasure you another way.

I lick lower and part your cheeks gently, reaching down to take the dental dam from where I've placed it under the couch, getting it out of the plastic bag, stretching it between your cheeks. My tongue finds your musky, puckered hole, wriggling inside as I feel it loosening up. You moan as I lick my way up and down your crack. I can tell you're ready for me, and I smoothly reach under the couch to where I've stashed the towel and the lube. I spread the towel on the couch, then lean back and look at you.

"You want this?" I ask, glancing down at my cock. "You want me to fuck you in the ass?"

You nod, hungrily.

"If you want to get fucked, get up on your hands and knees. Put that pretty ass of yours in the air."

You do it, positioning yourself over the towel the same way I've done more times than I could count. You gasp as you feel the cold dribble of lube between your cheeks; I rub more of it on my hand, warming it before sliding one finger into your asshole. You're really very tight; it excites me that you've never done this before. I put more lube on the head of my cock and rub it all over, then gently nuzzle my cockhead into the cleft between your buttocks.

I use one hand to guide the dildo and one to reach under you, stroking your cock as I press into you. "Breathe out," I tell you, and push the head in; you take a sharp breath as you feel it popping into you. I've selected a particularly small dildo, but it's still a big step for someone who's never been fucked like this. I feel your muscles tense underneath me; then slowly you relax and I sink into you, stroking your cock as mine enters you all the way.

Hearing you moan like this turns me on all over again. I could easily make myself come, but now I'm more interested in feeling your cock surge and spurt in my hand. I lift myself up with one foot on the couch so that I can have more control as I slowly give you my cock, stroke after stroke. I hear nothing but pleased noises from you, but I'm very careful to go slow—however much I want to fuck you harder and harder until you scream.

The whole time, I'm fondling your cock, feeling it hard in my grasp, feeling dribbles of pre-come running down from the head. It would be easier if I made you stroke yourself, but I want to feel it as you come with my cock inside you. I hear your breath quickening. I pump your cock harder, sensing your anus loosening as you relax into the sensations, then tightening as you get closer to orgasm. Then, all at once, I realize you're at the point of no return. Your body shudders, your cock throbs and spurts in my hand. I keep stroking, in and out of your ass, back and forth on your cock, until I hear a gasp from you and know you need me to pull out. I gently ease back, waiting for your tightened anus to release me of its own accord. My cock slips out and you let out a relieved sigh. I lay down on top of you, feeling you slump onto the couch. I rest my cock in the curve of your ass as I nuzzle your neck and whisper, "Now you're mine. All mine."

A Few Good Men

JASMINE HALL

We'd talked about it for years. You know, in the way that couples do. Almost shyly, confessing glittering secrets to one another late at night. Speaking softly of fantasies and daydreams. We'd shared just as much as we possibly could, pressing each other's boundaries. Pushing preconceived limits. Making sure that our desires overlapped, and that at the end of the day we were each getting exactly what we wanted.

This concept started out like all the rest—with me and Marc under the sheets in our tiny bedroom, limbs entwined, voices hushed. "You tell me, then I'll tell you—" was our game, a grown-up version of little kids playing doctor. When you're with someone for a long time—like ten years—having any sort of secret is difficult to fathom. So when Marc told me his brand-new fantasy, his number one jerk-off vision on the X-rated dial, well, I had to make it come true.

"But would you be jealous?" he asked, concerned.

"Me?" I asked, incredulous.

His eyes brightened at my response, and he nodded and said, "That's right. You're never jealous."

I'm not. I know that Marc and I are in it for the long haul. We have a bond that will last. Any other partners who happen to find their way into our boudoir—well, those are only small-time, bit-part players.

"How about you?" I whispered to him, trailing my fingers through the reddish fur on his chest. "How would you feel?"

He ducked his head for a moment, suddenly bashful. "I'd love it," he told me. "Every fucking minute."

So there it is. My defense. Why I did what I did. I knew exactly what would happen, planned in dreamy detail every single step of the way.

"Oh, fuck, you didn't," Marc said, his handsome face contorted in pain. His forehead furrowed, ginger-red eyebrows contracting as his green eyes squinted at me. I remained silent, waiting for him to continue. But he didn't say a word. He set his elbows on the table and then rested his chin in his hands, using his fingertips to gently massage his temples as if he had a seriously mood-darkening headache.

"I didn't mean to." There was a pouty edge to my voice.

"Lacey, I know you. I know all about your wicked sense of humor. Just tell me that you're teasing, all right? Tell me now, and I'll go easy on that sweet ass of yours later."

"Easy?" I asked.

"I'll only give you ten with the sole of my bedroom slipper instead of twenty." I was pleased to see that he hadn't entirely lost his sense of humor. "Sure, I can tell you that I'm teasing—"

His face brightened.

"—if you want me to lie to you."

He sighed, obviously accepting the fact that I was actually offering him the truth. "But how?" he finally asked. "I mean, Christ, baby. How could that happen?" He ran his hand through his thick red hair in a helpless gesture.

Now, I just stared at him.

"All right, I know how. I'm sorry."

We sat facing each other across the mint-green formica table. The videocassette case that usually held our favorite home-made X-rated creation was open. Inside rested a professionally made copy of *A Few Good Men,* the copy that belonged to our local video store. It was emblazoned with various messages in bold red ink: "Do not copy for personal use!" "Be kind, please rewind!"

"Just start at the beginning," Marc said, his broad shoulders sagging dejectedly, so I tried. Still, he knew the story as well as I did. We'd been watching our video together on the couch, already half-naked and in a passionate clinch, when one of my friends had come down for a visit from the apartment upstairs. Quick to hide the evidence, I'd popped out the tape and handed it to Marc, who had slid it into the container for *A Few Good Men.* His erection was a little more difficult to conceal, but he'd left the room for a few minutes, to get himself under control. Slightly disheveled, I'd managed to open the door for Darlene, who had eyed me coolly and asked if I'd forgotten about our date. Yeah. Totally. Sex makes my brain a bit addled.

We'd had drinks with Darlene, had played a round of pool at the café around the corner, then come home and crashed. In the morning, I'd returned the wrong film to the corner store. So maybe it was my fault—but at least on the surface it wasn't *all* my fault. Marc had been the one to put the video in that case in the first place. Sure, I knew what I was doing—but he didn't have to know that. At least, not yet.

"You're right," he agreed. "I should have reminded you this morning. But any way you look at it, the situation sucks, doesn't it? We'll never be able to go back there again. And we'll be god-damned lucky if the next person to rent the film doesn't upload our dirty movie and sell it for a million bucks on the Internet. I mean, we won't even get a cut of the profits."

"We're not Pamela and Tommy Lee."

"You're as hot as she is."

Charmed, I smiled at him, then ran my fingertips along the bodice of the pale blue halter-style top I had on. The one with the ruffle in the front and the tie in the back. I wanted Marc to notice what I was wearing, to pay attention to the fact that this story might not have such a devastating ending after all. I'd spent extra time this evening on my hair and makeup. A dark merlot hue glossed my lips. A silver band held my long hair up in a shining dark ponytail. My skimpy halter was on over no bra. My skirt was slightly more than semisheer and beneath I was completely pantyless.

"What?" he asked, catching onto some change of emotion in the air, but not able to fully identify what I was trying to tell him.

I just kept smiling slyly.

"Come on," he said. "Spill it, Lacey. I've had enough unexpected news for one day. And I'm serious about my slipper meeting your upturned ass."

"You know that guy who works there—"

"One of the metal-heads?" he asked, but it was obvious to both of us that he was intentionally playing dumb. Yes, there's a slew of dipsy-dyed, multiply-pierced youngsters who work the cash register at Red Rocket Video, but there is one young buck in particular who has caught Marc's eye in the past. Among the motley crew of video fiends, this attractive creature stands out. His build. His attentiveness. His way of cruising both Marc and me with his sexy, gray-eyed gaze. It's always been a dangerous turn-on of ours to imagine bringing a third partner into bed with us. A young male partner. A player whose sole purpose is to soak up our devoted attention. A lover like this one. This is the situation Marc had confessed to dreaming about late at night. This is the plan that I'd put into action.

At my unwavering stare, he answered his own question. "Alden?"

I nodded.

"What about him?"

I was about to tell, when the doorbell rang.

"We're not playing pool again with Darlene, are we? The girl can't hit a ball to save her life."

Shaking my head, I walked down the hallway. Before I opened the door, I looked back over my shoulder to where Marc still sat at our kitchen table. My expression should have told him everything he needed to know, but I gave him a clue just in case. "Alden's coming to change tapes," I said. "He caught the error at the rewind stage and is kindly giving us back ours—"

"And what are we giving him?" Marc asked, finally catching on to the fun. I pulled open the door, revealing

Alden standing outside in a red Sex Pistols T-shirt and skin-tight black jeans. He had our tape in one hand and a bottle of expensive vodka in the other. He didn't say a word, but followed me into our small apartment, then looked around the room and nodded in appreciation. The place is tiny bordering on mouse-hole minuscule. But it's classy. Vibrantly colorful art hangs on all the walls, and we have a multimedia center that would make most directors go green.

"Your tape," he said, placing it on top of the television set. I smiled when I noticed that he had rewound the cassette to the very beginning. To me, that meant he'd taken the time to view the piece in its entirety first. I also thought about the slogan: "Be kind, rewind." How kind was Alden prepared on being?

"And here's yours," Marc said, entering the room and handing over the video. Alden looked at it, then looked at me. He appeared slightly nervous as he set the vodka and the correct video on the coffee table. Then he waited. Was it my job to make the first move?

"I liked your movie a lot," he said, and that was all it took.

"Which part was your favorite?" Marc asked, taking a step closer. Suddenly, he was back in his own, rare form, taking the helm. I felt myself relax, knowing that he would be in charge. "This one?" he untied my halter as he spoke, and as the fabric fluttered forward he slid his hands under my small breasts, caressing my pert nipples with his thumbs. "Or this—" he continued, moving his hands now to the waistband of my feather-light skirt and slipping it down my thighs. I stepped out of the garment, then pulled my shirt over my head, so that I was entirely naked save for a pair of red, open-toed sandals.

I knew just how good I looked—my skin glistening from a shimmering body lotion, my pussy cleanly shaved.

"To be honest," Alden said, speaking to me, "I liked *your* role. High-class," he continued. "The way you looked right at the camera when he made you come."

"Ah," Marc and I sighed together. Alden wanted to be in the middle. In a hurry, we made our way to our tiny bedroom. The king-sized mattress takes up almost the entire room, but that's okay. The bed is the most important part. The boys were naked in moments, and Alden was in the center of the mattress, facing me. I felt his fingers wander over my collarbones, down my neck, over my breasts, toward my pussy as Marc got into position. I stared into Alden's cloud-gray eyes, then let my own fingers take a trip along his body.

Touching a new lover for the first time always brings out a wide range of emotions in me. I took in every part of Alden's face—his strong cheekbones, his high forehead, the light growth of raw whiskers on his jawline. I let my hands skim his strong chest, working my way down until I had a firm hold around his cock.

He let loose with a low, shuddering sigh, and that let me know exactly how to work him. Steadily. Firmly. A strong touch. A well-placed squeeze.

Marc was taking his time admiring Alden's backside. He'd begun by licking in a line down Alden's spine—I knew he was doing this, because Alden shivered and tensed at the sensation, which is exactly what I do when Marc kisses me like that. Then, with an anxious groan, he'd parted Alden's tight rear cheeks and gotten ready to start the fucking.

To ease Alden's suspense, I continued to play with his

prick. It was long and strong and I ran my fingertips lightly along the shaft, then cupped my palm around the head. When Alden suddenly gripped onto me, I knew that Marc had driven his cock home. I turned fully on my side so that we were creating a sinfully decadent sexual smorgasbord—Alden the filling in a hero sandwich, with me and my man the bread. As I parted my thighs, Alden slid his cock into the wetness of my pussy, so that the three of us were truly connected.

With each thrust of Marc's cock into Alden, the video store stud rocked his body into me. I held onto his shoulders, and Marc did the same, so that our fingers overlapped and our wedding rings made a light clinking noise. When I looked past Alden's glazed expression, I saw that Marc was watching me intently. What was he thinking? It could only have been what *I* was thinking—thank fuck that I'd had the nerve to switch those tapes, or we'd never have made it to this fantasy place. A place where Marc and I were both in charge of our own pleasure and Alden was the catalyst to take us there.

As I shifted my body on the mattress, Alden moved to bring himself above me. He did slow push-ups over my body as Marc took him from behind, doggy-style. With a grace that belied the fact that he was getting his ass fucked, Alden paid careful attention to my needs. When he slid his cock all the way inside me, he stayed sealed to my body, pressing up and back with his hips, so that he skimmed my clit with each rocking motion. I raised up to get the contact that I craved, and I groaned whenever Marc's skin brushed my own.

I was so turned on that I didn't notice immediately that Alden wanted my attention. Because suddenly, Alden was talking, surprising both Marc and me. "I couldn't believe it—"

he said softly, and I felt his cock swell and expand inside me.

"Which part?" I asked, staring up into his beautiful face.

"The way you looked when he fucked you like that."

"Like what?" I whispered, knowing but wanting to hear him say it.

"Ass-fucked you. And you looked as if it was the sweetest thing you'd ever felt."

"And is it?" Marc asked, before sinking his teeth into Alden's shoulder. "Is it, baby?"

"Oh, god," Alden sighed, "oh, yes."

The situation was suddenly more intense for me. I was getting to see Alden's expressions change as Marc took him fiercely. And I could just imagine what I looked like at that moment, the moment that Alden was talking about. Yeah, we made the film together—but this was somehow more true. A real-life enactment for my own viewing pleasure.

"You like that, baby?" Marc asked again, and this time I knew that he was talking to me.

"Oh, yes," I said, echoing Alden.

The strangest part was that I felt closer to Marc than I ever had before—closer, even though we were separated by a real human body. A living and breathing lover who continued to pump into me as my husband drove into him.

The situation was suddenly too powerful, and soon we were coming together—the three of us—making those rough, inhuman noises. More grunts than groans, yells than moans. When Alden collapsed against the mattress, Marc pulled out and took his spot on my left, so that now I was in the middle, bathing in the warmth of my two men. No one said a word. There are times when there simply are no more words left to say.

"So, Lacey—" Marc said softly after Alden left. His fingertips tricked along my slippery skin. "Did you enjoy the viewing?"

"Viewing?" I asked.

"You know, of *A Few Good Men*?"

I nodded happily.

"Really?" he murmured, obviously wanting me to talk more.

"Yes," I assured him. "Oh, yes. But you know how it is with the classics?"

Marc just waited, looking expectantly at me for the punchline.

"You need to experience them over and over to really appreciate the art form."

Now, Marc smiled, and I saw his gaze flicker over to the box of our home-made movies, as if trying to decide which one we'd return "by accident" next time.

Breakfast in Bed

EMILIE PARIS

Breakfast in bed was delivered to Marla by her handsome musician boyfriend. At the squeak of the bedroom door opening, Marla rolled over to see a nearly naked Zach carrying a carefully prepared tray filled with ripe, red strawberries, a well-endowed banana, a crescent of green melon, and a bunch of glistening-wet purple grapes. She looked up from the tray into Zach's feisty green eyes. He had plans. Marla could tell.

"Hungry?" he asked, grinning broadly at his blonde-haired lady.

"A little," she answered, honestly. Who wouldn't be ravenous after all the energetic activities of their wild, raucous night? As usual during one of their many ten-hour sexual tournaments, they hadn't gotten much sleep. There were too many ways to play, too many activities that they needed to try. But dream deprivation didn't matter much to either one of them. Dark under-eye circles were acceptable payment in exchange for the many decadent orgasms they'd shared. "You can sleep as long as you want when you're dead" was one of Zachary's favorite mottos.

While Marla waited to hear what was in store for her, Zach kicked out of his satiny black boxers and tossed them aside. The he climbed onto the mattress and began to prepare their feast. With extreme casualness, he lifted the lone banana and peeled it. His motions were slow and exaggerated, as if he possessed no ulterior motives. This was all about a healthy snack, right? Nothing could be more simple or elegant than breakfast in bed. That's what his calm expression said, anyway. But Marla was wary. She knew that she should be preparing herself for something unexpected.

Watching Zach strip the banana was like watching a porn show, live, happening in real time on the foot of her bed. Her boyfriend casually discarded the skin and then began to stroke the fruit up Marla's lean legs.

"What are you doing, Zach?"

"What do you think?"

She arched her brows at him, her body stiffening. "I don't know," she murmured. "But it's sort of strange—"

"Strange in a bad way?" he asked, watching her face carefully for her response. He trailed the banana to the very split of Marla's body, then ever-so-slowly spread open her kitty lips with his fingers and slipped the first bit of the fruit inside her. "Or strange in a good way?" he continued, his tone husky.

Suddenly, Marla found that her voice was gone. She wanted to tell him to stop horsing around and climb on top of her. She was wet and ready for him. They could start their morning off with a bang, no fruit necessary.

"Come on, Zach," she murmured. This was too bizarre, wasn't it? Even for Zach's standards, and he was a man who seemed to own no serious boundaries when it came to X-rated activities. She thought of their various escapades. He had no problem going down on her in a movie theater, making love in the single stall of a restaurant bathroom, doing it against his shiny vintage motorcycle on the side of a road. But this was different—this was brand-spanking new, and the oddest experience yet. Amazingly to Marla, as she turned the concept around in her mind, she realized that she didn't really want him to stop, did she? No, because she couldn't believe how it felt. Cool, moist, firm. What was happening to her? She was actually letting her boyfriend caress her with a piece of ripe fruit.

And it was turning her on.

With ease, Zach pulled out the banana, licked off her sex juices, and then slid the fruit back inside Marla, a little further. Oh, man, it was good. Who would have guessed it? She would never be able to make it through the produce aisle again without turning as red-faced as one of the vine-ripened tomatoes. Never would she be able to heft an innocent bunch of bananas without thinking of this moment, of what Zach had done, of how much she'd liked it. Oh, did she like it. Her body contracted on the yellow tubular fruit, searching for purchase. Her pussy squeezed tight on the impromptu all-natural dildo. Not quite yet ripe, the banana made the perfect sex toy—thick and hard. She had a collection of similarly shaped devices in her nightstand drawer. This wasn't so different from playing with a vibrator, was it?

Yes, it was. Because *this* toy was edible.

To calm herself, she grabbed hold of one of the down-filled pillows and held it to her chest, needing support. Her body came alive with the pre-orgasm shudders that always told Zach exactly how aroused she was. He knew, and he played with the fruit for a few more seconds, before discarding it in favor of a sliver of honeydew melon. What was he going to do with that? More of the same, apparently, but this was a different feeling entirely. The melon had been cut into a thick crescent, the rind removed, forming a pale green, watery spear. Again, Zach held her lips open with one hand and slid the length of the melon into her. It was colder than the banana, and the fruit's sweet juices seemed to bring forth her own, mingling together until she could feel them seeping to coat her inner thighs.

"You're so wet," Zach sighed, observing her sex before bending, licking her skin, pulling out the melon with his teeth, and taking one bite after another until it was gone and his lips were sealed for a moment to the bridge of her body. Marla felt empty without the fruit inside of her, and she hoped that Zach would have something else to fill her with. And quickly.

Instead, he leaned over the bed and plucked a strawberry from the white porcelain plate. Where he was going with the berry, she could only wonder. But she didn't have to ponder the impending erotic mystery for long. Zachary was already making commands. More than almost anything else, Marla liked to obey her boyfriend. When he issued sexual demands, the one concept in her mind was that she needed to please him.

"Spread your legs wide for me."

Was she ready for this?

"Do it for me, baby."

Something did a flip-flop inside Marla's stomach, but she

followed his request, parting her legs as Zach ran the bumpy edge of the strawberry along the split of her body. He worked gently at first, then used his fingers to squeeze a river of juice from the deeply ripe berry. As soon as she felt the cold drops falling like red rain onto her skin, Zach bent to lick away the liquid. Then he squeezed more, and licked more, until she could feel the climax building again inside her. Her body felt loose and long. She began to breathe more quickly, nearly panting. How many times would she be able to come in a twenty-four-hour period? Zach, the sexual scientist, seemed ready to find out.

Pulping the berry with his fingers until it was a sticky mess, he spread this fruity lotion along her skin and then licked Marla clean. She closed her eyes and gripped into the pillow, trying so hard not to come. She knew that there was more, waiting for her. With Zach, wasn't there always more? She didn't want to let him down, didn't want to let herself down. Knew there were other fruits waiting for her on the plate and wondered what uses they could possibly have.

Then she had to stop wondering about anything as Zach slipped his tongue between her thighs and began to tickle Marla on the inside. This was too good, too much, and she moaned and ground her hips upward. Hard. All she hoped was that he wouldn't stop. That he would continue with the inspired ministrations of his tongue for hours. Those dreamy circles, those endless spirals. But, of course, he did stop. Nothing was ever simple with Zach. He wanted to stretch out her pleasure, wanted to make everything vibrate within her. To do this, he had come well-equipped with several new playthings.

While Marla prepared herself to beg him, he pulled his

secret toy out from under the napkin on the tray. It was a can of whipped cream. Instantly, Marla realized that Zachary was going to turn her into a fantasy sundae, and she also realized instantly that she was going to like it.

"Ready, baby?"

Marla made some animalistic groan in response.

"Good girl." He started slowly, still wanting to play, pressing the nozzle on the can of cold cream and shooting a river of the sweet white fluff in a line down the basin of her belly.

Her breath caught in a half-sob, half-sigh as Zach devoured the cream and reached again for the can. It was like having a mountain of bath bubbles, of meringue, of the fluffiest white clouds, spread over her pussy. No other previous sensation that Marla had ever experienced was like it. She tried to think of true comparisons, but failed. The combination of the whipped cream and Zachary's warm tongue made Marla think she might actually faint with pleasure. She no longer wanted to come. She wanted to linger forever on the teetering precipice of pleasure. *Don't push me over,* she wanted to beg him. *Don't let me fall.*

Again and again, Zach brought the white corrugated nozzle forward, sprayed the whipped topping along the intersection at the tops of her thighs, and then licked it away with his perfect flat tongue. Marla felt the coldness of the whipped cream followed immediately by the heat of Zach's mouth, and she couldn't help but moan even louder. *This* was what whipped cream was meant for. The inventor must have known it from the start, must have thought "sex toy," as he or she named the tantalizing stuff "whipped cream."

But just when Marla thought she would come from this experience alone, Zach upped the intensity of the encounter. Now, he had Marla position herself on all fours, faced away from him on the mattress. As she was following his instructions, he removed one final hidden item from the second plate, not letting Marla see the item, but letting her hear the sound as he undid the cap.

"What is it?" she whispered.

"Guess—"

"Tell me, Zach," she begged.

"No," he said softly, his voice almost a laugh. "I'll let you feel it and then you'll know."

Whatever the mystery item was, it came in a jar with a screw-on metal lid. She heard the sound of the jar unsealing, and then she felt the thick liquid pour in a sensuous stream, slipping down her thighs, sticky and sweet.

"Honey," she said, naming the treat instantly.

"Baby," Zachary teased her.

"It's honey—"

"Yes, darling," he said, in his sexy, slight drawl. "Of course it is. Sweets for the sweet."

He topped it with more spritzes of the fluffy whipped cream and went to work. His full, hungry mouth tricked up and down her pussy lips, his tongue dipping forcefully between them to catch every last bit of the sweetness that lingered there. He wouldn't leave even one drop remaining.

She'd become a dessert, a fantasy confection, and Marla knew from passionate experiences in the past that Zach enjoyed desserts more than any other part of the meal. He truly savored his honey-covered lady, licking slowly at the decadent treat that had spread to her inner thighs, lapping his way up like a hungry cat, and getting his face wet and creamy with the mixture of sauces that included her own.

As the pleasure built within her, Marla realized that Zach hadn't brought her breakfast in bed—she *was* breakfast in bed. And she came when his tongue touched her center of pleasure.

Just touched it.

Cutting Class

XAVIER ACTON

"You ever fucked a virgin before, Mister?" the blonde asked me, her breath hot on my ear, the smell of grape bubblegum sickly-sweet in my nostrils. She was leaning against me, standing behind my chair. Her two friends, the brunette and the redhead, sat on the couch passing my $150 bottle of Scotch back and forth between them, swilling it and occasionally dribbling some on the sofa as they flicked ashes from their Marlboros onto the floor. The redhead with pigtails was sitting cross-legged, her thighs spread just wide enough so that I could see, as her plaid miniskirt skirt rode up, that she was wearing a Mickey Mouse thong along with her white stay-ups. The thong and stockings clashed with her pink lace bra, which I could see because the middle button of her white blouse had come undone right where the half-unraveled knot of her thin navy-blue tie dangled carelessly. The pigtailed redhead smoked her Marlboro absently, maybe not noticing that the ashes kept falling onto the couch between her legs. She was kind of distracted, after all, staring at the brunette.

The brunette had her mary janes up on the coffee table, leaning back hard on the couch as a dribble of Scotch glistened her red-smeared lips and ran down her chin and onto her pink-flushed cleavage, soaking the edge of her open blouse. Her D-cup breasts hung out of her black lace bra, and the nipples were still erect. I already knew that the brunette wasn't wearing panties. But in case I'd forgotten, she had her skirt pulled up and her legs spread, pointed straight at me. And her hand stroking lazily up and down in her pussy, up and down, to the rhythm of The Donnas on the Bang & Olufsen stereo.

The blonde smelled of my Cuban cigars and my ex-girlfriend's Chanel No. 5, and I had no idea what kind of underwear she had on under her school uniform—yet. I could feel her skirt draping against my hands, cuffed to the chair behind my back. I could feel her hair brushing against my shoulders, taste the blood in my mouth from where she'd punched me. The blonde leaned forward and curled her arms around me. She held up the switchblade, made sure I was watching, and pressed the button. It made a sharp, audible click, and five inches of steel hovered in front of my face, glittering and deadly. It swayed under my nostrils, smelling like oil and steel and death.

The blonde giggled, a musical sound, as she brought the blade closer and closer to my face, her other hand coiled in my hair and holding my head still—real still.

"You eat pussy pretty good, Mister—doesn't he, Amber?"

"Yeah," said the brunette, her voice hoarse and her breath coming short. "Pretty good."

The blonde giggled. "Yeah, you eat pussy pretty good. But how do you suck cock?"

She held the knife close.

I saw the redhead turn her head to look at me, her eyes wide as she caught her breath. She stared, fascinated.

"You want to see him suck my cock, Becca? You want to see him suck my steel cock?"

"Yeah," said the redhead breathlessly.

"How do you suck cock, Mister?"

"I—I don't know."

"I'd like you to suck my cock, Mister. Do you want to suck my cock?"

She stroked my lips with the tip of the switchblade.

"I think you want to suck my cock," she whispered to me, like a lover.

"N-no," I gasped. "Please!"

That musical giggle again, as the redhead watched me, transfixed. "Open up," she whispered, nuzzling my ear. "Open wide, Mister. Open *real* wide."

They'd caught me as I came home in the middle of the day, my arms filled with groceries. I thought Tricia was home already. I was wrong.

The satin pillowcase went over my head from behind. A hand hit me twice in the face. Somebody grabbed my wrists. I felt two bodies against me. Somebody kneed me in the crotch and brought me down, landing hard on top of me with their knee in my back. I smelled Love's Baby Soft and the trace of those scented markers you use on love notes. I heard the ratcheting of handcuffs as I felt them close around my wrists. Somebody was pulling off my shoes. I heard a click and felt something sharp against my throat.

"Don't move, Mister," came a feminine voice as hands fumbled their way under my body, undoing my belt. "That's a switchblade you're feelin'. You move or scream and we'll kill you, got it?"

"Why are you doing this? You girls cutting class?"

"Yes, we're cutting class," she said. "What are you, the fucking truant officer? You ain't dressed like a nun, asshole!"

"Take anything you want," I rasped, my mouth tasting of blood. "There's some cash in the top drawer of my dresser. My wallet's in my back pocket."

They pulled my pants down and kicked me in the balls. My head swam as the one with the knife sat straddling my back and slipped the knife under the neck of my shirt. She started to cut.

"Yeah, you bet we'll take anything we want, Mister. *And* you'll do exactly what we say. You cooperate real good and maybe we'll just waltz out of here with big smiles on our faces. And you'll have a smile too, Mister. That's if you cooperate *real, real* good. Otherwise the only smile you'll have will be across your neck, Mister. Understand?"

Panting, I nodded. My shirt was split down the back. The girl settled back onto me, straddling me, and I could feel her against my shoulder blades. Her crotch. Her pussy. She wasn't wearing any panties.

"You ready, Amber?" she asked.

"Ready as hell," a female voice chirped.

The one on top of me grabbed my wrists and wedged a knee between my legs. "Crawl," she growled.

"But my wrists," I groaned.

"Crawl!" she said again, kneeing me in the crotch, hard enough to make it hurt.

I started pushing myself forward, using just my knees, the naked top of my body rubbing against the carpet. I crawled about ten feet as the girl followed me, kicking me in the crotch to keep me moving while she laughed. Then she came down on my back again, grabbed the pillowcase, and yanked me up to my knees again.

She pulled the satin pillowcase off my head and shoved my face forward.

A second girl was in my big armchair, her legs spread wide, her plaid schoolgirl's skirt pulled up. She wasn't wearing anything underneath and her pussy was shaved. She had her hands between her legs and she was spreading her lips apart, showing me the glistening entrance to her young pussy and the hard, swollen nub of her erect clit.

I stared up at her face and she smiled cruelly back down at me. She was pretty—young, no doubt, but gorgeous. She had her dark hair in pigtails and way too much makeup on. My face was inches from her pussy, but I could still smell her perfume— Love's Baby Soft—even over the faint scent of her juicing cunt.

She blew me a kiss, and flipped me off.

The girl behind me bent down low and put the switchblade to my throat again. I could feel her loose hair dangling around my face and I could see that she was blonde. She didn't smell like Love's—she'd been dabbling around in my wife's things, and she was wearing Chanel No. 5. I saw

Christine's jewelry on her wrist. Out of the corner of my eye, I could see a third girl, sitting cross-legged on the sofa, her hair a pigtailed mop of flame. She looked younger than the other two. I could feel her bare breasts against my naked back as she growled in my ear.

"You any good at eating pussy, Mister? You like it? You like it a lot?"

I stared, hypnotized, into the brunette's shaved pussy.

"Well?" She jabbed the tip of the switchblade against my throat.

"Um, I don't —I don't know," I blurted. "I guess so, maybe, I don't know."

"Wrong answer!" giggled the blonde, and put the edge of the blade against my carotid artery. "Want to try again, Mister?"

Almost hyperventilating, I gasped: "Yes! Yes! I'm really, really good at eating pussy!"

"You like it?"

"More than anything!" I said. "I love it more than anything."

"More than getting your dick sucked?"

I hesitated, felt the pressure of the switchblade against my throat.

"Yeah," I said. "I love eating pussy way more than getting my dick sucked."

"And you say you do it real, real good?"

"Yeah! Yeah, I'm good at it! My wife comes all the time! She comes and comes!"

The three girls started laughing musically. The blonde was giggling hysterically. "That's a laugh! I bet your wife just pretends she comes!" They kept laughing, and the brunette blew me a kiss again as I looked up at her desperately. "But you better hope that Amber here doesn't hafta pretend, Mister, 'cause the only way we walk out of here with you alive is if she comes as many times as she wants to. How many times do you want to come, Amber?"

"Oh, I dunno," she said. "Five, maybe, or six."

"Amber here's never had her pussy eaten before, and you're gonna be her first."

"All right," I said, my voice shaking.

The blonde shoved my head forward and the brunette, Amber, took it away from her, her fingers tangling in my hair and dragging my face down between her legs.

"I think I'll give you something to remind you of your situation," said the blonde as she turned around and sat on my lower back, forcing me down into a prone position with my upper body twisted uncomfortably, face an inch from Amber's pussy. She grabbed my balls and jabbed them with the tip of the switchblade and I yelped. "You want to keep these, you'd better be the best pussy-eater in the world for the next few hours." The three girls giggled. "Remember, Mister, She wants to come five or six times, you keep eating her until she does. You poop out on us and we'll poop you out, Mister—permanently. You'll be the one wearing the skirt." They all giggled some more, and the blonde caressed my balls with the blade.

The brunette forced my face—hard—into her pussy.

My god, I've never eaten Christine out as well as I ate out that brunette. The taste of her pussy overwhelmed me and I almost choked—it was so different than my wife's, so much saltier, tangier, less musky. But I got used to it, helped along in no small part by the blonde's jabs with the switchblade into my balls.

As anyone who's ever tried it knows, it's not always easy to make a woman come from being eaten out. I'd bought the whole line of enlightened-sex-nerd, sensitive-new-age-guy bullshit: that orgasm wasn't the destination, sex was—and that orgasm was a stop along the way. Sanctimonious post-hippie garbage to begin with, but even if it wasn't, not relevant one bit here. I knew that orgasms—many of them, half a dozen, maybe more—orgasms weren't just the goal. They were my only ticket out of the eunuch club.

Lucky for me, she was moaning. Loud. I spent the first five minutes feeling her out, sensing what she liked, whether she dug the tip of my tongue under her clit hood or on the top or back and forth over the sides, whether she liked friction or pressure or a combination of the two, whether she liked her labia licked or my tongue to wriggle up in her pussy, whether she liked me to lick her thighs way up high or way down low, whether she wanted to feel my tongue swirling lower and lower until it neared her pert buns, near her asshole, whether she liked me to suckle on her clit when I tickled it with the flat of my tongue. Her pussy was so smooth that I could feel and taste everything, quickly learning the way she wanted it. I don't think she *knew* how she wanted it, never having been eaten out. But she learned—oh, how fast she learned. And I learned, too—every trick she responded to became my tool to save myself. Now I was focusing on her clit, with occasional licks down to her labia, and I could taste her pussy getting stronger as juices flowed out onto my tongue.

She had clamped her smooth thighs around my face and pushed her ass up off the chair, gripping the armrests and whimpering. Her whimpers grew to moans. I glanced up and saw that her nipples were poking plainly out through her blouse, that her cleavage was flushed and her eyes were dull with pleasure. I paused for just a second.

"Please," I said. "I'm not stopping, I just want to say—if I had my hands free I could do more."

"Oh yeah, asshole? What could you do."

"M–more," whimpered the brunette. "M–more. Don't stop."

"I'll show you. I promise I won't try to get away."

"M–more," the brunette growled, a cross between a sob and a snarl. "More!" She grabbed my hair and slammed my face back onto her pussy, grinding it so hard onto my tongue that it was all I could do to keep up.

"How about it, Amber? You want this asshole's hands on you?"

"Yeah," she gasped, and I heard the jangling of keys.

The first thing I did was slide my hands up her body under her white schoolgirl's blouse and feel her tits. They were big, maybe D-cups, and her nipples were so hard they felt like rocks. I pinched gently, tentatively—she let out a howl.

My blood ran cold. "Good?" I asked her.

"Don't stop! Don't fucking stop!" she cried, shoving her pussy hard against my face.

I pinched a little harder, caressing and gently squeezing her tits. She moaned louder, louder. Then the blonde was laughing.

"Look here! Mr. world-class pussyeater is enjoying himself after all!"

She teased the tip of the switchblade slowly up the shaft of my erect cock. I squirmed under the sensation, but didn't stop eating Amber or working my hands on her breasts.

"Looks like he's kind of sexually re-cep-tive—is that what Sister Bernice called it in Health class? He likes being taken, y'know?" She and the redhead giggled. Amber was way, way beyond giggling. She was about half a decibel from screaming at the top of her lungs.

That's when I felt the blonde's finger between my cheeks. She had licked it and it was slippery—just a little. So that when she pushed it home my back arched and my face pulled away from Amber as I groaned.

"Look at that! He *is* sexually receptive! How does it feel to be fucked, Mister? I know us girls are supposed to like it, so why shouldn't you?"

The two girls giggled as I squirmed, and Amber howled "M–more!" and shoved me hard into her crotch again. Her ass was off the chair, her legs were clamped around my face. She ripped her blouse open so fast the buttons went raining all over me. She grasped my hands and pushed them hard against her breasts, whimpered "harder! harder!" as she started to come. I pinched her nipples harder and licked her clit faster and faster as she let out a shuddering cry. The blonde drove her finger into me all the way as her friend came, and came, and came—until I felt a tiny trickle of ejaculate leaking out of her and onto my tongue. I swallowed, as I listened to the blonde's wicked, savage laugh overhead.

"I said open wide, Mister." I parted my lips and tasted the tang of the switchblade sliding into my mouth, lying easily on my tongue. She began to move it back and forth.

"You'll have to do it better than that if you want your reward," said the blonde. "See, Becca here has her eye on you. And you know what? She's never had a guy. She's a vur-gin."

Becca's face went red in an instant and she said, "Shut up, Crystal! I am not!"

"Oh yes you are," said Crystal as she worked her knife in and out of my mouth, fucking me with it. "Never even been fingered. But you aren't going to finger her, are you, Mister? You just want to stick your dick in and shoot your spooge, like all guys. Come on, suck it." She pushed the knife in deeper, almost to the back of my throat. I gagged, terror coursing through my veins. "Suck it better than that." I began to suck it, running my tongue all over it and kissing it with my lips as she held it in my mouth. "That's better," she cooed. "You want to stick your dick in little Becca over there? She's fif-teen, Mister. You want to stick your thing in a fifteen-year-old virgin?"

"I'm sixteen!" snapped Becca, rolling her eyes.

"Not until next week," said Crystal. "How about it, Mister? You ever popped a virgin before?"

I shook my head, moving it back and forth just a hair as I sucked the switchblade.

"Well, now's your chance. You can just stick it in and shoot it off, fill her up—ain't that the way you guys do it?"

I shook my head.

"Oh, is that right? You want to *make love* to her!"

I nodded, still sucking.

"You want to make our little Becca feel like she's the most special girl in the world? Suck faster, bitch. Remember, this is my dick."

I nodded, sucking faster.

"You want to make little Becca come, don't you, Mister?"

"Yeah," I said, the sound muffled by Crystal's hand on my face and the knife in my mouth.

"You want that, Becca? That hard dick of his look good to you? You want this filthy guy to pop your cherry?"

"I told you," whined Becca. "I'm not a virgin!"

"Yeah, sure, whatever you say, Becca, whatever you say. He'll just be another in a long line of conquests. You want to fuck him? You want him to make you come?"

"No!" she said, blushing deep, deep red.

The blonde giggled. "Too bad, Becca. Because you're gonna. This putz is gonna pop your cherry."

"I'm not a virgin!" she whined again.

"Yeah, we'll see," said Crystal, slipping the knife out of my mouth. "Take your clothes off, Becca."

Now her face was *really* red. Becca looked at the ground.

"Take 'em off!"

Wordlessly, Becca stood up and began to unbutton her shirt.

The bedclothes were dirty, tangled with sweat and sex. They made me change them, Crystal holding her knife at the ready in case I tried to make a break for it. They made me put on the satin sheets. Becca stood in the doorway, stark naked except for her white stay-ups and mary janes. Her pussy was as red as her hair. She had freckles all over her body and pert little C-cup breasts with pale pink nipples. She had a little heart tattooed on her left thigh. It had a banner that said "MIKE."

"Mike," I said. "Is that your boyfriend?"

"No!" spat Crystal. "That's her daddy! Get in bed, Becca!"

Becca sheepishly went over to the bed and climbed in. She pushed her legs together and looked up at me, terrified.

The brunette was slouched in the beanbag chair across from the bed, watching. Crystal held the knife in my back. "How do you make love to a woman, Mister? Especially if it's her first time?"

"I'd kiss her—"

She jabbed the knife into me a little. "Don't tell me, asshole! Show me! Show *her!*"

Gingerly, I climbed onto the bed. Becca was quaking.

"You don't have to do this," I whispered. "We can fight back against her."

"Shut up, Mister. You don't know her."

"You want me to do it?"

"Just *do* it!"

I put my arms around her. I let my hand trail up her body, pausing over her breasts. Her nipples were soft, silken. I put my lips to hers, kissed her gently. I kissed her some more. I let my tongue ease out into her mouth. I let it slide deeper in. I felt her nipples stiffen so suddenly in my grasp as my tongue plunged into her—then she was sucking on it, hungry for it.

"Never even been french-kissed, ain't that what you told me, Becca?"

"Uh-huh," moaned Becca. I pinched her nipple gently, teased it, played with it. She arched her back and pushed her thighs together. I slid my hand down her belly and paused over her thighs.

"Open your legs," I whispered. "Please. I'll be gentle."

She hesitated, looking up into my eyes dreamily, fear mixed with desire—maybe.

Crystal spat: "Open 'em, Becca! You want your cherry popped or not?"

Becca parted her legs, as wide as they would go.

I ran my hand gingerly up her thigh, slowly, savoring every inch of her smooth skin. I trailed one finger into her pussy—and she gasped so loud, twisted so hard, shuddered so powerfully, that I pulled my hand back.

But she was wet. I'd felt it, in that instant. She wasn't just wet, but gushing.

I brought my hand to her pussy again, gently teased her lips apart. When I did, I felt a dribble of juice running onto my palm. I slid one finger inside, and felt it so tight that I could barely penetrate her.

"She wet, Mister?"

I looked into Becca's eyes. "No," I said.

"Bullshit! Don't bullshit me!" She jumped onto the bed and kneed me in the balls again, wrestled me down on top of Becca. I felt the handcuffs going back around my wrists. She shoved me onto my side and pushed Becca's thighs further open with her knees, making the younger girl whimper. She shoved her hand into Becca's crotch, and Becca gasped and yelped as Crystal slid first one and then two fingers into her, eliciting a gasp of fear and pain—and then a low, slow sigh as the tension went out of Becca's naked body.

"Oh, yeah, Becca, you ain't no virgin! You've been with hundreds of guys! They just had dicks so small they didn't pop your cherry! What's that on my fingertip if it ain't a cherry?"

"I don't know," whimpered Becca.

"It's your fuckin' cherry! You're a virgin, aintcha, Becca?"

"Uh-huh," she groaned.

"Ever been kissed?"

She shook her head.

"Ever sucked dick? Been fingered?"

Becca shook her head, no.

Crystal waved the knife in front of my face. "Don't you ever fuckin' lie to me again, Mister. This bitch is dripping. Now put your dick inside her."

"But—"

"Oh, you want to eat some more pussy? Tough shit. Becca, next time when I ask you if you want to fuck, you say *yes, Ma'am,* understand? Especially when you're so wet you're dripping, understand?"

Becca nodded, trembling.

Crystal held the knife between us. "Now, tell me, Becca, do you want to fuck this asshole?"

"Yes, Ma'am," said Becca softly.

"Louder! Say, 'Fuck me, Mister!' "

"Fuck me, Mister," whined Becca.

"Louder! Say, 'Fuck me, Mister, stick your thing in my pussy, pop my cherry.' "

"F–fuck—"

"Louder!"

"F–fuck me—Mister, stick—stick your thing—"

"Louder!"

"Stick your thing in my pussy, and, and—"

"Say it!"

"Pop my cherry," shouted Becca.

"You heard the girl," said Crystal, crawling off the bed. "But suck his dick first, Becca. Look how hard it is."

Becca looked at me tentatively, terrified. I was lying on my back and my cock lay throbbing against my stomach. Trembling, Becca leaned down and took it in her hand.

"Put it in your mouth, virgin."

Becca opened her mouth and took it in slowly, gingerly. My back arched and I let out a moan as I felt her mouth enveloping my cock.

"Now suck it."

She started sucking it. Inexpertly, maybe, nervously, uncomfortably, but fuck! I had to hold back not to come. She licked up and down, her red pigtails bobbing against my thighs as she sucked my cock. After a minute, Crystal said, "All right, now. Time to pop Becca's cherry."

Becca took my cock out of her mouth, glistening with her spit. She rolled over and lay face up, her legs spread.

"Do it, Mister."

I crawled on top of Becca and kissed her. Gently, I nudged my hard cock between the swollen lips of her pussy. I could feel it slick with desire, dripping, hot. Gently, I began to slide it very slowly into her.

The head hadn't popped in before I felt the tightness— hard, thick, impassable. Becca looked up at me, scared.

"I'll try not to make it hurt," I whispered.

"No, Mister, make it hurt. She *wants* it to hurt! Or at least, *I* do!"

I pushed, gently at first, then more forcefully, as I heard Becca gasping. I pushed harder, harder. She strained up against me. I felt the resistance, pushing, hard, not wanting to let me in—then, all of a sudden, it gave way, and Becca's hymen broke as I slid smoothly into her tight pussy.

Crystal started cheering and whooping, and the brunette, having recovered from her orgasms, was laughing. The two of them applauded.

Becca was sighing, gasping, giggling a little, and then she was clutching me tight, moaning. I looked down and saw deep red blood leaking from her pussy, dribbling around my balls, staining the sheets. Becca began to push against me. She began to moan.

"What do you know?" laughed Crystal. "The little virgin is going to come!"

And then she did, about a half-second before me.

I was lying in bed, the schoolgirl's virgin blood sticky on my cock and balls, the scent of Love's Baby Soft and Scotch thick in my nostrils. I brought my slicked-up hand to my mouth, licked my fingers, tasted the chemical tang of artificial sweetener.

I heard the front door. I saw Julie outlined in the light of the door. She wore tight jeans, sneakers, and a T-shirt, but her flame-red hair was still in pigtails.

"How was that for a birthday celebration?" she asked.

"I would say unbelievable," I told her. "Except that I know you. And I know Steve. Where'd he get the switchblade?"

"He grew up Catholic. He probably bought it from a nun."

"And the blood? Your idea or his?"

"What do *you* think?"

"How'd you do it?"

"Trade secret."

"I could have sworn you really had a hymen there for a minute. I was beginning to wonder if you really were my wife."

"Vive le Kegelcisor."

I watched, enraptured, as Julie stripped off her T-shirt. She wasn't wearing anything underneath, and her breasts looked at once familiar and new with their pink nipples, freckles, schoolgirl pertness. She wasn't wearing anything under the jeans, either, I saw, as she kicked off her sneakers and dropped her jeans. Naked, she climbed into bed and nuzzled against me.

"Happy birthday," I told her.

"Thanks."

"Speaking of which," I said, stroking her hip, "I understand why you wouldn't let me see you naked for the last two weeks."

"That's *your* birthday present," she said.

"Six months early."

"Whatever."

Bad Doggy

JULIA MOORE

Late last night, I told him what I wanted: Dark. The type of dark that you don't talk about when daylight shines through your windows. The kind of dark dreams you're not even supposed to have when you're the fresh-faced girl that I am. Sweet and innocent. Pure and unmarked. Christ, people are so fucking dense. They get lost on surfaces. They look at me and see all the light and cheerful adjectives found on your average Hallmark card. But they don't see the real thing. They don't see the flaws or the bruises, or the desperate fantasies. Nobody sees the real me except Justin.

"You want to *what?*" my boyfriend asked, one strong, tattooed arm tight around my slender body. And when I didn't immediately repeat myself, he insisted, "Say it again."

"I can't."

"You'd better—"

"I want to be your pet—"

"You *are* my pet," he assured me, nuzzling his face against the back of my neck. His full lips parted, teeth spread, ready to bite.

"I'm not talking about being your *good* pet," I told him, eyes straight ahead, staring at the red-painted wall in front of me, focused on it so that I wouldn't have to look over my shoulder and see his expression change. "Not your sweet kitten. Not your puppy dog."

"Then what?"

"I want to be—"

"Say it."

"I want to be your bad doggy."

I felt him stiffen against me. In a single, silent frame, I felt his cock harden, felt his whole body change. From boyfriend to master in just one breath. He sighed, and I felt that warm rush of air against the skin on the nape of my neck, and then I sighed, too, with the relief of confessing. After that, everything happened so quickly that the actions were difficult for me to process. He was moving, standing at my side by the bed, and he was positioning me in the very center of our mattress, on my hands and knees, head up, shoulders back. I moved automatically, accustomed to obeying, but even so, I knew that this was different.

Justin admired my stance, and I felt more naked than I ever had before. The way his eyes roamed over my figure, as if he were a judge at one of those high-class dog shows, and I was just another fancy bitch in heat.

"You look good, Celia," he said before turning away and rummaging through the contents of my dresser, searching for something. I should have guessed what he wanted, but I didn't.

He came back with a rhinestone-studded pink leather collar, which he attached as tightly as it would go around my neck.

"Now, bark like a dog for me."

"A little dog or a big dog?" I said, and I giggled nervously, even though I knew how serious this whole thing was. I'd told him. I'd confessed completely. Now, he was giving me what I wanted. I should have been in the part already, not outside looking in, which is how I felt. Poodle-blonde hair tousled up in a high ponytail. That cute little collar around my slender throat.

"Your choice," he said magnanimously. "Whatever works for you."

I thought about it for a moment. But he was giving me too much freedom of choice. My thoughts wandered. What type of canine was I most like? A fiery-tempered dalmatian? A sweet-natured retriever? A carefully clipped high-end bitch with a haughty little wiggle? My golden-blonde bangs fell dramatically over my forehead, and Justin sweetly pushed the lock out of my eyes so that he could clearly see my face.

"I don't think I can—" I said, even though I heard the barking sounds in my head. The rough, low growls of a purebred. *Make me do this,* I wanted to tell him. *I can't do it on my own. You do it for me.*

Justin didn't say a word. Not one word. He simply waited.

I closed my eyes and tried to obey. But I couldn't. Here it was. Just the scene I'd begged him to give me. I was a bad doggy. I couldn't even bark for my master.

"You've already got the collar on," he said, his blue eyes shining as he tricked one finger beneath the thin leather band around my throat, "and you like wearing a leash when we go to S/M clubs, so what's the fucking problem?"

I didn't know. I just couldn't do it. I thought back to my high school days, when I'd gone with friends to a rowdy after-school football game. Everyone rooted wildly for the team, screaming whenever we scored a point, but I simply mouthed the cheers, unable to join in the chorus of happy yells. Even today, I find it difficult to raise my voice in public, and sometimes waiters have a hard time hearing me when I place an order.

"A simple yip," he tried next, climbing between my spread thighs and beginning to lick slowly up the inside of my legs. His ginger-red goatee tickled my skin in the most delicious manner. His tongue took tremulous, circuitous journeys on its way northward.

"Come on, Celia," he urged. "Come on, little puppy. Wouldn't you do anything you could to turn me on, Celia?"

Justin always knows how to bring me pleasure—pleasure that only comes from playing the most dangerous type of bedroom games. He's the one who turned me on to being tied down, the sole boyfriend who ever read the deep, dark wish in my gaze to be a submissive. Others pegged me for a sweet thing, a vanilla chicklet who wouldn't dare break a boundary. Not Justin. He raises the bar each time we fuck, and then he brings it right down on my naked hide, marking me as his own.

"*Woof,*" I said, and I would have collapsed upon myself in helpless giggles if I hadn't been so incredibly nervous. As it was, my body shook dramatically, but that might have been because Justin had reached my clit and was now centered on it with the full attention of his lips and tongue. He made slow, sloppy circles around and around, and I raised my hips up to meet his angelic mouth.

"*Woof, woof,*" I tried.

"No, you're not into it," he critiqued, lifting up to look at me. I saw the shimmering gloss of my sex juices spread on his skin, shiny in the light. "You call yourself an actress?"

"I've never played an animal before."

"But you've played a whore. You've played a coke-addict and a school teacher and an alien princess. All that's required of you is a little imagination. So what's the real problem?"

I didn't have an answer.

"You know what happens to naughty puppies, don't you?" Justin said.

Jesus, no, I didn't. But the way he spoke gave me an instant idea of how the night might wind up. I suddenly foresaw what lay in my immediate future: Embarrassment. Arousal. Pain and pleasure. My face pressed into my own filth. And all because I was being disobedient for my master.

"Bad doggy," Justin said, making a *tsk-tsk* sound with his tongue on the roof of his mouth. My heart did a flip-flop. My stomach clenched. I felt tears come to my eyes, because he knew. This is what I wanted. This is what I'd asked him for. "Such a bad little doggy—" he said, reaching up to tug on the collar around my throat, emphasizing his words with each firm pull. Why was I suddenly so wet?

"Please," I murmured. "Tell me what happens to naughty puppies."

"Try me," he said, "keep pressing my limits and you might just find out." And now he rolled me over in the bed. I heard the metallic click as he attached a leash to the collar on my throat, and then he was pulling back on the leather, forcing me to lift my head high. The fine muscles in my back tightened as I arched up. I could see my reflection in the round, gilded mirror over our bed, could see Justin take his position behind me. He was going to fuck me doggy-style. How appropriate was that?

"Head up," he insisted, and I worked even harder to keep my balance and stay tall and firm. "Belly up," he said next, tapping his fingers along my stomach. I took a deep breath, feeling my body respond to his commands. "Now, tail up," he said, a smile in his voice. "Come on, Celia. Tail up—"

I shifted my hips, raising an imaginary tail high into the air. Then I gave my hips a subtle swivel, as if wagging my tail back and forth. In my head I saw myself as "Best in Show."

"You're going to bark," he assured me now. "As I fuck you, I want you to bark."

Although I was getting into the mode of role-playing, I could feel tears streaming down my cheeks. This was beyond mortifying. How was I supposed to make a sound like a dog? Forget what I'd told him. Forget what I'd asked for, an image that I'd spent years coming to. Forget it. All bets off. My brain couldn't compute.

"You understand, don't you, Celia?" he murmured as he slid his hard, dreamy cock between my thighs. He'd gotten incredibly aroused simply from our bizarre conversation. That should have told me something. When I didn't answer, he pulled on the leash again, jerking my head up, and I nodded quickly. But that wasn't the type of response he was looking for. His hand came down hard on my rear, and I contracted instantly around his cock at the stinging sensation.

"Bark for me, baby," Justin insisted. "Be a good doggy, just this once."

I closed my eyes. Again, I tried to see the image in my mind. This is a trick I do at any audition: picture myself in the role. Lose myself firmly so that the "me" that is Celia Martin dissolves, to be replaced with the character I am going for. But now my character was a dog. Could I go that route? As I'd done before, I worked to get a feel for what type of mutt I'd be. A midsized pup, I decided. Well-groomed. Well-cared for. With a low voice and a high spirit. A dog who would play Frisbee in the park. Who would chase the neighbor's prissy white Persian cat up a tree. Who would bring the newspaper up to her master, but not release it upon request. A playful bitch, one that wasn't completely obedient—not out of disrespect, but out of sheer willfulness.

"Bark," Justin said, his cock driving hard, his hand slipping around my waist to find my clit. This was the missing link, the piece that I had needed to locate my center.

It wasn't a *woof, woof* this time. Not a *bark*, not a *yip*. I opened my eyes, met his gaze in the mirror, tossed my long turbulent mane of gold hair free from the ponytail holder, and gave a deep growl. Every vibration of the sound was animalistic. There was no pretty tow-headed girlfriend in bed with Justin anymore. There was only a canine, a sultry bitch in heat.

"That's it," Justin said, obviously surprised. He kept up the motion, his cock working steadily between my legs, but now he unfastened the leash and doubled it in his hand. "That's the girl," he continued, urging me on.

My next attempt was more dog-like, an urgent, insistent

barking sound. Justin rewarded me by fucking me harder and faster, his fingers plucking a melody out on my clit, taking me higher. And as I grew closer to climax, the barking continued. I couldn't believe it was me making these noises. But maybe it wasn't me. Maybe it was the pet that I'd become. As I got louder, Justin took on his proper role as my owner.

"Keep it down, girl," he said, a definite retraction of what he'd ask me for before. "The neighbors will complain. They'll think we actually have a pet in here. It might actually get to the landlord."

That only made me bark louder. I wanted to come. I wanted him to slam into me with everything he had.

"Bad doggy," he scowled, bringing the doubled-up leash against my ass. I whimpered at the punishing blow. "Bad doggy," he said again, smacking the other haunch with the leash. He worked me seriously with the belt, striping my hide over and over. I could picture the instant berry-red welts against my pale skin, and I rose up to reach each blow. Discipline is the magic that holds me together. "You listen to your owner. You be a good girl."

But I wouldn't. I growled and yipped. I pretended there was a full yellow moon outside, and I threw back my head and howled. Other dogs in the neighborhood answered my wails and soon there was a cacophony of canine noises filling the air.

"We're going to have to have a few solid lessons in obedience training," Justin scolded me as he dropped the leash and gripped into my hips. "A lot of long hours with your head on the floor at my feet, doing exactly what I say. You're going to have to learn to lie down. To sit. To stay. You're going to have to learn how to be a good puppy for me. Now, behave—"

But no matter how serious his tone of voice, I wouldn't behave as he demanded. I continued to bark, my voice rising, and Justin pulled away from the bed, a frown marring his handsome features. While I watched, he reached for the newspaper on the nightstand and spread the paper out on the floor. Then he glared at me.

"Down—" he said.

I didn't move. He let the belt land on my ass several times in a row in the hardest strokes I'd ever felt. Then he let up and gave me a second chance.

"Down," he said again. "Now."

Quickly, I started to move off the bed.

"Like a dog," he hissed through gritted teeth. So, like a dog, I moved on all fours off the bed to the paper-covered floor. "This is your bed tonight."

I gazed up at him, concerned, but he wouldn't say another word. Quietly, heart racing, I curled myself up at his feet. Justin gazed down at me, then nodded to himself and retreated to our bed. I heard the mattress moving as he jacked off, but he didn't ask me to join him. My eyes on the window, I watched the moonlight. My pussy throbbed, but I didn't touch myself. I lay there, breathing softly, until I fell asleep.

In the morning, I was surprised to find myself on the spread-out newsprint, surprised to see Justin with his leash in hand, standing at my side. I started to rise, and he put one hand on my shoulder, pushing me back down. With a firm gesture, he locked a leash onto my collar, then tugged me upright.

"Obedience school begins now," he said.

My lips parted, but he shook his head.

"You'll be punished," he assured me, "for each infraction.

Behave yourself, little doggy, if you know what's good for you."

I followed after him on hands and knees as he led me from our bedroom down the hall until we reached the French doors leading to our plush backyard. "You use the dirt out here, when you need to go," he said, showing me my spot, "and when you're finished, you wait for me here." He pointed to a rattan matt he'd set out on the wood porch.

His eyes were on me, staring hard, and I realized suddenly that he was actually waiting for me to pee in the backyard. Most bizarre situation ever. I wouldn't do it. But he was waiting, and I had to go. I *had* to. What kept me from standing up and walking down the hall like a grown-up woman to our bathroom? I don't know. The look in his eyes? Maybe. The fact that I'd confessed to him this very fantasy the night before? Probably. While Justin watched, I scampered off the porch to a square of dirt and squatted, pissing on the dark earth while he nodded his approval. When I came back to his side, he scratched the back of my head and led me back into our house.

I thought he would fuck me. I thought he would give in to the game playing and just fuck me. Rocket inside me and let me transform back into myself. But he was serious about his obedience training, and with the leash still attached to my collar, he led me back to our room and positioned me in front of our mirrors.

"Down," he said, and I humbly fell to his feet. "Now, sit," he commanded, and I easily obeyed. "Good girl," he said, "now go and fetch my slippers."

I crawled to the closet and nudged the door open, then reached for his leather bedroom slippers with my hand.

"With your mouth—" Justin demanded. I glanced over my shoulder at him, and saw that he wasn't kidding. I shook my head, and he was on me in an instant. "You obey me when I give you an order," he said, and the leather leash was unbuckled from my collar, and I found myself on the receiving end of the ferociously stinging blows. I bent down, cowering, as the leash found my bare ass again and again, and I realized just how much I desired the pain he rained down on me.

"Again," he said. "We try again." But I wouldn't put my mouth on those shoes, so he hauled me back in place for a second brutal encounter with the flailing leather strip of that leash. My ass was on fire. My thighs burning up. Each stripe of the belt made me more his obedient pet and less his girlfriend.

"Behave—" he hissed, and as something seemed to tear inside me, I lowered my head and took one slipper and then the other into my mouth, making two trips to bring my master his shoes.

The quality of my surrender made Justin harder than steel. He lifted me onto the bed and took me again, on all fours, exactly as I deserved to be fucked. My pussy was dripping wet; I was as turned on as I'd ever been in my life. Justin's cock drove inside of me with ease, and I saw myself as exactly who I was—who I'd always wanted to be: his pet. His puppy dog. Subservient to my master.

I looked into the mirror again and saw Justin reaching his limits. He lowered his head as the climax built within him, and he continued to fuck me just as hard as I needed it. Right at his peak, he touched my clit, just touched it, and I came with him, the explosions ricocheting back and forth between us.

He fell onto the bed and I curled up next to him, licking his lips with my tongue, kissing his face all over. I was still hungry, worked-up, and I moved down his body until my mouth was poised over his cock. I started slowly, licking the tip, then moving in a line all the way down to lick my sticky juices off his cock. Nuzzling my face against him, I lapped at his slippery pole. Then I took him into my mouth and felt his rod grow quickly hard again. I didn't speak, didn't make any noise at all. I was still his pet, but now I was his humble, subservient pet, and I worked as hard as I could to let him know how pleased I was.

He knew.

"Good doggy," Justin grinned as I sucked him. He petted my long hair as my mouth took him in. "Oh, Celia, you know you can be such a good fucking doggy when you try."

Curious

JULIE O'HORA

Over a few months' worth of sex talk, I made the quantum leap from curious to ready. Apparently, that's a finer line than one might think.

Brian had been my boyfriend for about two years. We had a good relationship—good friendship, good sex. Over time, as we got more comfortable with each other, we started sharing fantasies while making love. One night, I remember, we got talking about doing it on a sidewalk bistro table in Paris, naturally with plenty of onlookers. That was hot. I still think about that one, years later.

Anyway, one night he confessed that his biggest fantasy was to watch two women make love. No surprise there: He was a straight American male. He didn't want to join in, just to sit and watch and jerk off. The first couple of times he brought it up, I put up my mental shields. But deep down, I knew I liked to look at pictures of nude women. In fact, I preferred looking at women's bodies to men's. But have sex with a woman? That's a helluva leap, I thought.

Being a closet exhibitionist, however, I felt the idea of screwing around in front of an audience (even a one-man audience) had some appeal. It didn't take long for me to get on board with the girl-on-girl fantasy-weaving, so long as I knew he was watching. So long as he knew it was only a fantasy and that I had no intention of really doing any of it. We came up with some really sexy scenarios about camping with his college buddy and his wife, where the guys sat on a log jerking themselves off while us girls got naked on a blanket by the fire. Another story we created involved a woman he worked with and her husband. We'd have them over for dinner, then, when we were all sitting around the living room having a glass of wine, she and I would kneel on the big, oak coffee table and start making out, undressing each other and rubbing our tits together.

But, in the end, I guess I was no better than one of Pavlov's dogs. I had a couple of orgasms imagining it was a woman's tongue on me instead of Brian's, and lo and behold, I was feeling…ready. Before I knew it, we were scoping people out at clubs and taking a closer look at friends and colleagues. Unfortunately for us, this was the early '90s, before everyone with a telephone had Internet access. We soon discovered that the people who featured prominently in our bedroom fantasies were not really the people we could invite into our new reality. "How could I look my boss in the eye after you had sex with his wife?" he asked me once. "What if she hated it? He could fire me." "What if she loved it? He could promote you," I pointed out. It was a quandary.

We got the perfect idea while planning a trip for the holidays. We were going to spend Christmas at his parents' house outside L.A., then head to Vegas for New Year's Eve. That's when the neon lit up. What do they have in Vegas? Gambling, free alcohol, Siegfried and Roy. Yes, and what else? Legalized prostitution! Problem solved. Right?

Jesus, you can't imagine how hard it was to spend Christmas at his folks' house, knowing we were just a few days away from Really Doing It. Every time we made eye contact I could feel my face heat up as I read his mind. I know I got some gifts that year. No frigging idea what they might have been. Thoughts of our impending Vegas trip were all-consuming.

December 30th, New Year's Eve eve, found us on a plane en route to Fantasyland. As soon as we'd dropped our luggage in the hotel room, we raced down to street level, to those little sidewalk newspaper vending machines, and grabbed a rag from each box. Back in the room, we each sat on a double bed perusing the ads, discussing them as if we were looking for a dinette set or a used car. It seemed surreal.

"This one looks good."

"I don't know. That looks like a stock photo or something. What do they call it? Bait and switch?"

"What about this one? She has a money-back guarantee!"

"She looks like your Aunt Erlene."

Being fairly petite, I was hoping to find someone near my own size. I thought I'd be more comfortable with a brunette. (Don't ask me why—maybe because I'm a brunette and Brian was always into blondes before me. Maybe it was a jealousy thing; I don't know.)

Finally, we found her. She was just what we had fantasized about: long, brown hair; nice body; nice tits. (Sue me. Since discovering my bi-curious self, I'd also discovered I'm a tit-woman.) Brian placed the call. I sat nearby, nervously chewing a cuticle. There was something so unreal about the conversation, or maybe it was the culmination of all the months of story-painting and wondering. Whoever was on the phone quickly set Brian straight on the fact that he wasn't calling the woman in the photograph (shit), but a sort of hooker dispatch service. (My words.) The good news, however, was we could order up anything we wanted and they'd send her over. Brian essentially described the woman in the ad, gave our hotel info, and made the appointment for ten o'clock the following night, New Year's Eve.

When he hung up the phone, it was as if we'd spent the last couple of hours on foreplay. We attacked each other like rabid wolves. Instead of weaving a fantasy, we just kept panting, "Tomorrow." "Yeah, baby. Tomorrow."

To say I spent New Year's Eve day in a state of breathless anticipation would be an understatement. Dropping quarters into slot machines at an alarming rate, I'd occasionally forget, for a moment, our plans for the evening. Then something would trigger my memory (like this one cocktail waitress whose miniskirt was so short that when she bent to clear a table we could see her pussy through her panties), and my heart would race all over again. My cheeks would grow hot, my undies damp. I hardly ate all day, which was a shame because they had some really good deals at the casino restaurants.

The day dragged on, then suddenly it was time to get ready. I put on my black satin teddy, as planned, had a drink, and tried to relax. As if that was going to happen. At least I wasn't the one pacing a threadbare path in the carpet.

And then there was a knock at the door. I looked at Brian. He looked really sexy in loose, faded jeans and a black knit shirt. He still had the hard-on he'd been sporting since debarking the plane in Vegas. His eyes were kind of heavy and his lips looked full and flushed—sexy and cool. By contrast, I felt like a horny deer caught in the headlights—I imagine I looked like one, too.

Now, okay, I realize that New Year's Eve is probably the height of season for prostitutes, and maybe we didn't put our order in early, but the person at the door in no way resembled what Brian had ordered. She was tall, slightly overweight, with stringy blonde hair and the bored attitude of a grocery-store checkout girl with ten minutes left on the clock. At least she looked somewhat groomed. Brian and I had a whispered conference on the far side of the room, as she stood by the door staring at an ugly painting on the wall. I decided that we'd come this far, I wasn't going to back down now, even though I didn't find her remotely attractive.

Brian paid her $300 cash while I sat on the edge of one of the beds. She pasted on a smile for me as she approached. "Hi. I'm Heather," she said. Brian sat on the edge of the other bed as if he had a seat on the field at the Super Bowl. Without prelude, Heather reached out and unlaced the front of my teddy, taking a tit in each hand. More than a handful for Brian was much more than that for Heather. Brian breathed, "Kiss her." He already had his hand on the crotch of his jeans. Heather said, "I don't kiss clients." Which was really fine with me, since I wasn't attracted to her, but Brian was disappointed, I could tell.

Heather pulled my teddy down my legs, then removed her own blouse and denim miniskirt. No underwear. No surprise. She instructed me to lie face down on the bed. I snuck a peek at Brian, whose jeans were unzipped, hand working inside. Heather knelt over me and brushed her heavy breasts down my back. Wow. I couldn't see her, which was a good thing, but it felt spectacular and turned me on. It also gave me an idea of what Brian felt when I did that to him. Very cool. I'm sure I flinched a bit when she started fingering my pussy, but I was starting to get into it, knowing we were being watched—that Brian was watching us, getting off, just a few feet away.

Heather nudged me to roll onto my back and then she lay down next to me. She put my hand on her large breast and let me feel around a bit. While I explored another woman's chest for the first time, she started to finger-fuck me. Not my favorite thing, especially at the hand of a bored and jaded $300-an-hour hooker. I stole another glance at Brian. He was still working it, but his eyes didn't have that glazed-over look I expected to find. I did see his nostrils flare when Heather went down on me, though.

Poor girl. I bet she's still seeing a chiropractor. She must've been at it for forty-five minutes before looking at her watch and saying she needed to go. Just as well. I was about to give her "the tap" anyway. She was licking me numb and getting me nowhere. Who'd have believed a Las Vegas call girl would be so bad at eating pussy? Certainly we weren't the only people to think of this. Brian and I did, finally, have our orgasms, as we got soapy in the shower. I was glad to have him wash the tired hooker off me.

The next morning, Brian, salesman that he was, placed

a call to the hooker dispatch service. He explained that we weren't exactly happy with Heather and asked if they would honor their guarantee. Unfortunately, the guarantee was only good if we had sent her on her way before anything happened. They did offer, however, to send us someone else that night, at a $100 discount. When Brian relayed this to me, I shrugged. Why not? I'd tried it once and was nonplussed, but the idea still turned me on. Besides, we still had a couple of days left in the City of Lights.

We hung around the casinos again that day, mostly playing nickel slots since the bulk of our cash was earmarked for our lady of the evening. I didn't feel much of the anxious expectancy of the day before, probably because my hopes were so low. Or maybe more realistic. I was certain some tired career girl was going to show up at our door. This time, I told Brian, we send her back if we don't like her.

That night, I waited for our guest dressed-down, in a pair of jeans and a button-down shirt. My only concession to sexiness was a white lace demi-bra and matching panties, although I was sure Brian would be the only one to see them. Our eyes met when we heard her knock. Brian answered the door while I sat cross-legged on the bed.

She called herself "Sasha." She was gorgeous. A little shorter, a little thinner than I, she had a mane of wavy, black hair (yes, a mane—like lions have) and big dark eyes. Beautiful caramel-colored skin that proclaimed her to be half something-other-than-Caucasian. Brian glanced inquiringly at me and I glared back a "Pay the woman!"

Sasha greeted me with a hug and I felt the press of her smallish tits against mine. Looking at me, she told Brian,

174

"She's beautiful." Once again, Brian made himself comfortable on the other bed. Sasha and I sat on our bed and chatted a few minutes. She was nice, someone I could see being friends with under different circumstances. Apparently she was a dancer but took a few "odd jobs" like this on the side. She had a serious girlfriend who, she said, would like me, too. For some reason, that really turned me on.

As we talked, Sasha began unbuttoning my blouse. I guess she saw me watching her mouth, because she kissed me then. I'd never french-kissed a girl before. She slid full lips across mine in what I guess is called a "soul kiss." It was the softest kiss I'd ever felt. I pulled her knit T-shirt over her head just before she slid my blouse down my arms. I tossed them both on the floor. We made out for a long time in our bras and jeans, feeling each other through our clothes. I don't know how long we kissed and touched each other, I just know that the contours of her body—and being able to touch her, like in my fantasies—was amazing. Time stopped. I think Brian was having palpitations as he watched us.

Sasha unhooked and removed her own bra, then mine. Seeing her breasts was as much of a turn-on as touching them through her bra. She had my dream tits, the ones I always wished I had: small and perky with chocolate-kiss nipples. You know, the kind that look great in a tank top. We knelt on the bed and kissed softly. Her nipples were hard when they grazed mine—my first skin-to-skin contact with those fabulous nipples. It was as if an electric shock went from my nipples to my pussy. Our excitement cranked up a notch, and we both kicked off jeans and drenched panties and lay boob-to-boob on the bed. I could even smell how turned-on we were. Somewhere in the distance, I heard Brian grunt quietly. I knew without looking that he had his cock in his hand.

I hesitated for a moment. Understanding that I was new to this, Sasha directed me, encouraged me to take her nipple in my mouth. God, I felt like a teenager again! It is a completely different sensation to suck a woman's nipple when you're used to sucking a man's. Experimentally, I pulled on her with my lips, sweeping my tongue across the tip. She seemed to like that, so I did it again, just as Brian had done countless times to me. She brought my hand to her pussy and let me feel how wet I'd made her. It was a strange tactile adventure for me—the curly hair, moist folds, and hard clit felt familiar, like my own, but I wasn't touching myself. It was almost like being outside my body. And it was making my pussy pound.

After I'd had a few minutes to explore, Sasha smiled sweetly and pushed me back on the bed and set to work kissing her way down my body. I had never been so aroused in my life as I was with this beautiful woman licking my tits, her long hair falling all around us, and my aroused boyfriend looking on from four feet away. I'm pretty sure I heard a quiet whimper from him as she slithered down my body to bury her tongue in my aching cunt.

Holding my legs apart with small hands, she lapped at me, her hair brushing my inner thighs. I'd never felt anything like it—I was seeing colors, for chrissake!—and was powerless to do anything but buck against her mouth, caressing my own breasts. Brian was naked now, standing beside us, raging hard-on in hand. I turned my head a bit so that he could push the tip into my mouth a couple of times, before he retreated to a vantage point at the end of the bed. I was hungry for more of

him, and could've come easily with his cock in my mouth—
and my fantasy girl between my legs.

Sasha licked and sucked me for maybe another minute
before I shattered into a million pieces, all focused into Sasha's
pretty little mouth. I felt her move away, and Brian took her
place. He filled me with what had to be a painfully stiff prick,
and fucked me hard, and fast. When Sasha had replaced her
bra and panties, she came back over to me, cradling my head
and giving me hot, deep kisses as Brian pounded into me. I
came again on the fullness of his cock, lightheaded now, and
whimpering into Sasha's mouth. Brian moaned and came,
watching our tongues dance.

Brian and I just lay there, spent, entwined in twisted,
sweaty sheets, as Sasha finished dressing. After a few minutes,
she winked at me over Brian's shoulder and, with a small wave,
let herself out of our room.

"Well?" I asked, a bit muffled with my arm over my
face.

And Brian, purposefully obtuse, asked, "What?"

I rolled my eyes. "Was it good for you?"

"Shit, yeah," he grinned. "You?"

"Shit, yeah." I laughed. And then I said, "Let's do it again
sometime."

Aftercare

PETER ALLEN

Julie looks a little nervous as she gets out of the car.

I walk around the front of the car, take her in my arms, and fix her with that gaze that says, *Now or never.* I'm talking about her safeword.

She looks back at me, shakes her head. "I want to do it," she says. But her voice is shaking.

She kisses me once on the lips, and we walk over and knock on the door.

Eric unlocks the door. He sees Julie and smiles broadly. He's more excited about today's plan than Julie or I. After all, he's getting payment in trade.

"Hello," he says, and takes Julie's hand. He kisses her once on the lips, and I know he's soon going to be doing much more.

Eric leads us into the small waiting room. The tattoo parlor is warm; they always keep it warm because they do a lot of backroom jobs here. That's Eric's specialty. People tend to get chilled when they're laid out on a table, naked.

"You've already shaved?" he asks Julie.

She nods, her face reddening slightly.

"All right," says Eric. "Undress as much as you feel comfortable. You can leave your clothes on the pegs." It's what he always says, but this time he grins wolfishly.

Julie looks at me—as if to ask whether she really has to, but I know it's just for moral support. As if for show, she shyly steps behind the medical screen. I watch her shadow as she takes off her tight T-shirt, kicks off her shoes, unzips her leather pants and wriggles out of them.

I already know what she's wearing underneath: a white cotton thong under the pants. And nothing at all under the shirt.

Normally, she'd leave the shirt on while she was being tattooed. This, however, is anything but a normal tattoo.

I can see Julie's shadow against the screen as she bends over, taking off her thong and hanging it neatly on the peg.

She walks out from behind the screen and into the tattoo parlor. Naked and barefoot.

She looks at me shyly. She knows this is the moment when she should turn back, should utter her safeword. But she also knows she won't, because this is a turning point in our relationship: It's now or never.

I look back at her, love in my eyes—and something else. Lust. She's gorgeous, her slim pale body toned and pristine. She's never had a tattoo, never had a piercing. Despite her proclivity for pain, she's afraid of them. The idea turns her on incredibly, but she's afraid.

Eric looks her up and down, too. Normally, it would be highly unprofessional for him to do what he does. But this is anything but a normal day.

He whistles, showing his appreciation as he looks at Julie's firm tits, slender hips, long legs, and shaved pussy.

"Damn, Steve, I can see why you're marrying this fine piece of ass."

Julie blushes, but manages a shy smile. And I can see her nipples hardening, firm pink nubs even in the warm parlor.

Eric gestures toward the table. It's not a normal tattoo table; this one has a sling for her legs and stirrups for her feet. It reclines straight back and can be cranked up to put her in a half-sitting position or a position sitting straight up.

Now, Eric fits Julie's legs into the stirrups and buckles the leather bands around them. He sits her straight up. Then he cranks the stirrups wide apart so that he can stand between her legs while he pierces her.

There are also ring bolts on the side of the chair, so he fits restraints around her wrists and padlocks them to the chair.

Julie is a bondage fiend. I can tell she's already getting incredibly turned on. I move toward the table.

There's no need for Eric to turn his back. Instead, he watches shamelessly as I stand between Julie's forcibly spread legs and finger her bare pussy. I kiss her deeply, my tongue tangling with hers. I lift my fingers, slick with her juice, to her face. I put my fingers in her mouth and she obediently licks them. Then I start to play with her tits.

They're lovely tits, B-cup and firm. Nice, pink nipples. They always get hard when she's turned on. They're very, very hard now.

"You ready?" I ask her.

Breathing hard, she nods.

I step back and Eric takes my place. His tools are already laid out on the stainless-steel table next to Julie's roost. I take a seat on the counter and watch as Eric measures Julie's nipples with the calipers, makes some marks, and engages in some other puttering adjustments. Every now and then he looks her straight in the eye and smiles, his sadist glee showing through. When he does that, Julie takes a deep breath and shivers.

I'm rock hard.

Eric fits the clamp around Julie's right nipple. I've already told her that the right nipple will be first, because in the old days flagging on the right meant you were a submissive. And Julie, without a doubt, is my submissive.

Eric leans forward and presses his lips to hers. Julie, obediently, kisses him back. She squirms a little in her bonds. Eric holds up the bright needle so that she can see it.

"Want to hold her hand?" asks Eric.

I stand next to Julie and hold her hand, having to twist it in the restraints to get a good grip. He guides her through her breathing. Then he smiles. "It's all right to scream," he says just before he starts her on the one-two-three that will lead up to her piercing.

"One," he says, and Julie breathes in and out. "Two," says Eric, and I grip her hand. In. Out. "Three," he says, and when Julie breathes out the shimmering needle goes quickly through her nipple and stays there, menacing and beautiful.

Julie doesn't scream. Her eyes go wide, and she looks into my face. "Oh, god," she whispers. "Oh my fucking god."

"Keep breathing," says Eric as he fits the ring into the

end of the needle. "In, out. In, out."

"Those are her two favorite words," I say, and reach down between her legs to feel her pussy. She's even wetter than before, her clit hard and throbbing.

"This is next," I whisper into her ear. "As soon as we finish with your nipples."

Julie nods, her eyes sparkling with fear and arousal.

Eric draws the needle through, leaving Julie with a silver ring in her nipple. Then he starts on the next nipple, clamping it firmly and readying the needle.

Again, the breathing. This time, Julie is ready for it; perhaps that's why she screams this time. Not really a scream; more a moan. Perhaps a gasp. I kiss her deeply while Eric draws the needle through and marks her with the second ring.

"How do you feel?" he asks her.

"All right," she says. "It doesn't hurt as much as I thought it would."

"Steve tells me you're a pain pig. I think it'll start feeling good, soon."

"It already does," she breathes, smiling. "That was a disappointment."

"You won't be disappointed now," says Eric, reaching down to touch her clit.

I look into her eyes, smiling, seeing the fear and eagerness on her face. I am still rock hard; I could take my cock out and come in an instant. I watch and kiss Julie as Eric measures her clit, then says, "She needs to be fully erect."

I reach down and stroke her clit, listening to Julie moan as she writhes in her bonds. I rub her for a long time, making sure she's fully aroused.

"I think she's erect," I say.

"Me, too," says Eric, and fits Julie's clit between the teeth of the clamp.

When the needle goes through, Julie gasps, then wails. Her exhalation comes long and slow as Eric draws the needle through, fitting the ring into her clit. A single tear runs down Julie's cheek, and then she starts to moan softly as she rubs her face against my neck.

Eric finishes up with a few minor details, offering Julie a mirror to approve the placement.

Julie's eyes are glazed over, her whole body flushed with arousal and pain. She stares dumbfounded at the metal ring glistening through her clitoris.

"It's fine," I say.

"Time for payment in trade?" grins Eric.

I look at Julie. She's tranced out, fully overcome by the pain and sexual excitement. But I know her well, and she could still use her safeword.

Eric unclasps the buckles around her ankles, undoes the restraints around her wrists. He helps Julie off the table and leads her over, still naked, to the room's one armchair, a big one covered in leather.

Eric sits there and spreads his legs.

Julie gasps slightly as she lowers herself to her knees. She keeps her legs wide, hunkered down low, so as not to disturb her fresh piercing. She has more trouble with her nipple piercings, but she manages to arch her back and keep them clear of Eric's legs.

Julie knows what she is to do. Eric, our longtime friend, is receiving no payment for today's piercing. Instead, Julie's pretty mouth is the payment. She obediently unbuckles his belt and unzips his leather pants. She takes his cock out, finding it rock hard.

Without hesitation, Julie starts sucking him. I watch, my own cock hard as Julie's mouth slides up and down Eric's swollen cock. She whimpers slightly as she sucks it down, and I can tell she's hungry for it, hungry for his come.

Eric runs his fingers through her hair, his face blissful. When he's ready to come his ass lifts slightly and his hips pivot; Julie takes the cue and eagerly clamps her mouth around the shaft of his cock. He cries out, coming, filling Julie's mouth with his jizz.

When she pulls off of him and licks him clean, she looks up at me.

"Please, Sir," she says, her voice hoarse, her throat savaged by Eric's cock. "May I please suck your cock, too?"

Eric looks at me and smiles. This wasn't part of the plan, but clearly Julie's piercing has transformed her in ways none of us expected. And besides, I'm hard. I was already thinking fondly about pushing her head down into my lap once we got to the car.

"All right," I say, unzipping my pants and taking my cock out. "Come here."

I remain standing as Julie crawls to me, her body twitching with every movement that affects her freshly pierced tits and clit. But she makes it to me, and I lean my ass against the edge of the table where my slave was just pierced. Her mouth descends on my cock and she sucks it more eagerly than she ever has before—desperate for my jism. Hungry.

I look down at her and see her eyes glazed, blissed with

pain and sex. She sucks me as if she's been wanting to suck cock all her life, as if she's trained and planned for this moment forever. She pumps my cock into her throat and moans as she rubs it all over her face.

When I come, she swallows every drop, hot streams shooting into her mouth and down her throat. She licks me clean and tucks my cock back into my leather pants, zipping them up.

"Now that's what I call aftercare," says Eric, smiling.

I have to help Julie into the loose shorts she brought to replace her leather pants. She puts them on without underwear, and puts a clean undershirt on beneath the T-shirt she came in with.

Eric kisses her tenderly before he lets her go. I grasp his hand and say, "Thanks."

"Hey," he says. "Thank *you*. Anytime you want your little girl pierced, you know where to come."

"I think we'll be back soon," I say, patting Julie on the ass. "I've always wondered what it feels like to get your cock sucked by a girl with a tongue piercing."

I look into her eyes, still glazed over: There's a mixture of fear, excitement, and delicious anticipation. I know I can't fuck her for weeks. But she's already shown that there's plenty of other things she can do.

And I'm betting she can do them even better, now that she knows she's mine. Her devotion to me, her submission, has clearly gotten deeper with the piercing of her flesh, the insertion of rings to remind Julie who she belongs to.

I can hardly wait to get her home, and find out how deep that submission goes.

Good for the Goose

JESSE NELSON

Deep berry-red lipstick kisses mark my skin. When I see the imprints, I can almost feel Cameron's lips pressed against my body all over again. That gives me a powerful little thrill, and my cock hardens at the memory of what we've just done. How Cameron took her time kissing everywhere on me before finally rewarding my behavior with the sweetest, longest, most sensitive blow job I've ever had.

"Are you coming back to bed, hon?" Cameron calls from our room.

"Yeah," I answer immediately, "in a minute."

I stand naked in front of the full-length bathroom mirror, admiring the multitude of lip prints left by my randy girlfriend. Her kisses are like a road map of the places she's visited over the last few hours. My chest, my flat stomach, my cock and balls. The high-intensity red really stands out against my skin, and I realize that there are tiny sparkles blended within the color of the cosmetic, so that my skin seems to shimmer wherever the lipstick is smeared.

During our marathon sex session, Cameron would pause and reapply the gloss to her full mouth, then resume her position. She knows just how much I adore the echoes of her kisses to remain on me even after we're through fucking. But what she doesn't know is how much I really like her lipstick. The rows of tubes she keeps in the clear plastic box on the shelf by the sink always draw me toward them. Each time I enter the room, I run my fingers over her collection. There's magic in those dainty tubes.

I like to watch her put the lipstick on, charmed by the careful way she applies the color then blots away the excess. Sometimes, I sit on the cold porcelain lip of the tub and watch, pretending that we're simply having some normal conversation, but really paying careful attention to every last detail of her makeup routine. It makes me hard like nothing else. The way she drags the little mascara wand over her already lengthy lashes. The way she dips a sleek brush into a pot of blush and whisks it over her high cheekbones. She doesn't wear too much—just enough to enhance her already beautiful face. Pale pink on the apples of her cheeks. A silvery white on her eyelids. The perfect shade of plummy red on her lips. I don't know precisely what it is about the cosmetics that I like so much, but I find myself attracted to them. The way I've gotten around confessing my fetish to her is by having her put lipstick on herself when we fuck.

But what I really want is for her to put it on me.

I know just how Cameron looks when she reaches for the tube, purses her lips at her reflection, applies her favorite hue.

She's got so many different tricks. Sometimes she adds liner afterward, coloring in her lips rather than adding a cartoonish outline. Other times she swipes on a clear gloss—one called Triple X—that makes her mouth look like something right out of a porno movie.

Now, I want to see what the stuff will look like on my lips. Maybe it's because I'm still swimming in that hazy, turned-on, post-sex vibe. Or maybe my longing has finally gotten the better of my sense of preservation. I hesitate for only a moment before reaching for a black lacquered tube and removing the cap. What's the harm in trying it on? Just to see. Just a little bit. Really, there's nothing different from applying chapstick, right? And all sorts of men wear chapstick. Athletes. Businessmen. Nothing wrong with that.

With these bizarre mental words of wisdom urging me on, I undo the tube so that the lipstick extends upward. But I turn the cap too hard, and the column of color trembles unsteadily. I try to remember what Cameron looks like when she's manipulating one of these items. Does she only twist the tube a tiny bit? Does it go in this direction? I'm feeling exceptionally graceless now. My hand is large and clumsy in comparison to her delicate fingers. Then I hear her bare feet on the hardwood floor of the hallway, coming closer, and in my haste to hide my activities, I break the lipstick in half.

When she opens the bathroom door and catches me, I feel myself immediately start to blush. Does she know what I've been up to? Can she tell? I have her tube in one hand, but I curl my fingers around it, concealing the whole tube in my large palm.

"Admiring yourself?" she smiles, parking herself on the

rim of the sink and waiting for my response. She's wearing one of my white button-up shirts, and her long, coltish legs are bare.

I shrug my broad shoulders at her, and then nod because maybe if she thinks she's caught me, she'll leave. Then I can hide the evidence—the broken-off lipstick—and clean myself off. She won't know that one tube was missing from the masses, will she?

"I don't really think Peony Passion is your color," she says next, and I close my eyes to try to keep myself steady. How did she know?

"It's smeared all over your fingers," she says, before I can ask. "If I were choosing for you, I'd pick more of a true red—Crimson Kiss, I think. That one would look amazing with your dark hair and blue eyes."

I nod as if I understand what the fuck she's talking about. But I don't.

"You like it when I put on my lipstick," she says, "but you wish I'd put it on you instead." Was she in the bathroom with me while I was having these thoughts? Was she inside my fucking head?

"You're an easy read, Sam," she sighs, hand out, palm open, waiting for me to give over the crushed and broken tube.

"Sorry," I say.

"No," she shakes her head. "You aren't yet."

"Meaning...?" I ask, and she must see me puff out my chest a little bit, as if reminding her how much bigger I am than she is. Because I am. I tower over my finely drawn, slim-hipped blonde girlfriend.

"So tough," she grins. "With all your bulging muscles,

and your big hard cock, and your strong deep voice. But all you really want is for me to put my makeup on you and turn you into a pretty girl. Isn't that what you want, Sam? Tell me the truth."

I find myself nodding before I can have a mental debate about how to answer her question. She's caught me after all. There's no way to deny it.

"Here's the offer," she says. "I'll make you up, but you have to behave for me. You have to obey and do whatever I say. I promise you'll get a fair deal. But the thing of it is, what's good for the goose is good for the gander."

"I never understood what that meant, anyway," I tell her.

"It means if you get off, then I get off. Even-Steven."

"Anything," I hear myself saying. "Anything, yes, whatever you say."

Even as I'm still speaking, Cameron's in motion. She sprints to her closet and returns with a large silk robe in a pale blue the color of the morning sky. She holds it out for me, and I slide into the sumptuous creation, feeling the caress of the smooth, cold silk against my skin. Girls really know what they're doing, don't they? Dolling themselves up in these sweet, soft fabrics. Instantly, I feel more sexy for being in the decadent robe.

Then Cameron has me sit on the top of our hamper as she readies her supplies. "Close your eyes," she commands. I hesitate for one moment, but the look of power in her startling wide eyes makes me obey. When I do, Cameron uses one of her headbands to scrape my dark hair away from my face. I'm glad my eyes are closed so that I can't see how silly I look in this. But I can imagine the picture in my head—no problem.

I feel a cool lotion being spread onto my cheeks. Then her fingertips as they massage lotion into my skin.

And then she gets started. Brushes whir over my cheeks. Pencils color my eyelids and around my lips. She is working in fast motion, and each time she touches me, my cock stirs to life. I feel as giddy as I ever have. Maybe it's the silk robe, maybe it's the smell of the makeup she's using, but suddenly I am all girl. Cameron has me look up, at the ceiling, and I feel the brush of a mascara wand on my lashes. Then she has me purse my lips as she finally uses my all-time favorite of her cosmetic devices—the tiny little lip brush. There is something so sexy about being the object of her attention. When I look into her face, I see total concentration. She's not thinking of me as Sam, her hard-bodied beau. She's thinking of me as a canvas to illustrate.

"Yes," she says, stepping back and nodding to herself. "Lovely—"

Never heard that adjective used about me before.

"So lovely," she amends the statement. "Wanna see?"

I do and I don't. I'm actually terrified. But the way that my cock is scraping against the inside of the silk answers the question for her. I'm a tent in this thing. She takes that upright pole for the affirmative, and she steps out of the way of the bathroom mirror, revealing....

"Christ, I'm good-looking."

I mean it. I am. She's done something amazing with shadows and highlighter, with concealer. My strong bone structure had been transformed to something feminine, and even if I wouldn't fool anyone in the bright light of day into thinking I was a lady, I might definitely get chatted up in our favorite dimly lit bar. My blue eyes look brighter, my lips are suddenly bee-stung full.

It takes me a minute before I notice that Cameron has left the room. Where's my angel of transformation? I follow her to the bedroom, and then I see that she's made a transformation of her own. Where's Cameron, my femme little bunny? Nowhere to be seen. In her place is some young stud, wearing a fancy-looking harness and thick, hard cock. My lithe lover has got a ribbed white T-shirt on, and looks rock-hard and ballsy, waiting for me on the bed.

"Pretty thing," *he* says, eyes roaming up and down my figure. "Get over here."

For the first time ever, I play coy. I tilt my head, I run my fingertips along the sash of the robe. "Where?" I murmur.

"You know, Sammi, you know."

And I do, but I wait until this young stud leans up and grabs me, forcing me to come forward. "Kiss me," my lover demands. And now I know what she was talking about in the bathroom. She's in charge. She's making me wait. If I get off, then she gets off. But I'm hungry to please her, and I kiss from her collarbones down her neck, moving toward her cock. I want to suck it. Want that like I've never wanted anything before in my fucking life. When I get to the power of her pole, I bathe it in the wetness of my mouth. I slick my lips up and down, from the tip to the place where the cock meets her body. I bob on it, and I feel the lipstick start to smear.

Cameron instantly pushes me back and reapplies the lipstick, just as she does when she's the one sucking me. I feel the fresh coat of color on my lips, and I begin to intentionally leave marks on her. On the flat of her belly. On the skin of her inner thighs. I work her until she needs release, and suddenly she moves away from me and pushes me down into proper position over on the bed.

Then Cameron is behind me, lifting the robe to reveal my naked ass, and I feel the lube spilling down between my cheeks. I tremble, knowing somehow, an instant ahead of time, exactly what this is going to be like. My sweet pretty fancy girlfriend is going to fuck my ass and I am going to like it. How do I know? I've lived this scenario in jerk-off scenes my whole life.

"Ready?" my deep-voiced lover hisses at me. "Ready, Sammi?"

I think I say, "Yes." I must say something. But it's as if I'm already gone. Sam, the big hulking guy who was a wrestler in high school, who works as a volunteer fireman, who climbed Half Dome—Sam is gone. And Sammi has never been ass-fucked before and doesn't know how to relax.

Cameron knows what to do. One firm hand comes around my body, to play with me, and I close my eyes and pretend that I have a clit. That those fingertips are stroking up and down my clit instead of milking my shaft. Life is sweet as I feel myself getting wetter. I sigh as I finally start to let go. At that moment, Cameron pushes forward and enters me. A gentle press, a long slide. I lower my head to my chest and moan. The intrusion is welcome and breathtaking. Now, Cameron uses both hands to hold my hips, and I think of those hips as curvy rather than straight. Of luscious rather than hard.

With the slip-slide of the lube, and the pressure of Cameron's hands on me, I give in. I find myself working on the pole of my lover's cock, working myself, and then one of my hands is suddenly playing with my own sex. Taking over where

Cam left off. I probe between my legs, picturing my pussy as cleanly shaved, ready and wet. Even as my hand moves up and down my shaft, I think of my clit getting engorged, of the orgasm spreading through my body slowly, like rippling water, rather than rocket-fast and eruption-angry.

As soon as I come, Cameron pulls out of my ass and pushes me onto the bed. She pulls off her harness and slides her slippery-wet pussy in front of my mouth. I eat from her with abandon. I give over everything I have to the taste of her sweet cunt. All man again, I am. Or all woman. Or maybe both. Maybe it doesn't fucking matter what I am, as long as I get the taste of her on my face and in my hair, and on my skin. If I could, I'd climb inside her. As it is, I drink from her sweet-tasting pussy until she slams her hips against me, and then I keep tickling her clit with my tongue until she comes a second time.

When she reaches for me, pulling me up next to her, I know that she's ready for a breather, a little downtime between sessions.

Cameron looks down at the lipstick imprints that cover her naked body. "What's good for the goose—" she murmurs. She doesn't have to finish the statement. I already know the rest by heart.

Key Party

SCOTT WALLACE

He's not sure, but he thinks when he takes off the blindfold and holds up the key chain that he can see a hint of disappointment in her face. The room is filled with hoots and hollers as all the partygoers shout their suggestions to the new ad hoc couple. He glances around, seeing the men wink at him, the women cast flirtatious glances—he might have ended up with any of them.

He walks across the room to where she's sitting, looking divine in her long black skirt and sleeveless blouse, holding a glass of red wine. She fixes him pointedly with her stare.

"If you don't want to, we don't have to," he blurts. "I can put it back and pick another set of keys."

She sighs—again, disappointed, or is it his imagination? Then she sets her wine on the coffee table, stands up, and puts her arms around him, planting an open-mouthed kiss on his lips.

"I wouldn't dream of it," she says, amid the applause of all their friends. She plucks the keys from his hand. "Let's go."

A rhythmic and salacious chanting, strictly junior-high stuff, follows them out the door.

"Your place or mine?" She sounds sarcastic, but the smell of her perfume in her small Audi is exciting him.

"I have a reservation at the hot tub place near here," he says. "It's for nine o'clock. Two hours."

"You came prepared."

"I figured...I mean, if nothing else, we can just have a soak."

"I didn't bring my suit," she says coldly. "Besides, two hours in a hot tub and I'll be so wrinkly no one would *want* to fuck me. Not even my husband."

"Well...you know what I mean."

She shrugs, smiling wryly. "Then I guess we're skinny dipping. It's all right, I'm not shy. Besides, what's the point of going to a key party if you only get wet in the tub?"

"If you don't want to—"

"Oh, come on. Don't you think reluctance is kind of a turn-on? Wouldn't it be hotter if I didn't really want to but I do it anyway because I know my husband's getting fucked by my best friend tonight?" She laughs, leans forward, kisses him again. "Well, *I* think it's a turn-on. And you won't know if I really want it until I come—*if* I come."

"I guess not."

"Where's the hot-tub place again?"

He gives her directions.

Maybe it's the way they're dressed, but the girl at the front desk gives him a nasty look. He knows from rumor and innuendo that more than a few call girls use this place to avoid the expense of a hotel room. Does she look like a hooker, with her long black dress, a little too tight in the hips, and her blouse, tight enough to gap slightly between buttons where it pulls at her dress? He's wearing a tie, which he never does—so he feels more than a little like a trick.

"Now, you promise you don't have anything nasty?" she says to him in a stage whisper while the college student rings up his credit card.

"I promise," he says, and the college student turns several shades of red.

He's got to hand it to her—she doesn't smile.

The whole way down the sterile, chlorine-smelling tiled corridor, he's wondering whether he's supposed to take the lead. He picked the keys; does that mean he should throw her against the wall and tear her clothes off as soon as they're in the door? Or give her time to undress, put on a robe, get her bearings? Should he avert his eyes while she takes her clothes off? Should they flirt as they sink into the hot tub together? Should he wear his boxer shorts?

He's relieved when she begins stripping off her clothes before he's even locked the door. The room is furnished in tile and smells slightly dank and chemical; there's a hot tub, a sauna, and a waist-high padded vinyl table that, he's quite sure, was placed there with a single purpose in mind.

The blouse comes off and she hangs it on a peg; she kicks her shoes into a corner; she wriggles out of the dress and he sees she's wearing a thong and garter belt. No bra, which doesn't surprise him especially; he'd been able to see that from the way her nipples showed through the silk blouse. She doesn't even look at him as she unhitches the garter belt and pulls down her stockings. But she turns to look at him and holds his gaze like a cobra waiting to strike when she slides the thong off her body.

He feels his heart pounding, a sudden rush.

"Do those hurt?"

"Do what hurt?"

"Those Brazilian thingies."

"Like a motherfucker," she says, and tosses him her thong. He catches it and feels a wave of excitement as he realizes that it's damp. Sweat, maybe?

She sits on the vinyl table, leans back, and smoothly spreads her legs as wide as she can, her eyes locked in his, her knees bent, and her feet tucked against her firm ass. Now he can see the wax job up close, leaving every fold of her exquisite pussy revealed. She lets her hands rest on her thighs.

"But nothing beats the smooth look. Don't you agree?"

He agrees. Her pussy looks magnificent. His eyes flicker from her pussy to her eyes and back again; when he looks into his eyes, she holds his gaze. He understands that she was making it painfully obvious that she intends to fulfill every obligation of the key party—right here, right now, in these chlorine-choked environs. But however much her spreading her legs for him has broken the ice, they haven't yet made contact, and there remains in him that desperate awkwardness that comes from two people who have acknowledged that they are about to have sex for the first time—but who haven't yet touched.

So he walks over to her, leans up against the edge of the padded table, and bends forward to kiss her.

"No kissing," she says. "Remember? It's one of the conditions of the party."

He freezes, taken aback. He does remember, from the talk the host gave beforehand—it makes it easier for married couples to let their spouses fool around with each other, since kissing seems, to most of them, an intimate act reserved for longtime partners. But it hardly seems relevant. It's not like a serious rule—not when they are here, and she is spreading her legs for him, showing him her pussy, begging him to fuck her. Just the same, he figures, if she wants to be faithful to the agreement, he isn't going to argue.

So he does what he does when making love with his wife, when she seems even the least bit reluctant to make love. "No kissing on the lips, right?" he says, and drops to his knees.

The tile is damp, and he feels the moisture soaking the knees of his good slacks. Without pausing, he lowers his mouth between her legs, his eyes flickering up to meet hers just before his lips press against hers; the look on her face tells him that she wants this as much as he does, that she's been wanting this.

Something else tells him this: the slick feel of her pussy as his tongue wriggles between her lips, the sharp tang of her juice, full and ripe and abundant. She's wet—incredibly wet. His tongue-tip finds her clit and she leans back on the massage table, moaning.

She seems to taste so different, stronger than his wife, perhaps because she's shaved—but to smell milder, or perhaps it's just the overwhelming aroma of chlorine blotting out her scent. Nonetheless, she tastes good. He licks hungrily, devouring her pussy as she brings her legs together slightly so that her thighs caress his face. He licks from the entrance to her moist cunt up to the firm bud of her clitoris, then presses his tongue hard against it, feeling her body jerk against him as he works her. He feels her fingertips running through his hair, encouraging him to stay right where he is. He focuses his tongue on her clit as his hands come up underneath her and cup her firm buttocks, holding her lower body in place for him. Her feet tucked under her ass, she lifts her ass off the padded table and grinds her body more firmly onto his mouth.

His wife usually doesn't come this way, not from getting eaten out. So he's a little surprised when he recognizes the sounds of her breathing quickening, when he hears her whimpering and begging him not to stop. It sounds like she's going to climax, and he sees her playing with her breasts, pinching the nipples, getting close to orgasm. He reaches up with one hand to caress her tits, but she looks down at him and shakes her head.

"No," she says. "Put your fingers inside me."

His hand moves back down her belly and finds her entrance. Two fingers slide in so easily, and it's only a few thrusts later, her pinching her nipples hard, now, really hard, that she throws her head back and comes, her body pushing itself onto his fingers as if of its own accord.

He keeps licking her until she's shuddering, overwhelmed with the sensations. Her thighs come together and she gently pushes his face out from between them. She looks at him, her face overwhelmed with hunger.

"Take your clothes off and get on the table," she tells him.

He strips his clothes off quickly, not bothering to hang them on the pegs provided. He's hard—he always gets hard when he's eating pussy.

When he's naked he recognizes the look of open lust in her face. He stretches out on the table lengthwise, feeling awkward now that he's naked. He's almost afraid to look at her, she's so gorgeous in the strange light of the white-tiled room.

But his awkwardness goes away when he feels her weight on top of his lower body, when he feels her mouth descend upon his cock and take it easily in her mouth. She starts sucking him as if she doesn't care whether it feels good, as if she's not interested in his pleasure—only her own. She's desperate for his cock in her mouth, and that's what always turns him on the most when he's getting a blow job. His hands rest gently on the top of her head as he moans. She devours his cock greedily, her head bobbing up and down as she rubs it all over her face, licks his balls, lets her lips and tongue pulse up and down the length of his shaft as if she's eating corn-on-the-cob. One or two times it almost hurts, she's sucking him so hard. But the pressure turns him on, the tension of having her seem as if she's about to eat his cock whole and swallow it with a smile on her face.

Usually, when he's ready to come, his wife just licks and sucks around the base while she strokes his shaft with her hand, sometimes working her thumb against the glans. When he comes, she usually lets him shoot on his lower belly, occasionally offering a tentative lick as if to see whether she likes it. This woman, though, keeps sucking him, pumping his cock into her mouth.

"I'm about to come," he tells her breathlessly, expecting her to take it out so that she doesn't have to swallow. But she's not interested—or maybe she *is* interested—and he wonders if he heard her. He tries to hold back, desperately fighting his orgasm, telling her again: "Oh fuck, I'm about to come—"

And then he does, her lips still clamped halfway down his shaft, her tongue working him as he arches his back and lets himself go in her mouth. She doesn't pull back, not even a little—she doesn't even flinch. She sucks, hard, drinking every last drop of his come. When he's finished she licks his softening cock some more, as if unhappy that there's no more to drink. In fact, she continues licking him way past the point where he could stand it, way past the point where he would have delicately pushed his wife away and asked her to stop. But he lets this woman do it, until he's writhing in pain, half wanting it to end, half wishing it would go on forever.

When she's had enough—for now—she kisses his thighs and stands up.

"Let's have a soak," she says, and he watches her naked body as it descends into the water of the hot tub.

The conversation is awkward—they're two people who don't know what to say to each other. The hot water feels good to him, every nerve of his body alive after the intense orgasm. She props herself against the jets and rocks back and forth while they talk, and he recognizes that the jet is squarely hitting her pussy and clit.

"What *is* it about having sex with a stranger?" he asks at one point.

"Or a neighbor's wife?"

"Yeah."

"I don't know," she says. "It's forbidden."

"But this isn't forbidden. We got permission and everything. It was all so fucking negotiated."

She shrugs. "It's still forbidden. How many of our friends do you think actually went through with it?"

"You mean how many of them do you think did what we did?"

"Oral sex?" She bobs against the water jet, her face flushed with the heat of the hot tub—and probably with the feel of the jet against her clit.

He smiles, then frowns.

"I think most of them probably made out like teenagers," she responds. "A little fingering, maybe a hand job, but I doubt they went all the way."

"You don't think so?"

"No, I don't think they would go that far. But it's kind of a turn-on. All those friends and neighbors making out in the back seat of their cars, afraid to go all the way."

"I guess so," he says. "But doesn't it seem kind of a waste?"

She leans forward, her body distended awkwardly as she puts her face close to his to the point where he thinks she's going to kiss him, a forbidden act.

"Are you saying you're going to fuck me?"

"No, no," he says quickly. "I didn't mean that—we don't have to...."

"Yes, we do," she says, smiling, her lips so close to his that he can smell the faint hint of red wine on her breath. "Come on. We'll never forgive ourselves."

"I'm...I'm really...that was an incredible blow job. I'm happy just doing this, if you like...."

She tucks her head against his neck, her lips caressing his skin. Her breasts brush his arm and her hand slips under the frothing water, her fingers wrapping around his cock. He's hard in an instant.

"I'm not," she said. "I want you to fuck me."

Then she's out of the hot tub, her glorious body swaying as she walks to the massage table, the perfect height for her to bend over. Her belly rests flat on the table when she spreads her legs wide and looks at him over her shoulder.

He gets out of the water, his hard-on bobbing as he looks at her pussy. He wants her now, and there's something exceptionally wicked about knowing he's going to have her, without effort, without transgression. He gets behind her and the head of his cock meets her pussy.

"We have to use condoms, remember?"

"I…I forgot. Are you sure you want to?"

"It's part of the agreement," she says.

"I haven't used condoms in years."

"Neither have I," she says with a smile. "But it's part of the agreement. There's one in my purse."

"All right," he says, and gets it. It feels awkward unrolling over his cock, and a couple of times he catches his pubic hair. It's been a long time since he used condoms. He loses his hard-on.

"Sorry," he says.

She gets off the table and drops to her knees in front of him, holding the half-unrolled condom as she starts licking his balls. He starts to get hard again. She rubs her face over his thighs and licks the lower part of his shaft. When he's hard all the way, she positions the limp rubber at his cockhead, then slides her mouth over the top of it and unrolls it using her mouth.

Her fingers wrap around the hard shaft, feeling strange as they caress him through the latex. "Wow. That's a neat trick. I didn't know you could do that."

"You wouldn't have any reason to know, would you?" she said. "Unless my husband's been talking about me in the locker room. Besides, I haven't done it for years. I'm a little surprised myself. That I can still do it."

He finds himself wondering how many condoms she's put on with her mouth, but then she slides up his body, caressing his balls with her hand. She turns around, bends over the edge of the table, and spreads her legs.

He comes up behind her and guides his cock between the lips of her cunt. It feels bizarre with the condom between them, conjuring up memories of college trysts years ago. She's more than a little dry, probably from the hot water washing away her natural lubrication.

"Do you want some lube?" he asks.

"No," she says. "It'll be okay once it's in."

He enters her, and he feels her body tensing, hears her gasp. Where she was dry on the outside, her pussy feels exceedingly tight, but as he slides out of her he feels that his cock is slick with her juices. She pushes back against him, meeting his second thrust with her own.

"I was pushing up against the jet," she says breathlessly.

"I know," he says.

"I'm really, really close."

"I don't know if I can come with the condom on," he says.

"I don't care," she says. "Just fuck me."

He starts fucking her faster, each thrust meeting one of hers until she can't match his motions in that position. She leans heavily against the table and lifts her ass in the air; he grips her thighs as he fucks her.

"Harder…harder…harder," she keeps begging him, and as he focuses on making her come he realizes that he's getting close, too. He starts pumping her as fast as he can, and it's only a moment later that he feels the tensing in her naked body that spells her orgasm. A fraction of a second passes before a loud, low moan escapes her lips, telling him that she really is coming, and even through the condom he can feel the violent contractions of her pussy around his cock.

She comes for a long time, and he keeps fucking her until she's well past finished. He's close, really close, but he doesn't think he can come with the condom—it's too unfamiliar, too diffuse a sensation. She seems to sense this from the way he's fucking her, but what he does next surprises him.

"Take the condom off," she begs him.

"But I thought you said…."

"Do it," she moans softly. "I don't care. Take the condom off and come inside me."

He wrestles with his conscience for a moment—now that he's committed to the terms of the agreement, it seems strange to violate them. But he wants her—he wants to feel her pussy naked around his cock. He pulls out of her and rips the condom off, yanking out several strands of his hair and not giving a shit. When he enters her again he knows it's going to happen fast.

"I'm coming," he says with his second thrust, and then

he does, barely moving inside her as he climaxes. She wriggles her body against him, moaning softly as she coaxes his semen into her body—forbidden, so forbidden, and hot.

When he slides out of her, his cock feels slick with come and her juices. She climbs onto the massage table, exhausted, and he joins her.

Their bodies pressed together, they lie immobile, spent.

"Are you disappointed?" he asks.

"Like, duh," she says.

"Were you disappointed when you first saw it was me?"

She sighs.

"Why the hell do you think I've been carrying around that stupid teddy bear key chain for weeks? I was afraid you wouldn't get the hint."

"Oh," he says. "I didn't."

"Dense, but faithful."

"Would you have gone along with it if someone else had picked your key?"

"Luckily, I'll never have to answer that. Thanks for making the question irrelevant."

And, strangely, he feels okay with that.

He kisses her on the lips.

Doing Eighty

COREY SAWYER

I'm speeding again. I don't want to; I don't mean to. But ever since Daddy bought me this little red convertible for my sixteenth birthday, I can't stop myself. I put on a sexy outfit and slide into the bucket seats, smelling the new leather, and next thing you know my heart is pounding and I'm hurtling down the freeway doing eighty. Daddy knows I speed; I've got three tickets already. He tells me I shouldn't, and I promise I'll be good. But there's one thing Daddy doesn't know: Speeding like this makes me wet. There's something so hot about pushing the petal to the floor and feeling the engine rev while I'm playing Madonna at top volume on the extra-premium stereo, loud enough to blast through the sound of the wind as it whips through my long hair—it just drives me crazy. It makes my pussy wet in my skimpy thong; it makes my nipples poke out hard from my push-up bra. It makes me want to fuck. It makes me want to *get* fucked.

It makes me so hot, I can't control myself. It makes me so hot—sometimes I come while I'm driving. And I mean come *hard*.

That's why I cut down these country roads rather than taking the Interstate, because I know the cops never patrol them. Sure, it's more dangerous hitting the curves at speeds like these. But it turns me on so much that I start rocking against the seat. I push myself hard against it, trying to rub my thighs together to stimulate my clit. I know if I could I would straddle the gearshift and push it into me, shifting with my cunt, fucking my virgin pussy until I come all over it, my juice dripping down. I want to pop my cherry on my little red sports car, let this baby fuck me until I'm a whore. I'm so wet I can't stand it, and I know I could come any minute just from rocking back and forth on the seat.

That's when I see and hear you: red lights, siren howling in the dark. It's after midnight. I feel a rush of terror as I glance at the speedometer—eighty miles an hour. The posted limit is thirty-five. I keep driving around a few more curves, faster and faster, pushing the needle, hoping I'll lose you or you'll lose interest. But I know it's hopeless; after the next bend there isn't a hiding place for miles.

I pull over, feeling my heart pound in time with my pussy. You park your big bike behind me and climb off, tall and imposing in the headlights of your Harley. I can hear your motorcycle boots grinding the gravel as you approach the car. I feel myself quaking—what is a lone highway patrolman going to do to a rebellious little slut dressed like I am, doing eighty on a country road after midnight?

"Evening, Ma'am. Do you have any idea how fast you were going?"

I stare at you, surprised. You're too tall, too built, too muscular. Your voice is almost too low, husky, authoritative—but I know it's true: You're a woman. I feel a rush of relief—at least I won't be raped.

I shake my head. "No, officer."

"How old are you?"

"Sixteen," I tell you.

"What's your name?"

"Corey," I say.

"Well, Corey. You're about to lose your license."

"Wh–what?"

"Driver's license and registration, please, Corey."

"I—I wasn't—"

"Save it," you say. Silently, I hand over the license. You look at it, your face registering shock as you see the name, the details. You look at me with distaste on your downturned lips.

"Get out of the car, Sir."

"But I—"

Your gun comes out of its holster; you point it at my head.

"One more word and you'll lose more than your license."

I step out of the car, shaking. The convertible's top is down, so you push me against the hood, growling at me to put my hands on the car. And when I don't comply fast enough, I feel your knee in my crotch and one hand on my hair, the other hand clapping the handcuffs on my wrists faster than I can even realize what's happening. Then, while you're still holding me close, I fee the gun pressed close to the back of my skull. I begin to beg.

"Please, please don't—"

"Speak when spoken to," you growl. "You should know better than to lie to a cop. Your name's not Corey."

"Corey's my name—I mean, it's the name I go by—"

"In those whore clubs you go to? You on your way down to the city now, to check them out? You have to blow the bouncers to get in?"

I feel tears rolling down my cheeks as you grind your knee harder into my crotch, making me gasp. I can feel it pressing in—I'd been so close to coming, I could almost go off right now. The fear isn't making me want it less—it's just making me scared, mortally terrified, that I'm gong to come while you slap me.

You kick my feet, hard, wide apart, throwing me off balance and pitching me forward against the cold metal. You twist your hand in my hair, and it comes off in your hand, bringing a yelp from me as bobby pins scatter across the hood of the sports car. You toss the wig away and reach down between my legs, shoving my tiny spandex micro-mini and white lace thong out of the way and grabbing hard.

You grab my balls and twist.

"Please," I gasp. "Please don't—"

"You a virgin, 'Corey'?"

"Yes," I gasp. "I've never—"

"But you suck lots of cock, don't you? You suck cock to get into those clubs of yours, don't you? Those special clubs they have in the city, right? How many bouncers have you sucked off, Corey?"

"I've never—"

"Don't lie to a cop," you snap. "How many, Corey? How

many cocks have you had in that virgin mouth of yours?"

"Lots," I whimper. "A whole lot."

"Yeah, I thought so. You want another one tonight? You ever suck off a cop to get out of a ticket, Corey? To keep yourself from losing your license?"

"But you're...you're—"

That's when I feel it. You've got your knee out of my crotch now and your boots planted firmly on the insides of my feet, forcing my legs apart. You're leaning harder against me, forcing me roughly onto the hood of the sports car, almost lifting me off my feet.

And I can feel your cock.

It's rubbing against my ass, between my cheeks, each thrust you're grinding into my body forcing the spandex micro-mini a little higher, yanking the string of the thong deeper into my ass, making it rub my asshole and my balls.

"You ever suck off a lady cop, Corey? It's all the rage in those clubs you like, and I promise I won't come in your mouth. You think you'd like that, or do you just suck boy cock?"

"Please," I gasp. "Please don't make me—"

"You've got two choices here, Corey. You can get on your knees and suck my cock, or I can hold you down and pop that cherry of yours. You think your daddy would like that if I spoiled his little prize?"

"No, no, no," I hear myself moaning. "Please don't make me—"

"Or maybe your daddy doesn't know he's got a little sixteen-year-old virgin on his hands. Maybe he thinks you're his tough football player son. You think he'd like it if I let him know you're a little debutante whore on weekends? Maybe then he'd want to pop your cherry himself. Only thing is, I kind of like getting head. If I have to fuck you, I'm definitely going to take away that license of yours. You were doing eighty in a thirty-five, Corey, and I already ran your plates. This is your fourth violation. You'll never drive this sexy little car again, and everyone at school will know you're a little tranny slut. I think that'll make you real popular in high school, Corey. Don't you think?"

"Please," I begged. "Please don't tell them—"

"You know what to do, then, Corey. Make me like you. Make me like you a whole lot."

You pull me off the car and spin me around, shoving me back against it so that I feel the cold metal on my ass as the spandex rides up. You stand there, your cock bulging in your tight riding-pants.

My top has come undone and I can feel my nipples poking through the bra. Tears dribble onto them as I look up at you. My cheeks are wet with tears and I can feel the caked-on makeup running. I would wipe my face, but I'm still handcuffed.

I realize you're not even going to give me the dignity of forcing me to my knees. You're going to make me get down on them myself.

So I do.

I feel the asphalt, still warm from the long day, rough against my knees through the thin white stockings I'm wearing. I stare at the ground, too ashamed to look up at you.

"Take off the dress."

I begin to protest, but when your hand lingers over your side and caresses the butt of your pistol, I know better than to continue. Down on my knees, I wriggle out of the tiny dress and feel you pluck it out of my hand. You toss it on the ground behind you.

Now I'm clad only in a push-up bra, thong panties, garter belt, stockings, and high heels. It feels strange to be dressed like this without my wig; I've been down on my knees like this, cock in my face, so many times before—but always with my hair hanging down in my face. Always with my long hair hiding me, concealing my humiliation.

"Looks like it doesn't take anything but a hard cock to get you going," you tell me. "Doesn't matter who it's on."

In case I don't understand what you mean, you lift your boot and nudge the base of my balls where they strain against the silky lace.

Making my hard cock jiggle and bounce as it sticks out of my panties.

It's hard. Rock hard, throbbing hard. I don't know why. I don't want it to be. I don't want to want it this much. I don't want to be humiliated by you knowing how bad I want it. How bad I want your cock in my mouth.

"Suck it," you tell me. "Show me what you do when you're on your knees in those clubs in the city. Suck my cock."

I take the head of your cock in my mouth, and the touch is electric. You're thick, much thicker than any cock I've ever sucked. I have to open my mouth wide to take it in, and I'm not even halfway down the shaft when I feel your thick head pressing against the entrance to my throat. I've sucked cock often enough, felt the urgent thrust and demanding force of a stiff tool with no conscience, to recognize what it means when you tangle your hands in my short hair. It means you're going to fuck me. You're going to fuck my face; you're going to fuck my throat.

I barely have time to take a deep breath before I feel you forcing it down my throat. I swallow, and gag—it's too thick. But you're not interested in whether I can take it or not; you hold me tight and grind your hips forward, pushing your cock into my throat as my muscles convulse around it.

I feel it going in, feel you sliding down into my body. My lips stretch around the base of your cock, touching the leather harness. I can smell your pussy, all around me, filling my nostrils.

You begin to slide out. Then back in.

I have to gasp to get air between your thrusts. You're pushing deep with each pump of your hips, and I can tell the base of the dildo is pressing against your clit, like I read about in one of the porn novels someone in the club loaned me. You're fucking my face as if you're using me with a real cock, waiting to come down my throat.

Your cock fills me as I hear you say: "Touch it. Touch your cock."

My hand moves of its own accord, as if it's been waiting for the command. My fingers wrap around my hard shaft, gripping it tightly.

"Now jerk off."

I can't even believe I'm doing it; stroking my cock like this means I've finally admitted to you how bad I want it. I've finally admitted to you how hard it makes me to suck your cock, down on my knees. How bad I wanted you to pull me over for speeding, how every push on the accelerator was a wriggle of my butt, a sashay of my hips, a flirtatious flutter of my eyelashes.

I pump my cock as your hips force your cock in and out of my throat. Every thrust down my throat feels like a stroke on my own cock, and my hand matches the rhythm perfectly. You know it—maybe you know it better than I do. That's why you fuck me harder, forcing the dildo against your clit, using my throat to jack yourself off. I hear your moans coming faster, louder—and then you come, gripping my hair as you fuck me. Your body shudders against mine, and the feel of your hard, orgasmic thrust sends a surge through my cock. I'm going to come, too. I'm going to come very, very soon.

One hand still holding my head down on your cock, you bend over and tug my cock down, growling at me to keep stroking it. You cup your hand and tell me to come. I try not to—I don't want to, but I can't stop my hand. I feel the pleasure exploding through me as my cock opens up and I shoot, pulsing hot semen into your hand.

Then you pull your cock out of my mouth and I feel it, pressing against my face. Your cupped hand, slathering my come over my face. Ruining my makeup. Caking my hair. You force my mouth open and press your fingers in, filling my mouth with the taste of my own come, your fingertips prodding my throat—which is so open that I take your fingers right down my throat, without gagging. I feel my come dribbling down my gullet.

You rub your cock all over my face, coating me with semen. Then you pry my lips wide and make me lick it clean. I taste my come stronger than ever, and it feels like I'm licking it off your cock.

I look up at you, eyes wide, my carefully painted face ruined with my own desire.

You bend over, the key to the handcuffs jangling as you fit it into the lock. My wrists come free and I slump forward onto my hands and knees.

"You're on your way to one of those clubs tonight, aren't you?"

"Yes," I say.

"What are you going to do tonight, Corey?"

"I'm going to suck cock," I whisper.

"Say it louder."

"I'm going to suck cock."

"That's good. Make sure you drive fast to get down there on time, Corey. You want to make it by last call."

You pull away from me, tucking your cock into your pants and zipping up.

"And besides, I've got a lot of friends who work this road. The faster you drive, the more cock you'll suck before you even get there. You'll be in good practice by the time you get to the club. You can suck cock all night long."

I look up at you as you turn and walk away, leaving me kneeling with come all over my face, dripping down onto my small breasts, soaking my push-up bra. I kneel there, watching you as you climb onto your bike and speak into the radio.

Then you start the engine and roar away.

I know you'll be waiting there, in bed when I get home, probably still wearing your strap-on. I know that I *will* suck cock all night long—your cock, stretched on our bed, hungry for it, coming again and again as you use my pretty face.

I get into the sports car and start the engine.

I do eighty the whole way home.

Wine with Dinner

ERICA DUMAS

You told me what to wear tonight. I followed your instructions to the letter. I wore my sexiest dress, a little black number so tight that it shows every curve of my body. You told me not to wear a bra, so I didn't, my firm nipples tenting the fabric of the dress as they harden in anticipation of your arrival. On my lower half, I wear only the skimpiest of thongs, black mesh, see-through. It's already soaked before we reach the restaurant.

The maitre d' eyes me provocatively, and I see several eyebrows go up as we walk to our table. The waiter holds my chair for me. I don't even open my menu; you order for me and choose the wine. I sip it as we wait for our salads.

You drink your wine fast, starting on your second glass before I'm halfway done with mine. I also notice that you've drained your water glass. You see my eyes lingering on the empty glass as the busboy hurries over to refill it. I look up and your eyes seize mine, hold them.

"Do you know why I'm drinking so quickly, Erica?"

I feel a bolt of emotion and sensation go through my body. What am I feeling? I don't even know. Fear, terror, apprehension, yes—but, without doubt, there's excitement, arousal, surrender mingled in there too. I feel my body react as if you've just touched my clit, as if you've just kissed me so hard that I melt. My pussy goes all liquid, pulsing and aching. My clit hardens in an instant, pressing firm against the tight satin of my thong. My face reddens as I become increasingly aware that my nipples are hardening, showing through the dress.

Breathing hard, I shake my head.

You smile, tip your glass toward me. "You will," you tell me.

Through the rest of dinner, I'm so turned on I hardly eat a thing. I can feel my heart pounding in my chest, pumping blood straight to my nipples, my pussy, my clit. Every time I look at you, I'm fixed by that dominant glare of yours, telling me that you're utterly in charge—that you own me. For tonight, at least.

As we sip the coffee, I clear my throat.

"I...I have to go to the ladies' room," I tell you.

You smile.

"May I go to the ladies' room?" I ask meekly.

You lean forward over the table, very close to me.

"You may go to the ladies' room," you say to me, your voice a low growl of force. "If you take your wine glass and drink every drop you put out."

My head spins and I feel short of breath. I feel myself dissolving into the sound of your voice, the humiliation of what you've told me to do creating fiery conflicts between my pussy and my head. I can't possibly do such a thing. It's much too filthy. Too, too filthy, dirty, disgusting. I've never done such a thing before.

"Do you still wish to go to the ladies' room?" you ask.

I feel like I'm in a trance. I shake my head.

"That's too bad," you say. "Because you're going. Drink every drop, Erica. And no holding back. When you walk out here again, I want you empty down there."

Fear and heat wrestle in my body. My safeword is on my lips: your middle name, such a familiar word on most days. But now my mouth is frozen around the syllables, my throat thick as it closes, my mind shorted out as my pussy grabs hold of it and refuses to let me speak my safeword, put an end to the scene. I even open my mouth to utter it, but as I do I feel a greater surge of fear in my belly, and my pussy floods anew as I realize that I'm going to surrender. I'm going to do what you've demanded.

"Here," you say. "I'll help." You dump the remainder of your wine into your water glass, reach under the table, and take my purse. Under the table I hear the zipper, and you tuck the wine glass into the cramped space. You hand it back to me.

The wine glass is too big; my purse won't quite close. I clutch it nervously and look at you, pleading, not knowing if I want you to rescind your previous order or reaffirm it, reassure me that I have no choice at all in the matter.

But I already know which you're going to do.

"Go," you tell me. "And when you come back, I want your panties in your purse."

I take my purse, stand up awkwardly, my bladder feeling

full and bloated. I wish I hadn't waited so long. I wish I hadn't drunk so much wine with dinner, nor had so much water. I wish I hadn't asked to go to the bathroom.

The simple act of my thighs rubbing together as I walk is enough to make me feel weak. I can feel the cold sticky moisture at the tops of my thighs, feel the damp cling of my tiny thong molding to the crease of my pussy. I feel your eyes on me, hot, watching me as I disappear into the hallway.

I feel my heart sink as I walk in. I have to wait for a stall; there are two women in front of me. When I finally enter the stall, I feel my safeword again, filling my throat, refusing to come out. What would it matter if I said it now? You wouldn't be there to hear. Better yet, I could just walk out and tell you I want to go home. I wouldn't even have to say my safeword… would I? You would know that I want you to stop. You would know that I want the scene to be over.

Except that I don't.

Slowly, I put my hands under my skirt and pull down my thong. It falls unbidden to my ankles, laying inert between my feet on the tiled floor. I step out of the thong, leaving it like a limp, wet rag next to the toilet. I feel too weak to bend over and pick it up.

I take the wine glass out of my purse. Breathing hard, I set it on the toilet tank.

Slowly, my hands shaking, I pull up my skirt until it's tucked over my waist. I look down at my pussy, shaved at your insistence. I slide my finger between my smooth lips, and the second I touch my cunt I see stars. When I draw my fingertip up to my clit, I almost pass out.

I'm so aroused I could come right now. I could rub

myself…two or three strokes is all it would take.

I could lie to you. I could go back to the table and tell you I drank it. You'd believe me…wouldn't you?

Hands still shaking, I reach behind me and pick up the wine glass. Hearing the rich ladies mingling by the mirrors as they fix their makeup, discussing eyeliner and lipstick, I spread my legs and hold the wine glass in position.

My whole body shudders as I let the dribble begin. My eyes roam unfocused around the tiny stall, wondering if the women can hear the sound of it, hear that it's different than it should be.

The wine glass is full so soon. It's hard for me to stop the stream, but I force myself to do so, remembering your order to drink every drop. My pussy throbs, my muscles clenched tight with resistance to my need to let it all go.

I bring the wine glass to my lips. I'm not prepared for the smell; it hits me like a wave of force. Again the mingled sensations, emotions, reactions are exploding through me. I want to scream. I want to go running. I want to run to you, curl up in your arms, cry for you. I want to give up, admit that you've shamed me, confess that you've brought me to the brink of utter humiliation.

That moment, the moment of knowing you've won, you've destroyed my will, you've subjugated me—that's when I bring the wine glass to my lips and drink.

It's so different than I thought it would be. My throat closes tight around it and for a moment I'm afraid I'm going to throw up. But I think of you, imagine you holding my head there, your fist tangled in my hair, forcing me to drink. That makes me wet all over again, and the warm liquid flowing down my throat seems to pulse into my body, making me want you—and making me want this. My throat still closes, and I fight not to gag. But I manage to swallow it all.

It takes three more glasses to empty my bladder. The first glass and the last glass are the hardest, my body resisting as I open up for it, and as I finish. I feel bloated again, my throat burning with the salty taste. I wipe myself, wipe the glass, and tuck it back into my purse. I pick up my thong and put it in my purse, too. It's so soaked it's dripping.

Outside, there's still a line. I stop and rinse my mouth in the sink, praying no one can smell me. I fix my lipstick and walk past the line of women waiting for the stall in which I've just done the most decadent, filthy thing I can imagine. I blush a fierce red as I pass them.

As I go to sit down, you seize my hand and pull me over to you.

"Kiss me," you say.

I bend down, my heart pounding, my legs weak. I kiss you, your tongue forcing its way into my mouth. I wonder if you can taste it.

You can. You smile, telling me that you know—you know I followed your orders. That sends a warm flow of pleasure through my body as I realize I couldn't have lied to you—if you hadn't tasted it on my lips and tongue, you would have known I was unfaithful.

I see the check sitting on the table, ones and a five neatly stacked: the tip.

"It's time to go," you tell me, and the double entendre is not lost on me. It sends heat into my pussy, and I know I could still come with just the barest of touches.

The waiter retrieves our coats; you lead me to the door.

There's a cab already waiting. It smells like smoke and filthy sex. On the way home you kiss me again, tasting me hungrily as if to prove to yourself that I really did what you asked—what you ordered. Your hand creeps up my thigh and under my skirt. I feel your fingers entering me and I gasp with pleasure as you find that I did the other thing you asked. You finger me slowly in the back of the cab, not even caring if the driver notices. By the time we get to our apartment, I'm right on the edge—just another thrust and I'll come. But you know my limits, and you stop before you satisfy me. Tonight you'll satisfy me in another way.

The moment we're in the door you push me up against the wall, grab my dress, pull it down over my shoulders, then over my bare tits. Then you force it down over my hips and it falls like a pool of shadow around my feet. You tell me to kick off my shoes, and I do. Now I'm naked, at your mercy.

"Go into the bathroom," you tell me. "Kneel in the tub."

My pussy feels so hot that just the act of walking to the bathroom is more than I can take. I drop to my knees, grasp the edge of the tub, and have to crawl awkwardly into it and force myself back up onto my knees.

You walk in a moment later, nude, your cock half-hard and your belly seeming swollen, distended. My eyes follow you, wide with fright and arousal. You step into the tub and tower over me, your cock semifirm, inches from my lips.

You grasp my hair and pull my face forward onto you. With your other hand you guide your cock into my mouth.

I begin sucking obediently, hoping for a moment that you'll let me get away with just giving you a blow job, something I have no ambiguous feelings about—something I love. Then I feel the first hot squirt into my mouth, abortive in its pressure.

I swallow, my body quivering as I accept you into it. I can feel my own bladder, swollen with its recycled liquid, my lower belly painfully hard and full.

"Drink it all," you say. "Swallow."

Another hot squirt comes out, resolving into a stream as I open my throat and desperately try to gulp. I feel warm liquid leaking out from the corners of my lips, my filling mouth swollen with your issue. The balmy droplets hit my breasts, dribble down over my stomach, and tickle their way over my pussy and down my thighs. I moan low in my throat, whimper as I gulp down your pulsing flow. I feel my cunt warming in response. You hold my head, your fingers tangled in my hair. I only miss those few drops, and you regulate your stream so as not to choke me.

The flow comes to an end. I wait for more, but it doesn't come.

I look up at you brightly, realizing you're empty. You look down at me with obvious pleasure on your face. I feel a warm glow of pride that I drank it all.

Then I feel your cock growing in my mouth and I realize there's more to drink.

When my lips start working up and down on your hard cock, it feels like I've come home. That cock that just filled me up with the hot, humiliating jet of liquid now sends a hunger into me, a hunger to feel your cock in my cunt. But I want to drink you, drink all your come, swallow everything you have for me.

You gently pull me off your cock, looking down at me as I pant, my lipstick smeared all over your shaft.

"Turn around," you tell me. "Hands and knees."

I obey, and you drop down behind me and put your cock against my dripping entrance. You take me in one hard thrust, making me gasp, and as you start to fuck me I know you're going to make me come. But you're not finished with me yet.

You reach underneath me and touch my belly, feeling how hard it is—filled. You push on it and I gasp in pain, moaning as the hard pressure forces my filled bladder against my G-spot. It's a different kind of orgasm I have when I'm full like this—strange, frightening, almost a little bit painful. And I know, as you rhythmically massage my belly, that there's no way in hell I'm going to be able to stop it.

I come so hard I don't know whether I'm urinating or ejaculating, but I feel the heat squirting all over my thighs. I try to stop it, but the spasms of my lower body have a mind of their own, and you increase the pressure on my bladder so that I can't stop—no matter what I do. I surrender, feeling my pussy and thighs flood with it, feeling it spray onto both of us, feeling the thickness of my swollen urethra forced wide by the pressure inside me. By the time my orgasm and the ecstatic feeling of release have dwindled deep inside me, I'm gasping and sobbing with an almost violent catharsis.

You pull out of me, turn me around, pull me up on my knees. You put your cock in my mouth, making me taste both parts of me—salty and tangy, both hot.

I love sucking your cock. But this time it's more than that—I want to thank you, love you, worship you for giving this to me. I begged for it so many times, in hastily penned fantasies emailed to you at work, in lovingly composed notes tucked into your briefcase. I begged for it, and you told me you'd give me anything, anything at all—but not that. Maybe I have issues, you said. Maybe I'll get over them someday.

Or maybe you were just making me wait. For whatever reason, I love being your bottom more than I love anything. It took me a long time to fully accept your dominance, no matter how passionately I loved it and longed for it. And now, you've given me the greatest gift you could have given me: You've gone to that place I never thought you would. You've pissed on me. You've pissed in me. You've made me drink it, and an intense fantasy that I've been harboring for what seems like forever is now a vivid, explosive reality—a taste and feel and heat that will intoxicate me forever.

You're close to coming, now, and I suck you eagerly, desperate for your come to match the taste of your piss in my mouth. I feel tears running down my cheeks as your hot come erupts in my mouth, filling my throat, making me hungry for more. And you give me more—a long, rapturous pulse that tells me the long night of foreplay turned you on as much as it did me. Maybe even more.

I feel the hot water rushing over me as you rinse both of us clean. I'm so far gone I can't even stand as you pat me clean with a big clean white towel. You have to help me to my feet, and all but force me into my crisp white robe.

You take me into the bedroom and we curl up together. I feel surrounded by your warmth, sweetened by your merciless dominance. Freed by your humiliation—even though, now, cuddling and kissing, it's just the two of us, having shared something so sacred and so simple. Wine with dinner.

I want to tell you I love you, but I'm well beyond words. Instead, I run my tongue over the inside of my mouth and savor the lingering taste of you, its flavor a love letter from you to me and back again.

Even though I can't speak, you seem to get the message.

Your Secret and Mine
KC

The skirt is so short I'm afraid you'll find out my secret before I want you to. I can definitely tell that the length of my skirt has had the desired effect—you can't take your eyes off me. It gives me an added thrill to know that I'm about to blow your mind.

You've never asked me for it, and that's why I did it. Normally I'm a natural girl—you know, no perfume, no deodorant, no razors, no makeup, and only natural fibers, nonalkaline dyes, organic soap with all-natural scents. That's why, on special occasions like this one, it gets me so hot to tart myself up for you, shaving my legs, wearing rayon, showing off. Chanel No. 5, heavy eye shadow, push-up bra. Lipstick in cocksucker red.

We do it about twice a year, an early show at the symphony and a late dinner at Rivera's. By the time we get home, we're both always so horny that we fuck like bunnies.

This time, though, I've taken it one step further.

I know I'm bad. I know I'm really, really naughty, so bad that I don't deserve a trusting guy like you. But then again, you *did* say it was all right if I used your computer, and you didn't specifically ask me not to glance through your personal files. Besides, the folder marked DOWNLOADS wasn't in your personal folder…at least, I don't think it was, though by now it's all lost in a haze of surreptitious masturbation sessions at your desk while you were out. I guess I don't really know if it was personal or not. But I'm about to find out.

Because there in that DOWNLOADS folder I found something I thought I'd long ago lost—something that could shock me about you, something that could surprise and delight and terrify and excite me.

Something that could make me wet.

There, tucked amid a meager hundred or so downloaded images of cute girls in lingerie and sunning themselves nude at the beach, there was a single folder into which you'd separated out what I can only assume were your favorites—your kink, maybe? The one kink you'd never shared with me?

I can't blame you, really. We all like variation, right? We all want something a little different than we're getting—not instead of, but in addition to. Vive le différence—that's the nature of the turn-on. So even though I know you love me, even though I know you want me, it shouldn't surprise me that some part of you also wants *that*.

As I said, I'm a natural girl. I don't shave my legs, I don't wax my bikini line, I don't shave my armpits—most of the time.

And I definitely don't shave down there.

That is, until I'd spent hour upon hour looking through

your collection. That is, until I found out in a rush that I'd discovered something I could do that would shock *you*, that would—I hoped—give you something you'd fantasized about, something that turned you on, something that made you so hard you couldn't control yourself. Something you'd never had the gumption to ask me about.

And that's why I'm so wet, right now, under the short skirt. That's why my nipples are hard in the tight cocktail dress.

That's why my clit is so hard it's throbbing. And why I can't wait to get you home.

I decide that the right moment is while we're waiting for dessert to arrive. It's a small table, a crowded restaurant, and the tablecloths are long. So it's really only a small matter for me to scoot my chair closer, lean over near to you, as if I'm telling you something I want to whisper.

It's a slightly more difficult trick to take your hand in mine and guide it to my thigh to press the fingers splayed over my flesh—and then inch it up. The skirt's very short, so your instinct is to pull back when I slide your fingers underneath it. I don't let you. I wriggle my body forward, turned toward the table so that the tablecloth hides us, as I push your hand under my skirt and spread my legs a little.

I feel your fingertips caressing me and I swear, I could come right then. I'm dripping, and that's the second thing you notice. I kiss you, unable to suppress a little moan and a sigh as I feel two fingers sliding into me. Your fingers curve, and I feel you pressing against my G-spot as your thumb savors the smooth feel of my shaved pussy, your face showing its struggle as you try to remain nonchalant. But I can tell that I've had the desired effect—when I casually brush your thigh under the table, I can feel the lump in your pants.

Your thumb touches my clit, and this time there's an instant when I really think I *am* going to come. I don't—not quite, but I'm close.

"Oh, look," I say. "Dessert's here." The waitress brings our chocolate mousse, and your hand slides out of my smooth pussy.

As she sets down the dessert, I bring your hand to my face and kiss it—a casual gesture of affection to everyone else in the restaurant. But I can smell my pussy, ripe and salty and invigorating. And I can taste it when I let my tongue drift along the tip of your finger. It makes me want you even more. It makes me want to fuck you. Now. It makes me want to feel your cock sliding into my pussy—this pussy I've shaved smooth and pink for you. Just for you.

We've just paid the check when I stand up, walk over, and lean very, very close to you.

"I've got to use the ladies' room," I say in a low, sultry voice, making sure my breath caresses the back of your neck.

"Me, too," you say.

That's one of the things I love about this restaurant— private restrooms. I've fantasized about doing you in one of them so many times I can't count, and I know tonight nothing in the world is going to keep that fantasy from coming true. I can feel the moisture running down my inner thighs, can feel the ache where your fingers were a moment ago. I can feel my thighs trembling as we edge down the line.

I leave the door unlocked and pull up my skirt. It's tight,

so it's not hard to tuck it over my waist, leaving my lower half bare except for the garter belt and stockings. I stand in the mirror, leaning forward awkwardly on my high heels so that I can take a look between my legs, at the way my pussy looks as it waits for you—smooth, shaved, hungry. I sit down on the toilet and spread my legs.

It takes you a while to get in; the line was so long that you had to wait until everyone who saw me enter this restroom had gone into the other. You knock on the door; when I don't answer, you offer some feeble comment, making a show of suddenly realizing that there's no one in here. That means there are other people still in line. That means there are other people waiting outside, waiting for this restroom that we're going to monopolize with our fucking.

Knowing that sends a surge through my clit.

I lock my eyes on yours when you enter the restroom. Your cock is still hard in your wool slacks. I want it so bad I can feel my mouth water, feel my nipples stiffen painfully in the cocktail dress. Your eyes drift from my hungry face to my hungry pussy, taking in the way I've shaved it for you. You walk over to the toilet, where I'm sitting.

I'm on you like an animal. I don't even kiss you; you don't lean down to kiss me, either. I've got your pants open in moments, and I'm bending forward, not even teasing you in the slightest—I've been teasing both of us all evening, after all. Your cock glides down my throat effortlessly, its taste mixing with the taste of merlot. I hear you suppressing a moan as my mouth lingers around the base of your cock. I savor the feeling of you thrusting deep inside me. Then I come up for air and swallow you again, whimpering slightly as I do. I'm hungry for it. My hand rests absently on my shaved pussy, stroking it, loving the way it feels, loving that it turns you on so. I want to rub my clit but I know if I do I'll come, so I don't. I just stroke my lips, caress the opening. And suck your cock.

You have to push me off you to get your turn. I know this is all about my pussy, but it's so hard for me to give up your cock. You drop to your knees, not even caring that your face hovers inches from the toilet bowl as I spread my legs still wider and feel your mouth descend onto my pussy, your tongue caressing the smooth flesh. I run my fingers through your hair and tell you that I'm going to come. I'm going to do it fast, so fast—and when your tongue finds my clit, I know from experience that nothing in the world will make you stop before I do. I lean back on the toilet seat, my hips rocking slightly as I mount toward orgasm. When I come, I have to bite my lip so hard to keep from screaming that I'm afraid, for a moment, I've drawn blood.

Part of me worries that you'll be satisfied, that you'll be quick to leave now that you've made me come—knowing that other people are waiting, that it's rude to monopolize the restroom. But that seems to be the furthest thing from your mind. Instead, you slide your arms under my shoulders and lift me off the toilet, turning me around like a rag doll as you tell me what you want. This pussy is yours, you know, and you're going to take it. You bend me over the toilet, my arms resting hard on the toilet tank. I lift my ass in the air and spread my legs, tottering on my high heels. I wriggle my butt, begging for it. But I know you don't need me to beg—I've been begging all night.

I feel your cock sticky with my saliva. It meets my

pussy, sliding easily between my lips and entering me. I gasp as you thrust in; at this angle, with my ass so high in the air, the head of your cock hits my G-spot and continues deep to press against my cervix. My whole body shivers as I feel it. You don't give it to me slow; you don't want to take your time. Not because time is so short, but because you can't bear to wait another instant. You give it to me hard, fast, demanding, as if you don't care about anything but taking this smooth, bare pussy that belongs to you. And that is what makes me come, even harder this time, bent over the toilet tank and moaning softly, wishing I could suppress the noise issuing from my lips—but totally unable to do so as the pleasure explodes through my body. I look at you over my shoulder, locking eyes with you, and whimper that I want you to come. I want you to come inside my shaved pussy.

You do, your hips pumping quickly as your cock explodes inside me. I push back onto you, knowing that you're filling me up with your come, knowing that I don't have a pair of panties with me. That thought almost makes me want to come again, but all I want right now is for you to fill me all the way, pump me full of you.

Your cock slides out of me; your fingers give me one last fleeting caress and you fasten your pants.

Without kissing me, you move toward the restroom door. You give me a final lingering look as I stand there, high on my heels, bent over, naked pussy exposed as it drips your come.

"I'll get the car," you say.

A Very Naughty Girl

SEAN EVANS

I've been anticipating this all day. Throughout my boring meetings, the dull paperwork, what kept me going was the tingling of my palm as I anticipated the feel of my wife's ass underneath it. The commute home was torture. As I sat in traffic, my hand on the gearshift longed to have her bum against it instead.

When I arrive home Sarah is already dressed for me, as she is every night. Her commute is shorter, so she always has plenty of time to change. Her blonde hair is in pigtails, her C-cup breasts stretching the white lace bra so that it shows through the thin white blouse, the mounds separated by the trail of a blue tie. Her curvy hips are clad tightly in a plaid skirt, too short for a schoolgirl but perfect for Sarah. She has on knee-high white stockings and mary janes. She's holding a Scotch on the rocks.

"Did you have a good day?" she asks me.

"Boring. But I was thinking about you. How was your day, Sarah?"

"Very good," she says meekly, looking at the floor, her face flushing red with imagined shyness.

I accept the drink, go into the living room, and sit down in the middle of the sofa. Sarah follows me. I sip the drink and hold it out for her. She takes it from me and sets it on the coffee table, sitting down next to me on the sofa.

"Do you know what I was thinking about you all day?" I ask her.

She shakes her head shyly.

"I was thinking about spanking that pretty ass of yours."

She flushes deep red, and I can see her nipples hardening under the white blouse.

"But I've been good," she says.

"I know," I tell her. "That's why I'm spanking you. You know you enjoy it."

She covers her giggle with her hand. "But that would be bad of me," she says. "I'm not supposed to enjoy spankings."

"But you do," I tell her. "Lie across my lap."

Meekly, she obeys.

I'm already hard when her belly pushes into my crotch. She wriggles slightly as I edge up her skirt.

"Spread your legs," I order.

She obeys, parting them just enough for me to slip my hand under her skirt and feel her smooth-shaved pussy. It's dripping wet, and as I slide two fingers into it she whimpers and squirms, her belly rubbing my cock.

"You're not wearing any underwear," I comment.

"I know," she says. "It…it got wet. I had to take it off."

"Why did it get wet?"

"I…I was thinking about you."

"What were you thinking about me?"

"About your cock."

"What about my cock?"

"Your cock…sliding into my ass."

I chuckle, easing two fingers deep into her pussy and letting my thumb travel up to linger between her cheeks, rubbing her tight anus. She gasps.

"That's very naughty," I say. "I thought you'd been good, but now I don't think you deserve a spanking."

"Oh please," she sighs. "I…I tried to be good. It's hard not to think about your cock."

"Because you want it so much? You want it in your ass?" I push harder on her anus, feeling it stretch gently around my thumb.

"Yes," she gasps.

I reach underneath the cushions of the sofa and find the lube she always plants there before I get home. I squeeze some lube out onto my thumb, a little more between her cheeks, and slide my thumb into her without preliminaries. She gasps again, louder this time, and then moans, long and low in her throat, a bestial, helpless growl of desire.

"You've been a very naughty girl," I tell her. "Thinking about my cock in your ass all day. You definitely don't deserve a spanking. But you don't deserve to get what you want, either."

"Please," she begs. "I want it so bad.…"

"If you want your spanking, you're going to have to earn it. Do you know how you'll earn it, Sarah?"

She shakes her head.

"Take my cock out."

She hoists herself onto her hands and knees, my thumb still planted deep inside her ass. She gropes at my belt and unzips my pants. She takes my cock out and, without being instructed, begins to suck it. Her lips slide up and down on my shaft, and I wriggle my thumb back and forth in her ass, making her whimper as she sucks my cock down her throat, breathing deep between thrusts.

"Very good, Sarah. Now sit on it."

I slide my thumb out of her ass and she climbs on top of me, straddling me as she lifts her skirt and guides my cock up to her pussy. She works it up and down her smooth, shaved slit, and then fits the head into her tight notch.

Then she settles down on it, moaning as her pussy accepts my hard shaft.

"Does that feel good, Sarah?"

"Uh-huh...." She can barely nod, so overwhelmed is she by the sensation. She reaches down and begins to rub her clit.

"Naughty girl," I say, grabbing her wrist and taking her hand away. "You don't get to come until your spanking. You don't get to come until Daddy does."

She slides up and down on my pole, her breasts swaying close to my face. I grab her blouse and rip it open, popping her full breasts out of the white lace bra. I start to suckle her nipples, eliciting moans as her hips rhythmically pump up and down, forcing my cock into her pussy with thrust after thrust. I'm very close to coming, even though it's always hard for me to get off in this position. I know it's very easy for her to come when she's on top like this, hand or no hand—my cock hits her G-spot firmly, and her clit, pushed out by the stretching of her lips, rubs against the base of my cock as she comes down on it. She's fighting not to come, even though she wants to. I grasp her pigtails and pull her head back.

"Very good, Sarah," I tell her. "You're not being naughty at all."

"Th–thank you," she gasps.

"Get off me and lie down on your belly."

She pulls herself off my cock with difficulty and as I get up she lies down, face pressed to the sofa's pillows, exposed breasts pushed against the cushions. She lifts her ass high in the air.

Her asshole is still lubricated from the thumbing I gave it earlier, but I add a little extra lube just to be sure. I've taken her ass so many times before, but I know it always scares her just a little bit. I part her cheeks with my thumbs and push my cockhead into her asshole. She moans loudly as I force it into her. She starts to come almost immediately, and I fuck her fast, making her climax intensify as I take every inch of her asshole. Within moments I'm shooting, groaning as I fill her ass with my come. Sarah's whole body is shaking, her orgasm mounting and peaking as I finish with her tight back door.

When I pull out of her ass, I say, "Very good, Sarah. But you came before Daddy did."

"I…I'm sorry," she says.

"I'm afraid you've forfeited your spanking," I tell her.

She sits up, rolls over, and grabs my arm, tucking her head against my chest. "No," she begs. "Please, please, Daddy…."

"Unless…."

"Unless what, Daddy? I'll do anything…."

"I'll spank you if you take a caning first."

She breathes hard, her hands shaking. She looks up at me, and I can tell she wants that spanking pretty goddamn bad. We enact this ritual all the time, almost every night. When she's naughty, a caning. When she's good, a spanking. The spankings make her come. The canings make her walk funny for days. She tries very, very hard to be good. She hates canings more than anything.

She nods. "All right, Daddy. If it'll make you happy."

"Go into the basement and take your clothes off."

She knows the scene is moving to the next level. She's no longer a naughty schoolgirl; she's now, indisputably, my slave.

"Yes, Daddy," she tells me. She stands up and walks toward the basement door. I hear her footsteps, heavy in the mary janes, as she goes down.

I take a moment to compose myself, taking off my work clothes. I put on my high boots but don't don pants, shirt, or underwear. When I go down the stairs into the basement, she's already stripped naked and pressed herself up against the St. Andrew's cross, legs and arms spread. She's holding onto the wrist restraints, the ones with the handles.

"I'm ready, Daddy," she says softly.

I approach the cross and fasten the restraints around her wrists. I know there's no need to padlock them. I slowly walk to the toy rack and select the long, flexible wooden cane. I swish it through the air a few times as I look over her glorious body, naked and pale in the warmth of the basement. She turned on the heat before I got here—she knew there was a good chance we'd end up here.

"Each cane stroke equals a stroke of my hand on your

ass," I tell her. "How many do you want?"

I see her struggling with the fear, fighting to count how many spanks it usually takes her to come. She's rarely in any state of mind to count accurately when she's over my lap, but I am. I know it's usually twenty.

"Twenty-five," she says, her voice quaking.

"Good choice," I say. "Are you sure you can take it?"

She nods. "I'll try, Daddy."

I start out slow, hitting the sweet spot of her ass firmly but without too much intensity. She whimpers and squirms against the restraints, pulling hard as I increase the intensity. When I give her the first truly hard cane stroke, she's warmed up, but it still makes her whole naked body explode with shudders. Soon she's writhing and moaning, her ass swaying back and forth and making a difficult target. Nonetheless, I hit her right on the mark every time.

"Count down the last five," I tell her.

I can hear the tears brimming in her voice as she whimpers "Yes, Daddy. Five more."

I hit her hard, the cane leaving an angry stripe across her pale ass. She shrieks and moans in agony, "Four more, Daddy," her voice choked with pain.

By the time she reaches "One more, Daddy," she can't hold the tears back any longer. They explode from her and she collapses against the St. Andrew's cross, weeping. I come up behind her and run my hand over the textured stripes with which I've adorned her ass.

"Just one more, Sarah. Ask for it. Remember, you decided how many you could take. You asked for twenty-five."

"Please, Daddy," she sobs. "Give me one more. Hit me

one more time."

Her body twists and spasms as I land the final blow on her ass, and she hangs limp in the grip restraints. I unbuckle the panic snaps and carry her over to the leather sofa tucked into a corner of the basement.

"Still want your spanking?" I ask her.

"Yes, please," she sobs. "Please, Daddy. Spank me."

I go slow at first, making sure to hit her in places that won't drive her over the edge. She squirms in my lap and moans, her belly rubbing against my cock, which has gotten rock-hard despite my recent orgasm. I build gradually, hitting her sweet spot when I'm sure she can take it. The feel of the raised welts is erotic to me, and as Sarah's sobs turn to whimpers and moans of orgasm, I grind my hips against the smooth flesh of her belly and tits. I'm so hard that I know I'm going to come again, maybe without even fucking her. She knows it, too. I've passed twenty-five long ago and I'm hitting her sweet spot passionately with my open palm. Sarah is edging into her orgasm, getting closer and closer, her climax ready to overtake her when I give her the rapid series of strokes right on her sweet spot. She bucks like a mare, thrusts her ass into the air, pushing it back against my hand. Her legs spread, pussy exposed, she shakes back and forth, screaming as she comes. I grab her hair with my free hand and push her down against me, both to increase the contact of our skin and to exert my dominance in this, her final moment of surrender. And there's a third reason: because I'm damn close to coming myself. I grind my cock against her tits and keep spanking her as she keeps coming. I shoot hot, thick come all over her tits and she hungrily rubs her breasts against the slippery liquid as it erupts all over her.

When she's finished coming, her breath comes in great ragged sobs, her whole body aglow with warmth.

"How do you say 'thank you' to Daddy?" I ask her.

She climbs down off me, her breasts slick and glistening with semen, her face flushed with orgasmic release. She bows down before me and presses her face to my high leather boots, starting at the tops and licking her way hungrily down to the toes, polishing me all over.

When she's finished, she licks her way up my legs and kisses my cock, lapping at the oozing remains of my semen. She puts her face in my lap and says three words I've wanted to hear for as long as I can remember.

"Thank you, Daddy."

I stroke her face tenderly and say, softly, "You're welcome."

Paying Customer

THOMAS S. ROCHE

I slip into the booth and put a five-dollar bill in the slot. I feel a quickening of my pulse as the screen slowly goes up; for a moment, I think I've miscalculated and chosen the wrong booth—it's not you. It can't be you. You look so incredibly different on the other side of this dingy glass panel, in your black G-string and hot pink go-go boots with your JUST DO ME baby tank stretched across your teacup breasts, pigtails dangling around your shapely shoulders, sex toys fanned before you like an array of forbidden fruits offered for twenty-five-cent temptation. I feel my cock start to stir before the first wave of recognition flickers through your eyes, before you grab the telephone and press it to your lips.

You say my name, incredulous. Part of me thought you might not recognize me, that I might just be a faceless trick on the other side of the glass. But the masquerade is incomplete, and I take off the baseball cap and sunglasses, tuck them into my jacket.

I pick up the telephone, smiling.

"Hi, baby."

"You know this is against the rules," you say with a faint, mischievous smile on your face.

"I'm a paying customer, aren't I?" I take a twenty out of my jacket pocket, hold it up so that you can see it, and feed it into the slot, seeing the glowing readout change from 3 to 25. "And here's something else to make it worth your while." I stuff three more twenties into the tiny slot under the glass pane.

You look strangely young as you smirk and sigh, tugging on your pigtails coquettishly.

"I can't take your money," you say, whining a little.

"Why not?" I ask you. "You're going to put on a good show, aren't you?"

You laugh behind your hand. I could see this any day of the week at home, but lately you've been talking a lot about your job. How it sometimes turns you on, but it annoys you that there aren't more guys coming in that you're attracted to. I figure this will take care of both the positive and negative aspects of this.

"Show me your pussy, Candy."

"Fuck, it's weird to hear you call me that," you say.

"Why? It's posted on the door right outside. That's who you are here, isn't it?"

"Kind of," you say.

"Then show me your pussy."

You sigh, half defeated, half excited. You wriggle out of your G-string and spread yourself wide, pointing your glistening, smooth-shaved pussy at the plastic panel. You start to stroke your cunt, your fingers working smoothly up and down in your gleaming slit.

"Yeah, you're nice and wet, aren't you?" I growl into the telephone. "It really turns you on to show a stranger your pussy, doesn't it?"

"Yeah," you smile. "The lube I put in there before I started work doesn't hurt, either."

"Hey!" I laugh. "I'm a paying customer. I don't need to know that. Tell me it makes you wet."

You roll your eyes. When you speak again, your voice is transformed, the day-to-day girl I see at home become a flirtatious, barely legal slut, begging to show her pussy for a stranger.

"Yeah," you whimper. "It makes me so fucking wet to show you my pussy."

"That's more like it," I say. "What does it make you want to do?" My cock is hard now, throbbing in my pants. I unzip and take my cock out, standing up so that I can show it to you as I lean against the panel. "It makes you want to get down on my knees and suck my dick, doesn't it?"

"Yeah," you moan.

"Do you suck your boyfriend's cock real good?"

That catches you off guard, but it brings a slight flush to your neck. You've told me more than once that the one thing that always turns you on is when guys ask about how your boyfriend fucks you. It always makes you think of me, and that turns you on as you give them every detail of our kinky games—details they no doubt think you're making up, but are absolutely true.

"Yeah," you tell me, your voice thick with arousal. "Especially when he ties me up and makes me."

"I would have thought a slut like you would want to suck

247

your boyfriend's dick," I say. "Show me your tits, Candy."

You pull up the tight baby-T, obscuring the PLEASE DO ME message and replacing it with the sight of your perfect apple-round tits, B-cups looking just large enough on your slender frame. I see I was right about your being turned on; your fair skin always flushes deep red when you get aroused. Your nipples stand out firm and hard from your breasts.

"I want to," you coo into the phone. "But it turns me on when he forces me."

"He can't force you if you want it, can he, Candy?"

"No," you moan, your hand going to your pussy and starting to stroke it. "I can't."

"You just want it that way so you don't have to admit how bad you want it, Candy, isn't that right?"

"Oh God, yeah," you moan. Your hand lingers over the largest of the dildos arrayed before you. "Can I fuck myself, Mister? Please let me fuck myself. I'm getting so fucking wet."

"Yeah," I tell you. "But shove it into your ass."

I see the flush between your breasts deepen, glowing hot and red. "But Mister," you whimper. "It's too tight back there. I've never done it that way."

"You want to fuck yourself, Candy. I want to see that cock in your ass. Now put it in there."

You pinch your nipples. "Can I slide it in my pussy first?" you beg. "To get it a little wet."

"Your pussy looks more than a little wet," I tell you. "It's fucking dripping, isn't it, Candy?"

"Yeah," you whimper. "Please, Mister. Please let me get it wet in my pussy before I put it in my ass. I've never been done that way before."

"Two strokes," I say. "Just enough to get it wet. Two strokes in your pussy, Candy. I don't want to see you fucking yourself."

"Please, Mister," you moan. "Please, I've got to fuck myself...."

"Just get it wet and then put it in your ass."

Two strokes is all it takes. When I see you slide the big dildo into your pussy, I recognize the sign of impending orgasm. You always come quickly when we play this game, and my suspicion that you'd come even faster if we played it here was correct. On the second stroke your body shudders and I hear you whimpering into the phone. Then the phone is gone, dropped as you twist and writhe in rapture.

"You just came, didn't you, Candy?"

You grab the phone and cradle it sensuously. "I don't know, Mister," you whimper. "It felt kind of funny."

"Put that cock in your ass."

"Do...do I have to?"

"Yeah," I growl. "Shove it in there."

You roll onto your belly, lifting your ass high in the air and reaching behind you, your dancer's flexibility showing itself as you position the dildo at just the right angle. I know you do lots of anal shows, so I know you've probably inserted a squirt of lube into your ass before the curtain went up. But when we play at home it turns you on to pretend it's just your pussy making the cock so wet. You work the dildo into your rear hole, wriggling your butt back and forth as you force it in.

"It's so big, Mister!"

"Shove it in," I demand. "Shove it in harder, Candy!"

With a great trembling rush, you push the dildo all the

way into your ass. Your moans rise in volume as you hump your body back onto your hand. Then you inch your ass back and press the suction cup of the dildo up against the panel, where it suctions firmly even as you start to hump back onto it, rubbing your cunt.

"Feels good, doesn't it, Candy?" I murmur into the phone.

"Oh god, yeah, Mister," you moan. "Feels so good. It's so fucking big...."

"Fuck yourself onto it. Harder!"

You obey, pushing your ass back onto the shaft of the dildo so that I can see it stretching the tightness of your ass. From this angle, it looks so much bigger than my own cock, which I've watched and felt stretch your ass numerous times.

"It kind of feels like I'm going to come again," you whimper into the phone.

"Yeah," I say. "Make yourself come again, Candy."

Your fingers zero in on your clit in exactly the way I've seen them do so many times before—I know you're not faking. This is the way you make yourself come at home, in our bedroom, whether I'm watching or not. As you pound yourself back onto the dildo, I start to pump my cock rapidly, watching your beautiful ass separate around the long hard dildo as you shove yourself onto it again and again. Then, as I hear you moaning into the phone, moaning in orgasm, I quicken the pace. Just as you finish coming, you look back at me in time to watch my cock explode, shooting streams of hot jizz all over the plastic panel.

You tug your body forward, slipping off the dildo.

"Did you like that, Candy?"

"Yeah," you whimper. "I love it when I make you come."

Without warning, the dark panel goes sliding down. You blow me a kiss just as your face disappears.

I tuck my cock back into my pants, zip up, buckle my belt, and hurry out of the booth. I'm already late for work, so I'll have to take a cab.

There's going to be hell to pay when I get home, I know. You'll tease me mercilessly, maybe even be a little bit mad that I dropped in to see you without letting you know I was coming.

But then, you have only yourself to blame. After all, you were the one who gave me the idea, showing up at the All Male Theater like that, wearing your stupid fake mustache and baseball cap, sitting there amid the sleazy, closeted bridge-and-tunnel queens while they watched me strut my stuff on stage. That night you were so wet, you fucked me so good, how could I bear not to give you a little payback?

Payback's a bitch, hon. And you'll always be mine. I'm sure you wouldn't have it any other way.

About the Authors

XAVIER ACTON—"X" to his friends—has written for Gothic.net, Necromantic.com, and the first edition of *Sweet Life*. He lives in San Francisco and is at work on a horror novel and more erotic short stories.

PETER ALLEN wrote "Aftercare," inspired by his polyamorous lover's experience of being pierced by another longtime lover while Allen watched. Although it didn't turn out exactly the way it does in the story, it certainly was fodder for ongoing fantasies, and helped convince him that not only can polyamory work, it can also be hot.

ELIZABETH COLVIN'S nonfiction writing has appeared in *Sinister* and *Good Vibrations* magazine. This is her first published piece of erotica.

FELIX D'ANGELO is an East Coast drug program counselor who writes erotica in his spare time. Although he's been writing for years, "Special Occasion" is his first published story. It was written for his girlfriend, Katrina.

DANTE DAVIDSON is the coauthor of the best-selling anthology *Bondage on a Budget* and the self-help guide *Secrets for Great Sex After Fifty.* His short stories have appeared in anthologies including *Sweet Life, Bondage,* and *Naughty Stories from A to Z,* and on the websites www.goodvibes.com and www.tinynibbles.com.

ERICA DUMAS'S poetry and fiction has appeared in *Allusion, Calico, Broken Dances, Fear Time, Seduction, Sweet Life, Best Bisexual Women's Erotica, MASTER,* and *Slave.* A native Californian, she now lives in New York. She is at work on a collection of short stories.

SEAN EVANS is the pseudonym of a well-known erotica author who saves his most taboo fantasies for private consumption. "A Very Naughty Girl," though embellished, is a description of a real-life relationship. Evans's stories have appeared in the anthologies *MASTER* and *Juicy Erotica.*

ELLE MCCAUL'S erotic short stories have appeared in collections including *Girls on the Go* and *Naughty Stories from A to Z.* Currently, she is working on her first novel.

JASMINE HALL is the pseudonym of a journalist who writes for several national magazines, including *Parenting* and *People.* Her celebrity interviews have appeared in several Los Angeles weekly papers. She lives with her boyfriend and their video camera.

KC is the pseudonym of a San Francisco Bay Area erotic writer who believes that some things are too naughty even for the usual nom de plume.

ROSE KELLEY works in a café in San Francisco by day, and by night she writes for local zines, goes to bars, and has hot affairs (in person and via the Internet). She believes that the ways you can express erotic ideas are infinite. This is her first published story.

ALEXANDRA MICHAELS has had her short stories published in various *Penthouse* publications. Her work has also been published in *People* magazine.

JULIA MOORE is a coauthor of the best-selling *The Other Rules: Never Wear Panties On a First Date*. Her short stories have appeared in *Sweet Life* and *Naughty Stories from A to Z* and on the website www.goodvibes.com.

N.T. MORLEY is the author of ten erotic novels: *The Parlor, The Castle, The Limousine, The Contract, The Office, The Circle, The Appointment, The Nightclub, The Library* and its sequel *Borrowing Privileges*. In progress are volumes 2 and 3 of the *Office* trilogy, volume 3 of the *Library* trilogy, and a volume of short stories.

JESSE NELSON lives in Santa Monica where he spends too much time surfing and not enough time working.

JULIE O'HORA'S stories have been featured in the *Erotica Readers and Writers Association Gallery, Adult Story Corner,* and *Amoret.* She spends most of her time writing screenplays for romantic comedies and looks forward to being produced someday soon.

EMILIE PARIS is a writer and editor. Her first novel, *Valentine,* is available on audiotape. She abridged the seventeenth century novel *The Carnal Prayer Mat.* The audiotape won a *Publisher's Weekly* best audio award in the "Sexcapades" category. Her short stories have also appeared in *Naughty Stories from A to Z* and in *Sweet Life.*

GISELLE PARKER, also known as Mistress Giselle, is a real-life player in S/M, especially gender play, with her partner and others. Although she has written her fantasies down and distributed them on the Internet, "Girls' Night Out" is her first story published in print.

THOMAS ROCHE'S most recent books are *His* and *Hers,* two books of erotica coauthored with Alison Tyler. He has written more than 200 published short stories and 300 published articles that have appeared in many websites, magazines, and anthologies, including multiple volumes of the *Best American Erotica* series, the *Mammoth Book of Erotica* series, and the *Best New Erotica* series. You can find him at www.thomasroche.com.

PAUL ROUSSEAU'S poetry has appeared in the zines *Intelligentzia, Confab,* and *Prestochango.* This is his first published piece of erotica.

COREY SAWYER has written for *Good Vibrations* magazine and numerous underground zines. A sex educator from rural Missouri, he now lives in Chicago.

SIMON TORRIO is a keyboardist and underground music writer in Seattle. His work has appeared in zines such as *Downbeat, Re:Play, Hard Trance, Throb,* and *Miracle.* This is his first published piece of erotica.

ALISON TYLER is undeniably a naughty girl. With best friend Dante Davidson, she is the coeditor of the best-selling collection of short stories *Bondage on a Budget.* Her short stories have appeared in *Erotic Travel Tales, Sweet Life, Wicked Words, Best Women's Erotica, Guilty Pleasures,* and *Sex Toy Tales.* She is the author of a collection of short stories, *Bad Girl,* and novels including *Learning to Love It, Strictly Confidential, Sweet Thing,* and *Sticky Fingers.*

CRAIG T. VAUGHN is a musician living the Hollywood lifestyle in Los Angeles. His work has appeared in a wide variety of music zines. Look for him hanging out at the Kings Road Café, Swingers, or Book Soup Cafe—but not before noon.

SCOTT WALLACE'S work has appeared in *Underground, Myriad,* and *After Darque.* This is his first published piece of erotica. He lives in New York City.

About the Editor

VIOLET BLUE is senior copywriter at Good Vibrations where she writes book and video reviews, which has her watching an awful lot of porn and reading virtually everything imaginable written about sex. She is a sex columnist and a sex educator, and was the founding editor of *Good Vibrations* magazine. She is the editor of *Sweet Life* and the author of three books, *The Ultimate Guide to Cunnilingus*, *The Ultimate Guide to Fellatio*, and *The Ultimate Guide to Adult Videos*. When not thinking about, writing about, or having sex, she spends her time turning a wrench in the world of mechanical art and robotics as a member of Survival Research Laboratories. Or sipping delicious inebriants from the belly button of a squirming lover. Visit her website, tinynibbles.com.